Book Cover by Evelyn Render-Katz

First edition 2023

Skin in the Game

E.G. Rutledge

For Joyce, who heard the first version of this story and for Mom, who loved mysteries.

*To have "**skin in the game**" is to have incurred risk, by being involved in achieving a goal.*
   Attributed to Warren Buffet

✳✳✳

I can calculate the movement of heavenly bodies, but not the madness of people.
   Sir Isaac Newton

Chapter One

Alive, he was almost handsome except for the weak chin. Now, his lips were blue, and a trickle of blood had pooled in the corner of his mouth, just short of escaping.

The snare left an uneven, smear of deep purple over Craig Vitale's Adam's apple. The wire had compressed the windpipe without cutting the skin. A point of pride. It took skill to apply the right amount of pressure, strength to keep the victim between life and death until the right moment, even with him sedated nearly to the point of unconsciousness. A miscalculation. Still, the act had been satisfying—the anticipation, preparation, then triumph watching the bleary surprise on Craig's face turn to panic as his feeble movements only pulled the snare tighter.

The wire transmitted sensation, turned the snare into an instrument of pleasure. It ended in a moment of release, accompanied by a flood of memories of that first time. A volcano of need and fury contained for so long, channeled into ecstasy. If only that moment could be recaptured. Each kill had been an attempt to experience the same intensity again. But for now, this was enough. It was time to go.

First, a sweep of the scene and one last look at the body. The recessed lights in the high ceiling were turned off, but light from the street below found its way through the tall windows of the living room.

There were no curtains to detract from the clean look or spoil the view. Pale light spilled across a photo of Craig posed with his parents and their golden retriever. The Eames leather chair Craig was trussed in faced away from the windows, leaving his body half in shadow.

A button from his expensive shirt had been lost as it caught on the snare. No point wasting time over a lost button. The only prints on it would be Craig's or that of the laundry service. Everything else was in place, wiped down, or stowed in the black plastic bag. Except for the memento, which was less a memento than insurance. The micro cassette was carefully placed in an envelope and tucked in a compartment of the messenger bag.

Craig's corner apartment was conveniently located across from the stairway, which although well lit, remained deserted. Exiting the apartment and inching open the heavy door to the stairway, it was a dizzying ten flights down, then into the camouflage of the alley.

Chapter Two

Sheila's morning began early and wrong. She needed to be out the door in twenty-three minutes to catch the crosstown bus, then change to the subway.

She wasted time wrestling her hairbrush free from a drawer. "Damn you, Hemnes," she cursed her nightstand, using its IKEA name. The bent bristles caught in her hair halfway down the back of her head. Another bad hair day, but who would notice?

Sheila slipped on a skirt, pullover, and jacket. Three shades of beige. Not counting her once-white underwear. *Please don't let me get hit by a bus and wind up in the ER.* She promised herself to ditch her granny panties and buy some sexy lingerie again. Even if she was the only one to enjoy it.

Now to grab her trench coat, messenger bag, and get out the door. She zipped up her serviceable knee-high leather boots. Remnants of the April 6th blizzard with ten inches of snow—a belated April Fool's had lasted a week—into the first Passover seder. Snowballs, then matzoh balls. She'd even braved the remaining slush to attend a singles seder. Another prank of nature: women outnumbered the men three to one. *I try, Mom, honest.*

But Sheila hadn't come to New York to find a husband; she'd come to be a writer. From the time she'd been able to hold a pencil in her chubby fingers, she knew that was what she wanted to be when she grew up. And she'd dreamt of living in New York, a real city with a real skyline, not grain silos and endless fields. Okay, so her job as a copywriter wasn't her dream job, but it paid the bills.

Yesterday had felt like a day and a half at Hummingbird, the new PR firm where she worked. The firm was aptly named—although she was a senior copywriter, her job seemed to consist of frantic darting, hovering, and flying backward in pursuit of her clients' satisfaction. Today: yesterday, part B.

The commute was her time for reading and catching up on the news, but Sheila had an open mic that night at the Comedy Cellar in the Village. She ran through her routine in her head. It wasn't quite *there* yet.

Why did she give her precious spare time to stand-up comedy, after her unimpressive one-minute tryout in high school and some tortuous open mics at Grand Daddy's and Maxwell's back in Iowa City? Simple—she'd needed to write something different after her day job. Something for *her*. She still couldn't bring herself to write about Sam. *Would she ever?*

Getting up in front of an audience scared her, but it was an easy scare. If they didn't laugh, there was always another audience full of strangers. She was not her shyer, more introverted self on stage. Her onstage persona was the ballsy Sheila. The one who said what she thought, even though she'd written and edited and rewritten those thoughts. She found it easier to live with whatever happened during her five-minute set than the quicksand of grief and despair she found herself in when she thought of Sam.

She remembered every one of those days in the first year after he died. All three hundred sixty-five were the same. Wake up and expect to hear him in the shower. Reality hit and she would cry. Walk through the halls at school and expect to catch a glimpse of him. Reality. Pass the lockers in the hall where she used to see him. Every meal at the dinner table. Reality. Her mother and father staring at their plates. She would eat one bite of each food item on her plate: broiled chicken breast, mashed potatoes, and peas. Tough and tasteless or soft and bland. The seasoning of her tears made it even more disgusting. She thought of Sam, the bottomless pit asking for seconds. Reality. There were leftovers every night.

Whenever she'd tried to write about her brother's unsolved murder and the awful years that had followed, she'd come up against the wall of how little evidence had been found. She'd naively told herself—no *sworn*—that no matter how long it took, she would expose her brother's killer.

That promise had dogged her, taunting her from Delmont to Iowa City through her college years and all the way to Manhattan. Ten years, she'd felt it eating away at her from the inside. Not the gnawing in the pit of her stomach of self-imposed starvation but a desperate thing trying to claw its way out.

She closed her eyes, rolled her shoulders, and took a couple slow breaths. She was feeling more than her usual free-floating anxiety. Not just anxious. Today she had the old bad feeling.

Sheila got off at her stop and sprinted to the office. *Crap.* She'd be late for her first appointment. And Craig was punctual. He worked as an investment counselor for a private brokerage house. He'd come to her for a presentation and branding campaign for a new fund he was developing.

"Don't you have someone in-house who'd work with you on this?" she had asked him. He had told her this was something outside his regular work.

"Kind of a gamble," he'd said, and she'd felt his nervous excitement.

Sheila panted as she rounded the corner from the stairwell. She made yet another false promise to herself to get to a gym. She launched through the glass door of the office vestibule avoiding the eyes of Danielle, their receptionist and glanced at the Howard Miller clock on the wall that overlooked the warren of cubicles. *Not so bad. Only five minutes late.*

"Relax." Kevin, her coworker, poked his prematurely balding head up over the first cubicle. "Your first one's not coming."

"Oh, did he call?"

Kevin gave her a grim look and held out a page from the *Daily News*. She took the page of the morning paper and blanched as she read the headline: "Investment Wiz City's Latest Murder Victim."

She steadied herself on Kevin's desk, then stepped into the next cubicle, hers. She sat in the uncomfortable office chair, her bag in her lap. She felt a familiar the-sky-is-falling feeling descend. *That old bad feeling.*

"You okay?" Kevin asked. He disappeared for a moment, then returned from the water cooler with a paper cup. "Here, drink this."

She threw it back like a shot of tequila.

"Hey, I mean, you thought he was late, not *late*."

She gave him a stony look.

"Too soon, huh?"

"Too not funny."

"Listen, have Danielle call your clients scheduled for today. You look terrible. I can probably fill in on a couple. I'd like a crack at those candy bar peddlers."

"Thanks, Kevin, I'll be okay. I'm feeling a little off, and now this." She shuddered. "Sometimes the random violence in this city gets to me."

"Sorry. I know what you mean. But this one doesn't sound like it was so random. I mean, this guy lived in a real ritzy building. Secure, you know? Cameras, doorman, the works. Sounds like he knew his killer."

"And why do you say that Columbo?" she said in her best straight-man delivery while a drum began to pound inside her head.

Kevin tapped his fingers on his chin as he spoke, squinting to picture what had been reported. "The paper says there weren't any signs of forced entry. So, he must have opened the door and let the guy in. He was strangled."

Sheila reflexively put a hand to her throat. Craig had been strangled. She gave her head a little shake, trying to erase that thought and what would surely follow.

Kevin went on. "And the killer cleaned up after himself."

She tried for a wry smile, but she feared it was more of a grimace. "A clean fiend. Should I fire my maid? Oh, wait, I don't have one. Thank God."

Kevin brightened at her attempted smile and joke.

"Ha! Better, yes? I hate when you look like just another despondent writer here. Tell you what, I'll go get us some coffee. Good stuff, from the deli."

"Throw in an order of matzah brie and all is forgiven."

"Who?"

"It's French toast but with matzah instead of bread."

Kevin looked horror stricken.

"It's delicious. Boris at our deli knows."

Kevin cast a concerned glance back at her as he left. She gave him a little wave. But her hand shook, and the pounding in her head was more insistent.

She no longer cared about the fried matzoh; she wanted a few minutes alone. She wanted to scream. She'd been afraid she was going to lose it in front of Kevin, then it would all come pouring out. She'd be right back where she'd been ten years ago. Reliving that whole nightmarish time. She'd come so far. Run so far from her brother's murder.

Chapter Three

"Man, I'm beat, and we catch the new DB right before the weekend. Bonnie and I had plans. Damn, we were going to start painting the baby's room and maybe catch a movie."

Head bent over his keyboard, typing at a respectable speed for someone with so little clerical aptitude, Detective Mike Sloan leaned back in his chair and gave his partner a sympathetic nod.

"I had some plans myself," he said. "Hey, just another perk of being DI third class, Detective Corrigan." Burnt Folgers fumes wafted from the cup of black coffee on his desk, permeating their shared space.

Duane pulled a face, then asked, "Who called it in?"

"Business associate. Victim missed an eight o'clock dinner meeting in Union Square. Must have been pressing business because the guy went looking for him at his apartment. Found the super and convinced him to open the door."

"You like the business buddy for this?" Duane asked.

"I'd like anybody for this. I want it off our board. But we'll see. The victim has an office in the Trade Center. Some of these big-money types like to play in rough waters, but this?"

Mike fanned out four of the crime-scene photos next to Duane. A man who looked to be in his mid-thirties was slumped in an Eames chair. His dark, undercut hair was slicked back with gel that made it look wet. His hands were bound behind the chair with a necktie. Shirt unbuttoned; pants unzipped.

He looked surprisingly peaceful. Except for the bulging eyes—whites gone red from burst capillaries and the swollen tongue that lolled from his open mouth. The only mark on him was an ugly purple line around his neck.

"Looks a little like George Michael. Except this guy's got a weak chin."

"That's the least of his problems. He didn't die singing. Killer must have stood behind him, slipped the ligature around his neck, and pulled it tight. Steel or coated wire, no fibers."

Detective Mike Sloan looked at the close-up shot of the vic's hands. The tie around his wrists wasn't tight—it was a slate-blue silk Hermes necktie. He knew from the little horseshoes woven into the fabric that the tie was from the "Lucky" collection.

"No indication of a struggle. Toxicology isn't back yet, but my guess is he was drugged with an opioid or combination of alcohol and ketamine. Coroner's thinking death took place between nine at night and one in the morning," Mike concluded.

"Any drugs at the scene?" Duane asked.

"A little grass, some coke."

"Whoa, some cocaine? Captain Doby, I suggest you take this to the lab and have it analyzed this time..." Duane said doing his best Hutch imitation. Big and blond, Duane could pass for David Soul. Mike wasn't much of a Starsky, but he liked to play along.

"Recreational stash. No prescription pain meds or tranquilizers. This wasn't drug related," Mike said.

"Could be some sex thing, with the bondage, the pants open. You know, maybe he forgot their safe word," Duane said.

"Maybe he didn't get a chance to say it."

Mike felt the familiar churn in his gut. The crime lab provided close up photos of the ligature marks on the victim's neck. Ligature strangulation was less common than manual strangulation. That alone would have been enough to get his attention.

What had he told his partner about what had happened in his hometown, Delmont, and in those other towns in Iowa over the past ten years? He was sure Duane would dismiss any comparisons to those cases. Mike told himself *he* should focus on the present, this victim, this crime scene. But there was so little evidence. So little to go on. No weapon, no apparent suspects or motive. The same. Different time, different place, but to him it felt the same.

He needed to get his head straight, get back in the present. He needed to find out who Craig Vitale had been and who would want him dead before he went down the rabbit hole of why the killer had chosen to drug, humiliate and garrote him. Duane would help keep him on track.

Mike really wanted to be home with Ed, talking this over. Although they'd met nearly ten years ago, when Mike had been a freshman at Syracuse, they'd only been living together for the past year. Their relationship had evolved. They'd even managed to weather the challenges of a long-distance romance after he transferred to John Jay College of Justice, and later, a bad breakup. His "roommate" and lover knew when a case had him tied up in knots, so they'd made a pact to talk rather than bottle it up. Over the years they'd been together, and even when they'd been apart, Ed was the one person he could share anything with. Like the things that were already beginning to needle him about this case. Some of the things he wasn't quite comfortable talking about with Duane. He better mention the similarity to those other cases to Duane and get it out of the way.

"Duane, I don't know if you remember what I told you about a serial killer in Iowa in the seventies," Mike said. He tried to keep his tone casual, his breathing even.

"Hell yes. You couldn't shut up about it when you came back here. Meanwhile, how many murders were turning into cold cases right here in the city—hundreds? Thousands? But it was your hometown, Dilbert, right? So, I get it."

"Delmont," Mike corrected.

"Yeah, yeah. Perp used a ligature on his victims, and they were all men. Started in one corner of the state and worked his way east, along I-80. Never caught the guy. Am I right?"

"Damned right." Mike paused, his personal connection threatening to pull him down into places remote and dark. "You remember I worked those other cases too."

"This one wasn't bludgeoned first, though," Duane noted.

Mike took a swig of the cold coffee and grimaced.

"Come on Mike, get real. Odds are this case has nothing to do with those cold cases. You're not in Kansas anymore, Dorothy."

"Not in Iowa."

"Same difference."

Mike blinked at the beam of spring sunshine that cut through the streaked station-house windows. "You're right, buddy." He picked up his pen and clicked it a couple times. He began to trace a circle on his note pad, spiraling like a coil of wire. "So, what else do we know about the poor schmuck taking the long nap on the coroner's table?"

Chapter Four

Sheila closed her eyes and cupped her hands over them for a minute. She eased the stack of folders out of her messenger bag. Craig's was on top. She took a cleansing breath and let it out slowly, turning the folder over and relegating it to another pile of work at the far side of the desk. She'd do something with it, but whatever that was, it could wait.

Kevin would be back soon bearing coffee. Maybe even matzah brei, if it was still on the menu on this last day of Passover. She had a few minutes left. She needed to call Mike, her brother's best friend. She'd only spoken to him a couple times since he returned to the NYPD. He'd made detective. His folks must be proud of him. Sam would've been. She felt her eyes begin to fill. She'd save the hard call to Mike. Who could she call instead? She never felt comfortable talking to the friends she'd made here about Sam. She'd never even mentioned her brother to most of her girlfriends here. How could she begin now? Where would she begin?

Go ahead, call Billy. Guilt pinged her gut at that thought. She used Billy. She vented to him, revealed her insecurities and frustrations and he let her. Hell, he encouraged her. Yet she kept him at a distance, not wanting to fuel his forever hopes that they'd be more than friends.

Billy and her best friend, Nancy, had always had her back in high school. They had made Delmont tolerable. Nancy had married her high school sweetheart and stayed in the Midwest. It had been a wrench to leave Nancy, but even their friendship couldn't make Sheila stay in Iowa. Even her parents, especially her parents couldn't keep her there. Not after Sam's death. A year after she'd moved to New York, Billy had followed. Sheila was glad to have Billy here. After all the years, the countless arguments and apologies, he was still her friend. Sometimes more like faithful dog. Wagging his tail behind him. Was it conceit that she thought he'd come to New York to be close to her? After all, he'd earned a law degree and found a spot with a New York firm that specialized in financial law. Somewhere along the line he'd grown enough killer instinct to make his way up the ladder of that firm without anyone's help. Not bad for a small-town boy. The current financial crisis meant job security for the firm and therefore for him.

She got his answering machine and left a halting message: "Billy, it's Sheila. I need to talk to you right away. You know that young investment broker I've been working with, Craig Vitale? He's dead." Her voice shook with that last statement.

Her phone rang a minute later.

"Sheila, are you okay? I read about it. I knew him—sort of. His daddy's a big shot on Wall Street." Billy paused. "What I'm about to say isn't so nice."

"Then you're talking to the right person," Sheila said. It was their old joke, but neither of them laughed.

"Craig didn't inherit his dad's smarts. I heard he couldn't really cut it at the firm he started out at. Got booted downstairs when his boss noticed how strung out he was. It was costing the firm clients, not to mention what it looked like to anyone he worked with. Anyhow, Daddy sent him to a fancy rehab clinic, and Craig was back to making friends and influencing people, same as before. I heard Daddy wedged his size elevens in the door of a firm whose *values*, and I use that word loosely, were more in line with his ambitions."

"I was helping Craig with this proposal for some new investment tool. Was there something not kosher? I mean, something funny about this hush-hush project?"

"You're the comedian. But if you mean funny, as in not on the level, not strictly on the up-and-up, then I'd say yes."

"He said it was kind of a gamble, this new proposal."

"A Ponzi scheme by any other name…"

"Billy, I know what you're going to say when I tell you this, but I have a bad feeling."

"I know better than to argue with you. All I'm saying is maybe he was in over his head. Maybe he was screwing with the people."

"You're probably right, not that it makes me feel any better. Hey, will you come to the funeral with me?"

"Sounds romantic. Sure, I'll pick you up."

"Thanks, Billy. By the way, have you seen Mike now that he's back in New York?"

"He's busier than I am. And I'm busy. I talk to him now and then. He asks about you. You should give him a call. Who knows, maybe he'll be calling you. I think the murder took place in his precinct. Mike and his partner could be investigating Craig's murder as we speak."

She felt her throat constrict. "Right," she managed to say. "Thanks, Billy. Promise to call Mike. Talk to you later."

She had to get out of here. She wanted to be somewhere she felt safe, back in her apartment. Yes, she'd have to call Mike. Just not right now.

Chapter Five

Mike had only spoken to Sheila a handful of times since he'd returned to New York City. She'd come to the city after graduating from the University of Iowa, then working in Iowa City for a couple years. Had it been seventy-eight or seventy-nine? He knew she had worked on a local newspaper back then and it had been a far cry from the kind of writing she wanted to do. She'd been relegated to doing farm and livestock reports along with an occasional local interest story. Was her move to advertising and PR better or just different for her? Life happens and plans change. Mike knew that only too well.

He had found himself living in the city the first time after transferring from Syracuse to John Jay College of Criminal Justice. Living in Manhattan was even more liberating and overwhelming than leaving Delmont his freshman year. He'd joined the NYPD after graduation, but mass layoffs and cuts that same year had sent him back to Iowa until two years ago.

Sheila was his best friend Sam's little sister. She'd been like a little sister to Mike. They'd leaned on each other after Sam had been murdered. They were also painful reminders to each other of their loss and the fact that Sam's murder had gone unsolved for a decade.

When the Ross's had moved to Delmont in his senior year, Mike had felt drawn to Sam like the needle of a compass to true north. Seeing

Sam was like waking up on Christmas morning for Mike. Every time. Some days it was all he could do to keep from bursting with his feelings for Sam—feelings that threatened Mike to his core.

He and Sam had planned to go to the University of Iowa: Sam focused on pre-med, Mike on pre-law. Then Mike's athletic prowess, especially in basketball got him a full-ride sports scholarship from Syracuse University in New York. He could hardly believe his good luck. His folks would never have been able to afford four years of tuition, plus law school, even at a state school. Not on a small-town police chief's salary or his mom's earnings as a librarian. No, Syracuse had been the better choice. Going to Iowa with Sam would have been filled with mixed emotions.

A battle raged inside him between longing and shame, passion, and the sting of rejection. And anger, sometimes so much anger. At himself, and right or wrong, at Sam. Syracuse had been nearly far enough away from Delmont and Sam. Mike had figured he'd get over his one-sided infatuation and their solid friendship would survive. After all, their bond was forged of more sturdy stuff. Shared dreams and things that threatened to derail those dreams when you least expected it. Mike's secret would've been safe. So would Sam's.

Now he was at the start of an investigation that had brought him full circle and it wasn't a surprise to hear from Billy Miller. Billy's father, the county prosecutor and Mike's police chief dad had been friends. Mike had known Billy before he became Sheila's friend. Billy specialized in financial law. He'd made it into law school at City University of New York, after doing undergrad pre-law in Iowa. Billy had left Iowa after graduation just like Sheila.

New York was really a big, small town after all, but Mike *had* been surprised when Billy mentioned Sheila's connection to the victim. She must be reeling from the fact that this murder involved someone she knew, however superficially. He would set up a time for a formal interview with her after the victim's funeral. And while he pondered what a small world it was, he noted Billy's acquaintance with Craig Vitale. He added Billy to the list of interviewees.

Billy had called Mike before he had a chance to call him. Billy said both he and Sheila were planning to attend Vitale's funeral. Mike welcomed a reunion but not under these circumstances.

"Figured I'd be hearing from you anyway. I knew him enough to talk *about* him, not really *to* him," Billy said. "His father was the real heavy hitter, but Craig was determined to make his way to the top one way or another. He was involved in some unconventional financial practices."

"You're saying some of his business might have been illegal?" Mike asked. Before Mike could ask if Craig was being investigated, Billy hinted that risky practices in finance hadn't been Craig's only problem.

"Maybe. Craig had a history of other things that got him in trouble too. Nothing that a couple trips to rehab and his father's money and influence couldn't fix... until now."

"Like some unhealthy business relationships," Mike ventured.

"And some unhealthy recreational habits," Billy said.

"This one doesn't feel like a drug deal gone bad." Mike paused. "I can't get specific, but the case resonates with me. Not in a good way."

"I know, I know. Sheila said she had that old bad feeling. I hope it's not contagious."

Chapter Six

She'd told Danielle she'd be leaving after she made a few calls, so she was only putting off the inevitable. It wasn't going to get any easier. Sheila dialed Mike and he answered on the third ring.

"Sheila, how are you? I've been thinking about you," he said.

"Same. Same here," she said. Her voice felt tight, strained.

"I just got off the phone with Billy. We need to catch up. I imagine that's not why you're calling."

"Right. Billy told you that Craig was one of my clients. He had an appointment to see me this morning." Sheila felt tension creeping back into her neck and shoulders.

"But you didn't see him this morning. Sorry, Sheila. Sorry to have to ask you, but when was the last time you saw him?"

She let out the breath she'd unconsciously been holding. "Last week. We were making the final edits on the copy for the presentation on his investment project." Sheila closed her eyes and massaged the space between her brows. "He said he needed to check the numbers for earning projections with the investment analyst he'd been working with one more time, and if everything checked out, we'd finalize the copy."

"Did he mention the guy's name?"

"I don't remember." She paused searching her memory for a name, any name he might have dropped—*Einstein?* That was a nickname, obviously. She heard Mike clear his throat. "Mike, this has really thrown me. I might remember more later, but I can't concentrate right now. I've got an open mic tonight in the Village, and I don't even know if I'll be able to remember my material." Sheila cringed. "Does that sound obnoxiously self-centered or what?"

"Sheila, it's okay. You've already been a big help. I realize this is hard on you."

"The paper said he died of asphyxiation. They didn't give any details, but…"

"You understand I can't talk about the details with you. This is an investigation, and I can't compromise it. But I'd like you to come down to the station and make a statement, the sooner, the better."

The way Mike had sidestepped her question was all the answer she needed. Sheila took a deep breath and sighed. "Is tomorrow soon enough? I'm going home to try to relax before the club tonight."

"Tomorrow's fine. Sorry I won't be able to make your show—lots of paperwork on this case already. Break a leg."

"With my luck, I probably will. But thanks, Mike."

She'd let Kevin handle the rest of her schedule. Time to go home and pull herself together before she was due at the club. She had time to take a shower and fix her hair. She'd wear her jacket with shoulder pads. It made her feel tougher, less vulnerable. Even though at the moment she felt anything but tough. *The show must go on.*

Chapter Seven

She had thought concentrating on her lines, timing, and delivery would have been enough to keep her rooted in the present. In fact, she bombed in those five minutes at the Comedy Cellar. Her timing was way off. Her mouth kept going dry, and it was hard to get her lines past the tightness in her throat. Her normally mellow, slightly snarky voice sounded weak and high. The nervous energy that usually charged her performance had left her feeling too vulnerable and raw. What was she thinking—trying to carry on with a stand-up gig when all she could think about was Craig Vitale, strangled in his apartment?

Then there'd been that unexpected meeting. She still didn't know what to make of it. What to make of him. She'd gone back to her seat after her set to nurse her bruised ego with a glass of Blue Nun. She'd been staring into the abyss of her nearly empty glass when she'd caught the scent of his aftershave. She looked up and felt her pulse quicken. Warm brown eyes behind aviator frames met her wine bleary green ones as he held out his hand.

"Hi Ms. Ross? Marcus Kent."

She was caught off guard, but she didn't want to be rude. It might have been the wine or the fading adrenaline rush from her set, but her heart thudded in her chest as she shook his hand. He had a firm but not aggressive grip. He didn't take his eyes off her.

"Nice to... um... have we met before? I'm sorry, but it's been a sh—a tough day."

"I caught one of your stand-ups during an open mic at The Laugh Track last month. I was hoping to go up tonight but no room. I'm glad I stayed. I like the way your mind works. Good stuff. Your delivery needs work, though."

Sheila's face fell. That was not what she wanted to hear. She bit back a sarcastic remark that was on the tip of her tongue. *Don't shoot the messenger. Especially not a handsome one.*

"Hey now, don't be offended," he said. "I can be a little too direct sometimes."

She managed a smile. "No offense taken. I come from a family who has no unspoken thoughts." She, on the other hand, was having plenty of unspoken thoughts.

He laughed. *He has a nice laugh.*

"I asked the emcee about you."

Her breath caught. *Swell, a stalker.*

"I asked who he thought was a new talent. He said you were a funny girl."

Sheila exhaled. "As in Fanny Brice or just weird?"

He laughed and she laughed.

"I've got an idea about teaming up with someone for a comedy partnership. You know, a dynamic duo."

"Like Batman and Robin?"

"I was thinking more along the lines of Burns and Allen."

He looked into her eyes, and she was dumbstruck. Silence yawned between them. She let it. She was fresh out of witty repartee.

"Well Funny Girl, here's my phone number. If you want to talk about it or give it a try." He handed her a card, turned and walked back to the bar.

She slid his business card into her purse. A little half smile played on her lips as she ran her finger around the rim of her empty wineglass. She gave her head a little shake and stood to go, purposely avoiding looking in his direction. Only when she was to the door did she hazard a quick look back. He was talking to another comic.

Probably the last I'll see of him.

Even so, she half hoped she would see him again. He had an ease and self-confidence about him she found attractive. It was different from the arrogance so many of the men she encountered displayed. It wasn't the polished, hard shell that Billy presented to the world and even to her these days. Maybe she would call him.

Careful. People and things aren't always as advertised. If anyone should know that I should.

***

Marcus had been a pleasant distraction, a temporary reprieve from the old bad feeling that kept threatening to drop on her like a sandbag. That surprising tingle she'd felt when her eyes met his was something she hadn't felt in a very long time. Part of her wanted to hang onto any good feeling she had. *Just a little longer, even if it doesn't go anywhere.*

But the anxiety that grew in the shadow of death wasn't so easily banished. Onstage last night it kept popping into her mind. *Why is New York City like Delmont, Iowa?* It sounded like the straight line for a joke, but Sheila didn't have a punchline. All she had was a claustrophobic feeling that made her want to howl or punch a wall. It felt like being back in the tiny town she hadn't been able to get out of fast enough, because Craig's murder had brought back memories of

Sam's. Her brother, strangled in his own car. Discovered on a deserted stretch of highway only fifteen minutes from home.

Her last words to him: "What time will you be home, Sam?" yelled at the top of her lungs, not spoken as he backed the car down the alley. He'd been on his way to work at Tractor Supply. He was late.

"After dinner," he'd shouted back, annoyed.

When the doorbell rang that night, her mother had answered. Sheila had been up in her bedroom, working on a funny poem that included Billy, Nancy, and herself. She couldn't find anything to rhyme with Sheila that sounded funny other than "feelya." Maybe she'd change all the names to protect the innocent. Maybe a snack to stimulate her poetry brain cells. Sheila went downstairs to the kitchen. Her mother had put out more pinwheel sandwiches leftover from a bridge game. She was surprised to see Mike's dad, the police chief.

"Sheila, is your father home?" he asked as he took her mother's hand and led her into the living room. "Please get him, and the two of you come and sit down. I need to speak with all of you."

Everything that had happened after that was a blur. She thought she remembered screaming. Then she went silent—if she didn't say anything, it wouldn't be real. It would all go away. The last ten minutes in her life would break up into tiny particles and evaporate. And then, she could be a daughter sitting with her mother in a living room in a house in an awful little town in Iowa, waiting for the best, most annoying brother in the world to come home.

The scene replayed over and over in different ways and at unexpected times. Sheila's freshman year of college, her best friend, Nancy, was coming for a weekend visit. It was going on more than an hour past the time Nancy had said to expect her. Sheila heard her own voice asking Sam when he'd be home. Like a bad song she couldn't get out of her head. She was pacing around the dorm lounge, feeling caught between wanting to scream or pass out. When Nancy finally arrived, she took one look at Sheila and said: "What the hell is wrong with you? You look like you're ready for a straitjacket."

This time, she was waiting for her client. The one who would never walk through her agency's door again. She tried to tell herself it was *not* the same. This was someone she'd worked with, what, maybe four times? She couldn't even say she liked Craig. She still felt awful. Not liking him didn't make his death any less horrific.

She'd be seeing Mike tomorrow and she had nothing to tell him. That realization felt like cold water dashed in her face. Again, she thought of Sam's murder and her total uselessness in the investigation. Nauseating feelings of helplessness and guilt came flooding back, leaving her feeling weak, her limbs heavy. She tried to refocus. *This is now, be here now.* She repeated the mantra and took three deep breaths. Inhaling through her nose, exhaling through pursed lips. Slowly, energizing anger replaced the helplessness. If she wasn't going to sit on the sidelines wringing her hands again, she needed to do something. Where to start? She'd need to look up everything she could about Craig Vitale. *But where to look? Who's Who in the New York City Morgue?* Why hadn't she asked him more questions, pressed him for more background information about himself even if he wasn't willing to give her more on his special project? Maybe she hadn't wanted to know. She'd let herself think of him as his slick, Wall Street persona. Her job was to help him sell whatever it was he was selling. Not to judge his product or him.

That thought brought her up short. One of the things about this job that didn't thrill her was how far it was from what she'd learned to do as a journalist. She valued the chance for creativity that PR offered—coming up with punchy lines for ads, envisioning slick, eye-catching print and graphics for the campaign. But sometimes what she did smacked of sleight of hand.

Okay, so be objective. Try to get back in reporter mode. Concentrate on the facts. But the only facts she had were those gleaned from yesterday's newspaper article. Nothing she read in the tightly spaced columns of black and white print dispelled the suffocating feeling that descended on her.

***

Ten years and over a thousand miles separated the two murders. Was it all in her mind—unresolved grief and guilt making connections that weren't there? Was it some psychic-intuition thing going on? Some neurotic-Jewish thing. Feeling responsible for anything bad that happened. Ever. Even things that were clearly out of her control. She let her mind play back the old tapes she'd tried to erase. The old hurt she'd tried to let go. Back not long before Sam's death. There, somewhere, tangled in the mess of her teenaged angst and fury at being yanked out of St. Paul and dumped in Delmont in her sophomore year was something barely remembered. Something important. But she'd be damned if she knew what it was.

Her most vivid memories before Sam's death involved her own second-child insecurities and how he made her feel... like the proverbial chopped liver.

***

"Sam, hurry up. I really have to go."

Sheila pounded on the bathroom door.

No answer.

"What's taking you so long? You having fun reading *Portnoy's Complaint* in there?"

Her mother's voice made its way up from the kitchen: "Sheila, give him a few more minutes. And please don't mention that horrible book again."

"If it was me in there, you'd be telling me to hurry up. It isn't fair."

Sam's unmusical interpretation of this week's top ten hits had woken her up fifteen minutes ago. Now, he launched into a tortuous rendition of "Bridge Over Troubled Water."

"PS, you're using up all the hot water, and I've got to pee." She used her nickname for him at moments like this. PS: Perfect Sam, Perfect Son, take your pick. She didn't think he had a nickname for her. Unless it was sis—also the sound he made peeing.

"Chill out," he said as he opened the bathroom door, shaking off water like a wet dog. He loped down the hall, a towel casually draped around his waist.

"Yuck, I'm all wet now."

"Not my fault if you're still not potty trained, sis."

"Sa-a-a-am!"

He'd be going off to college next year. She could get out from under his big shadow. She might or might not miss him, but she'd have the bathroom to herself. Maybe more of her parents' attention too. Was it her imagination or did an A on her report card count less than one on Sam's? Didn't all younger sisters want to kill their brothers sometimes?

***

Knowing she'd see Mike the next day got her thinking about everyone who'd been important in her life a decade ago. Nancy and Billy had been her best friends from the first week she moved to Delmont. Nancy's boyfriend, Gregg, went into the mix too. Gregg was just your average jock, perfect counterpart to Nancy's cheerleader persona—at first glance. Neither were as vanilla as they appeared. That was the good news.

She smiled thinking of Billy. Loyal Billy, with his too-short hair and too-eager smile waiting as she and Nancy crossed the street to Smitty's Café. Smitty's with its flavored colas, hand-cut fries, and black-and-white-striped leather booths was the closest thing to a teenage hangout there was in Delmont.

Nancy had elbowed Sheila and whispered, "I told you Billy's got a thing for you."

"No doubt a *little thing*." Sheila crooked her little finger and giggled. Nancy guffawed and nudged Sheila in his direction. Billy gave a tentative wave as they approached.

Faces and scenes emerged and faded from her memory like aging Polaroids. There were gaps, and maybe what she remembered wasn't accurate. One memory in particular was missing some details.

Billy had offered to buy her a Coke that day by way of an apology. They argued as much as they laughed together even then. Sort of like her relationship with Sam. But what were they apologizing to each other for that day?

She remembered them saying at the same time:

"Sorry." then "Jinx," and finally "Cokes!"

Then they both laughed.

"No hard feelings?" Sheila had asked.

"Don't sweat it. We're friends, right?"

Sheila had smiled. "Right."

"Want to get that Coke? I think you said it first, so I'll buy."

Nancy smiled and arched an eyebrow.

Sheila ignored her. "Sure, let's go."

The scent of fries had made Sheila's mouth water as they worked their way to the counter and found three stools. Billy sat next to Sheila. Billy and Sheila each ordered a Cherry Coke; Nancy ordered a chocolate malt. Of course, she did. And of course, Sheila remembered what they used to eat. Always dieting, envying Nancy's perfect body and hating her own. What her mom used to call their family tendency to be a little *zaftig*. Pleasingly plump? Sheila had found nothing pleasing about it. Sam had never needed to worry about his weight. And he never would.

Who had been most important in Sam's life? Janice, Sam's sweetheart, and then Mike, his best friend. Anybody missing? Sheila ran through names and faces of classmates, teachers, neighbors that peopled that small town. Parents, teachers, and neighbors who had loomed so large in that part of her life seemed small and far away now. Talking to Mike face-to-face would bring some memories back into focus. But not without letting in feelings that came with those memories.

Chapter Eight

Sheila arrived at the station house to give a statement, her usual five minutes late. Mike saw her shiver and hug herself. It must have been the grimness of the place. He'd grown used to it. The squad room's nicotine-stained walls were covered with flyers, photos, and curling posters. She stopped in front of one: "Color of the Day: Forest Green." Mike wondered if she'd ask him about it. Undercover cops would wear an article of clothing that was the color of the day so that they could be identified by fellow officers.

Mike greeted her with a handshake that turned into a half hug.

"Sheila, welcome to the house." He looked her up and down. "You're looking quite svelte." His mother had once told him that was a polite way to acknowledge a woman's weight loss, but he probably should have kept his mouth shut.

"Thanks. I call it the 'death diet.' Your appetite gets buried with the victim."

She looked too thin. At sixteen she'd been a little chubby. Not fat but a contrast to Sam's lean, lanky build. In the months after Sam's death, she'd rapidly lost weight. Mike knew Sheila's mother worried that she'd developed an eating disorder, a grief reaction to Sam's murder. No doubt this latest twist of fate had taken a toll on her.

She had the same determined look in her eyes, but her usual wry smile was missing.

Mike pulled out a chair for her next to a metal desk. "How do you like the prison industry's handiwork? Our desks and lockers are compliments of inmates. Three of us share this fine desk. At least I got the top drawer."

"At least you didn't have to put it together yourself," Sheila said.

"Right. Welcome to the bullpen. Not exactly the corporate suite, but it's home."

"I wasn't expecting designer blinds on the windows. But this makes me feel like I should organize a bake sale or take up a collection for you." A smile quivered on her mouth, then vanished. "Enough about decorating. Let's get to it. What do you need to hear from me? Fire away."

"This shouldn't take long," Mike said. "Just the facts, ma'am, just the facts." He smiled hoping to make her feel more relaxed. "I've got your name, address, etcetera, so we can dispense with that." Mike had his notebook in front of him. He had a nervous habit of clicking the button on his retractable pen. The clicking sound it made was surprisingly loud. Sheila raised an eyebrow at him and looked pointedly at the pen in his hand. Mike cleared his throat and began. "So can you tell me the date you first met Craig Vitale?"

She pulled a daily planner from her messenger bag and flipped through it to find the first appointment he'd booked. She hadn't known him long. A month almost to the day.

"Sheila, what was your exact relationship to him, and do you remember the date, place, and time you last saw him?"

She'd seen Craig almost a week before his murder, in her office—cubicle, she corrected herself. He'd been prompt, as usual. He hadn't seemed on edge or worried that day.

"Disappointing how little I've got for you. Craig wanted my help with the narrative for his 'investing-outside-the-box plan.' He would seesaw between making me think I was barely needed on the project and then telling me that every phrase I suggested was pure gold. Not so different from working with every other client in my PR firm: 'love this, hate that, don't know what I want, but I'll know it when I see it.' We didn't waste time with chitchat. Craig was focused on the presentation. He did mention there was someone working on the financials and that he had enough juice to secure investors."

"You mentioned the financial analyst when we spoke before; have you remembered a name? Did Craig mention anyone else? Some of the investors?"

Sheila shook her head. "He shared an office with a partner. Of course, his name escapes me. Wait, Vitale and Serta. No that's the mattress. Something more exotic, romantic. Maybe Italian sounding. Sienna, that's it."

"What did he tell you about him?"

Sheila wrinkled her brow, "This guy was older. Like old enough to be his father. I got the impression he wasn't as much of a risk taker as Craig. Craig said he didn't want to involve him." She sighed.

Mike could see her winding down into silence. He asked her one last question.

"Is there anyone else you can think of we should talk to, anyone who might have had a falling out with him?"

"Sorry, no one comes to mind. If you threw out a few names, they might jog my brain. Otherwise, I don't know. Craig didn't talk about people with me. It was all about this project." She stared at her hands. A minute of silence passed, and she looked up at Mike, a pained expression on her face. "Not to speak ill of... it's just that I didn't find Craig particularly likeable. He struck me as greedy and arrogant.

I suppose that's in style these days, but I don't like it. Still, I don't think he was unlikable enough to get himself killed—not like that." She shook her head as if to erase an image. She seemed lost in her own head again for a minute. Then Sheila gripped the arms of the chair hard enough to turn her knuckles white. She rose and said, "Maybe he was plain unlucky."

Unlucky—that was what everyone had told them about Sam. He could hear his father, Chief Joseph Sloan, wearily proclaiming that Sam had been in the wrong place at the wrong time—plain unlucky.

Mike was on his feet. He put a hand on her shoulder and said, "Thanks, Sheila. We'll be in touch."

She nodded and walked to the door without looking at him.

He shook his head as he watched her walk away. It might be better to be lucky than smart, but in the absence of luck he hoped he was smart enough. This time.

Chapter Nine

Sheila had felt a prickle of dread as she pushed open the heavy doors of the station. It felt cold and dark inside for a spring day. Then her writer's curiosity kicked in, and she wanted a behind-the-scenes tour of the "house," as Mike had called it. But no, she hadn't wanted Mike to take time away from the investigation. Time was not on their side. A killer was out there. She knew she was letting herself get too wrapped up in Craig's murder investigation. But how could she be objective and detached? What if someone else, someone in Craig's circle, was in danger? One "you knew the victim" conversation with Mike was enough.

She'd left seeing Mike with no more understanding of what had happened to Craig than she'd had before. She could only hope something she'd told him would help. Now, she felt empty. Not just empty, she felt shaky. *Low blood sugar?*

Sheila realized she hadn't eaten yet and bought a big, warm pretzel from a street cart and sat on a bench. She bit into the salty, chewy crust and let her mind drift while the carbs kicked in. She sighed as her growling stomach silenced enough to allow her brain to focus. Chewing helped her think. *Mental-movie-rewind time. Start with the easy stuff. What did I notice about Craig?*

Every time she'd met him, he had worn a gray Armani power suit, colored dress shirt with white collar and cuffs, and silk tie. Monogrammed cuffs or cufflinks. The uniform. But it was never quite right. Not the clothes so much as the man. Craig didn't have that slightly aloof but dynamic aura Sheila associated with Wall Street. He'd struck her as more desperate than dynamic. *Think of his words.* Snippets of their conversations came to her. Mostly bullet points he wanted to use in the presentation, small talk about the weather, and if the market was up or down that day.

Words from a man and woman at the pretzel cart drifted into her brain. The woman's voice: "That jerk has no business leading a new sector of the fund."

She wondered who they'd been referring to. Why didn't she know more people involved in Craig's world, the way Billy did? *Because I never asked, damnit. Okay, so all I know of Wall Street is how many shares I own of a worthless stock my dad invested in years ago. Do savings bonds count?* She had to admit she'd had little interest in things financial so long as her checking account wasn't overdrawn. She'd need to pick Billy's brain to see if there'd been talk among his coterie of finance lawyers about fallout from Craig's death and who profited, or was it who benefited? Whatever. It was the age-old question in any suspicious death.

What about the other cliche, *cherchez la femme*? Craig had a woman in his life, but damned if Sheila could remember her name. Would his girlfriend have had anything to gain from his death? She'd guess he was worth more to the girlfriend alive—alive and dragged to the altar anyway. Ring on her finger, house in Scarsdale. But Craig acted like a player. Maybe his girlfriend was the jealous type. Jealous and psychotic? She was worth looking into.

And what about the fund? Craig had said this was his baby, but this project hadn't sprung from his forehead fully formed. He was no Zeus. Surely he hadn't been working alone. Working on the funding pitch didn't involve her alone. She contributed to the high-level summary slides. She helped him articulate the problem and how this fund would solve it. They both had ideas for marketing strategy. Her writing set the tone. The financial projections were the work product of other parts of the team. Again, she drew a blank when she tried to recall any mention of the others on the team.

Chapter Ten

Three days after Craig's death Sheila rode with Billy to the church in Hampton Point. She hadn't attended the viewing and mass the evening before. One schlep out there was enough. She still hated open caskets. And more and more she felt like she knew less and less about Craig. She didn't feel comfortable saying anything beyond: "I'm so sorry about Craig" to his relatives and close friends.

She flashed back to Sam's funeral and the people who didn't have more than a superficial connection with her brother. The ignorant things they said to her and her parents. But she wanted to pay her respects to Craig. And she had to admit to her own morbid curiosity. She signed the funeral guest register, and as she put the pen down, Billy and Mike came up on either side of her. They walked into the small chapel together. She was grateful for their company.

At first, there weren't that many pews filled with mourners. Female representation was also sparser than Sheila had expected. Mostly young men in fine business suits. Craig look-alikes. They sat down a few rows behind the "Craigs." Sheila reached into her purse for a cough drop and popped it in her mouth. Mr. Hinkley had coughed all through Sam's funeral, and that had really pissed her off.

The empty pews began to fill, and bits of whispered conversation seeped into the echoing quiet of the sanctuary. Craig's family entered with the minister, and a hush descended. She looked around the room and felt a chill. She'd been to other funerals over the past decade, a great aunt, parents of friends, and every funeral had felt like Sam's.

***

Sheila stood between her father and mother with her grandma, Bubbe, seated in a folding chair in front of them. Like they were posing for a family photo. They were in the room reserved for family at the Mason Funeral Home. Even though they had requested "in lieu of flowers we suggest donations be made to your favorite charity," the room was filled with gladioli and lilies. The scent was overpowering. Sam's best friend, Mike, his girlfriend, Janice, and Sheila's best friend, Nancy, stood in front of family, each touching the hand or arm of the person next to them, completing a circle of grief.

Mike's father and Billy's stood at the door like sentries, backs stiff, mouths set. Their wives, Sharon and Eileen, were at the front of the chapel, standing in front of the closed casket with the rabbi who had come from Council Bluffs. They explained to people who had expected a viewing that open caskets were not a Jewish custom. "Remember Sam as you knew him in life," the rabbi offered when people filing past the casket had given him a searching look.

The small chapel was packed. Sheila had looked up at the front of the room, relieved not to see a big crucifix. Although if Sam could, he'd have made a joke: "If it was good enough for Jesus, it's good enough for me." A smile crossed her face for a moment, then her eyes flooded with tears. She stood when the rabbi motioned them to stand and sat when everyone else was seated. The rabbi read the Psalm 23 and the "El Maleh Rachamim," the prayer for the soul of the departed.

Her uncle Isadore had come from Des Moines. He praised Sam's intellect in his eulogy, as well as his ambition, good-natured sense of fun, and most of all Sam's concern for others. Mike spoke through tears of Sam's devotion to his family, friends, and desire to be a doctor, not for status but to help others. When it was Sheila's turn Nancy stood next to her. Sheila cleared her throat, then stood in silence. Nancy cupped Sheila's elbow, and she began.

"Sam was my big brother, but he thought he was everyone's brother. You could ask him for any favor, and he'd do it for you... unless you were me asking him to get out of the bathroom fast." Sheila stopped. Her body began to tremble, and she thought: *Was it one of you? Did one of you kill him?*

She took Nancy's arm and let her read the rest.

She recited the Mourner's Kaddish with her family as the rabbi lead them in Hebrew, and she closed her eyes as he read the English translation:

"*May His great Name grow exalted and sanctified.*
In the world He created as He willed...
Blessed is He.
Beyond any blessing and song,
Praise and consolation that are uttered in the world...
He Who makes peace in His heavens, may He make peace upon us..."

Sheila wanted to feel consolation and peace. She only felt hollowed out by her anger and despair.

In the cemetery they sat on folding chairs under a canvas awning as Sam was lowered into the ground. The rabbi read Psalm 91; Sheila only heard the rumble of traffic on the highway that ran past the cemetery. It sounded like distant thunder as she sat wrapped in fog, heavy and gray as the sky.

The sky sifted rain over them as the rabbi put a shovel full of earth into Sam's grave. He placed the shovel in a mound of dirt for each mourner to use in turn. The shovel felt impossibly heavy to Sheila as she lifted a clod of dirt from the pile and let it fall onto Sam's coffin. She looked up to see Jane Brown, a girl in her class. She was standing outside the awning, well away from people filing past the open grave. Rain ran down her face and wet her thrift-store dress. She met Sheila's eyes, nodded, and turned away. Sheila had felt momentarily disoriented at the unexpected sight of her.

***

A woman sat down at the far end of the row in front of them, next to the last Craig clone. She looked familiar. *Jane? It was Jane.* Jane Brown from Delmont. Sheila nearly swallowed her cough drop. She couldn't help but stare. Beyond weird, seeing her here, of all places. Jane must have felt her stare. She turned and looked at Sheila. Sheila could feel Jane's eyes as she homed in on her. Sheila touched Billy's shoulder. "Weird Jane." Sheila regretted using the moniker she and Nancy had given the poor girl in high school. Kids had called her *Plain Jane* before that. Jane had been different. Super smart, but a social zero. A girl nerd. They'd both gone on to the state university. Sheila's last memory of her had been Jane suppressing a yawn as she patiently took Sheila through an equation for the third time. Math class had always been where Jane reigned supreme. Definitely not Sheila's forte.

He whispered, "What the fuck? Excuse the cursing."

"Love the cursing."

The service seemed to go on forever. When it ended, Sheila hesitated, for a beat. The woman walking in their direction was Jane. Sheila felt her face flush with guilt. They hadn't exactly been friends. Still, Sheila's curiosity won out. She closed the distance between them, Billy and Mike behind her.

"Jane, it really *is* you! This is one of those *Ripley's Believe It or Not!* moments, isn't it? I mean, that we're here. You remember Billy and Mike Sloan too."

That sounds as awkward as it feels.

Jane blinked and looked from Sheila to Billy and Mike. A slow smile came to her lips. She nodded at them.

"Sorry, but this is such a coincidence," Sheila rambled on. "Do you live here, in Manhattan? And Craig, how did you know him?" She was nervous. She needed to shut up.

Jane said, "I've been in New York since we graduated. I work in finance. Craig and I worked for the same firm when we were starting out. Small world." She looked Sheila up and down. "What have you been up to since our Hawkeye days? Still a journalist? That must be a tough game, especially here."

"I must admit, I left journalism for PR work here. I feel lucky to be at Hummingbird."

She fumbled in her purse for a business card and handed it to Jane. *Am I trying to impress her?* It had become habit: see someone, hand them a business card.

"What a cute name." One side of Jane's mouth curved up like Mona Lisa. "So, how did you know Craig?"

"I worked on a presentation with him. Pitch deck, branding, that sort of thing, For a new project launch." Sheila said. She felt a pinch of regret, as if she'd overshared. Her old habit of talking too much when she felt nervous or awkward had taken over.

Jane nodded and said, "Ah. Well, good to see you."

"We should have coffee or something. Catch up," Sheila offered.

Jane gave her head a little toss and smiled, "Sure. I'll call you. Take care of yourself," then strode away like a runway model.

Mike had been silent during the whole exchange, a look of concentration on his face.

"Mike?" Sheila said, "You're awfully quiet."

"Just thinking what a small world it is."

Billy took Sheila's arm and walked her out of the church. "That's one person I haven't thought about since graduation. Of course, I didn't think much about her even then. She's fixed herself up. Wowsa. Don't think I'd have recognized her if I passed her on the street."

Sheila hadn't thought about Jane either. Except for once recently. She'd stood on the subway platform and looked across to the uptown side. She'd seen a woman who looked familiar. She'd probably only noticed her because there'd been so few people waiting on the platform. She'd stood apart from the rest of the passengers, half in shadow. Sheila had strained for a better look at the slim figure standing, aloof and solitary. She'd racked her brain; she knew that woman but from where? But a train passed between them, and when it was gone, so was the woman.

Chapter Eleven

M ike had gone to Craig's funeral in hope of getting information. Being there gave him an idea of who Craig's friends, and even his possible enemies, were. Sometimes killers really did attend their victims' funerals. *I should get so lucky.*

He visualized the surprisingly scant attendees of Craig's service. His eye had been drawn to Craig's father, a distinguished-looking man who Mike knew only by reputation. A mover and shaker in finance, Carl Vitale was respected and, to some extent, feared by those who entered his orbit. Mike wondered how many times he'd had to call in favors to keep his son's ass out of a sling. Yet, in the end, he hadn't been able to prevent this horror. Carl looked stunned and defeated as he'd stood, arm protectively encircling his wife, Laura. Although her black suit was definitely not off the rack, it hung on her, and no expensive cream or makeup had been able to erase the lines of grief from her face. He'd given them his condolences and his card after the service, but they'd both given statements to his partner earlier.

Then there were Craig's contemporaries. Was it accurate to call them his friends? Some attractive-looking young women were sprinkled in the pews. One sat close to Craig's parents, dabbing at her pretty face to keep her mascara from running. That must have been Sarah, Craig's girlfriend. He imagined the other women were ex-girlfriends or colleagues. And their male counterparts, all meticulously dressed, filled in a pew. They'd cared enough to show up, but had any of them cared enough to kill him? Among them sat the guy who'd missed Craig at their meeting and gone looking for him. He looked a little rougher around the edges than the rest of Craig's friends. He had known Craig well enough to worry he'd gotten into trouble. *Albright? No, Althorpe.* He'd had an alibi—witnesses who could place him in a Union Square bar at the time of Craig's death. Enough to rule him out—for now.

Craig's business partner's absence was conspicuous. Alfred Sienna had been out of town and wasn't expected back until next week. He'd returned Mike's phone call sounding shocked; still there was something cold and rehearsed in his words. They'd need to check out his alibi through phone, credit card records, and reservations. Airlines, hotels, and restaurants should be able to verify Sienna's whereabouts.

He'd been surprised to see Jane Brown. Billy had been right; he wouldn't have recognized her. She wasn't the "plain Jane" he remembered growing up in Delmont. No limp, mousy brown hair—it was sophisticated, blond streaked, and just grazed her collarbone. It was held back on one side with an expensive looking hair comb. And her clothes were not from any thrift store.

She'd known Craig through work, she'd said. Mike wondered just how well she'd known him or if they'd had anything other than a business relationship. She hadn't seemed very broken up about his death, but the Jane he remembered had always presented a cool, dispassionate face. Even during that spring and summer in Delmont when a young couple, the Mahoneys had gone missing. Jane had been their nearest neighbor. Mike had a special attachment to Mary Mahoney. Mary had been like an older sister to him. Mike's mom had mentioned that Jane used to hang out at the Mahoney house. She must have been freaked out by their disappearance. Even after Sam's murder, when it seemed everyone else in town was losing it, gathering and placing flowers where Sam's body had been found. Jane remained apart, on the periphery of activity. Maybe she'd busied herself with other things.

Mike remembered running into her at Hinkley's in Delmont one Christmas when he'd come back for a visit. Fred Hinkley's little store reminded Mike of the neighborhood stores in New York, with crowded aisles and limited, out dated stock. He took the cranberry sauce and sour cream up to the counter to pay for it and noticed the young woman in line ahead of him. It took him a minute to recognize her. Jane Brown, taller, her figure more mature than when he'd last seen her. From a certain angle she reminded him of Mary Mahoney. She paid for her purchases and turned to face Mike. She looked surprised to see him, but she only nodded and went on her way.

"That Jane, she's a very bright young woman. Started a house-cleaning business. I let her advertise, right here." Hinkley nodded to the cork board by the door where flyers and business cards were tacked. "Business minded, like her father," Hinkley remarked as he put Mike's items into a bag.

"I don't really remember her father," Mike had said.

"Course you don't. You were a kid when he left. Old Al Brown." Hinkley shook his head. "He was a fast talker and a fast thinker. Left here in a hurry to get to the big city. I can just see him in Chicago or New York. No doubt, he's making money hand over fist. Even with this so-called financial crisis, I bet he's sitting in the catbird seat."

Chapter Twelve

Ed was in their galley kitchen making coffee and eggs for what they both hoped would be a leisurely Sunday breakfast. Ed's practice in labor law was keeping him nearly as busy as this case was keeping Mike. By the time they both got home from work, often long after traditional office hours, they were too tired to do anything more than sit on the sofa and fall asleep.

Mike had been drawn to Ed because his dark, curly hair, strong profile, and likable goofiness reminded him of Sam. It still took him by surprise sometimes, a bittersweet thing. And it had been a sensitive spot in his relationship with Ed. Ed had seen a graduation picture of Sam that Mike kept in a drawer—seen it when he'd been packing to move from Syracuse to New York City.

He and Ed had been apart for four years. Those years had not been happy ones for Mike. But in that time, he'd realized that what and who he really wanted was in New York. He'd found his way back, and reunited with Ed.

"More eggs?" Ed offered and reached for Mike's plate.

"I don't know how you do it," Mike said.

"The secret is to cook 'em low and slow," Ed said with a smile.

"Not just the eggs." Mike reached across the table and put his hand on Ed's. "Somehow, something as ordinary as eating breakfast with you makes me happy. Even though work is making me, and some people I care about, miserable."

"No movement on the Vitale case?"

"Not enough to keep the big boys off our backs. But it's more than that. I've had to question Sheila, and Billy. It brings up unpleasant memories for them."

"For you too." Ed looked at him, face full of concern. He seemed on the verge of saying something, but he had the good sense not to.

"Yep," Mike said in a clipped tone that cut off discussion of his feelings. "What's bothering me most are the coincidences—that they both knew the murder victim, yet he didn't have any ties to Delmont. And there are similarities between Vitale's death and Sam's..."

Ed frowned and took a sip of coffee. "That really doesn't make sense, does it? I mean, what would those two have had in common?"

"Nothing. Absolutely nothing. Sam and Craig were different as two people could be. Another thing," he took a breath. "In the ten years between those murders, I've turned up three more murders with the same MO. Victim taken by surprise or incapacitated so there wasn't evidence of struggle, and strangulation with a ligature. No synthetic or natural fibers from rope or cloth on the body or the scene. Killer used some sort of wire."

"Piano wire? Like the hit man in the *Godfather*? Didn't find a fish wrapped in brown paper in his kitchen, did you?"

Ed smiled. Mike gave a nervous chuckle. They shared a dark sense of humor, and at times like this it surfaced.

"Craig wasn't sleeping with the fishes. He was dead in his fancy leather chair. We haven't identified any mob connection, although I've heard he had dealings with some 'associates.' Got me thinking about that killing involving a guy near Iowa City who ran an illegal high-stakes poker game. But that didn't figure in Sam's case or in the other two cold cases I investigated during that time. Least not in any way I could see."

"Three murders?"

"Yep. Murders always come in threes and sixes."

"If those cases weren't related it seems even less likely that they could be related to Vitale's.

"Maybe not, but that's not how it feels," Mike said. "I know I need to separate those from the Vitale case, it's just. . ."

Ed's warm brown eyes looked into his. "Mike, do you think it would help to talk to Duane or maybe your superior about some of those cold cases?"

"I've talked to Duane about them."

"Have you told him everything?"

Mike took a deep breath and let it out. "Not everything." *I haven't even told you everything.*

***

He'd met Cory at a Gay Alliance meeting at the University of Iowa when he'd returned home after the big layoff in New York. Cory had befriended Mike, unaware that he was a cop. Flying the freak flag, flirting with Mike, in full regalia, including a Dolly Parton wig. "Call me Coralee, sugar pop," he simpered to Mike.

Mike admired that unfiltered, uncensored persona. But there was a more vulnerable Cory underneath, who Mike caught a glimpse of when the drugs and alcohol wore off. Mike tried to get Cory into treatment. Or at least a twelve-step program. But Cory stepped to another drummer and wasn't ready to leave the party, yet.

"You want to bust me because I'm fabulous. Don't deny it, I'm having more fun than you are. Don't hate me because I'm beautiful, Mike-a-licious. You gotta let it go!"

Mike never found Cory with drugs on that fabulous person. Attempts to badger or cajole someone into sobriety were useless. Mike worried. He could see Cory deteriorating, more emaciated and desperate every day.

One night, Mike found Coralee in the squirrel cage, wig askew, makeup smeared. Bruises bloomed through the carefully painted face.

"What happened? Stanley said he busted you for turning tricks. He saved your skinny ass from being beaten." Mike looked at the bruise darkening Coralee's high cheekbone. "Well, from a worse beating."

"Hey! Stan the Man hurt me while he was pulling my date off me. Police brutality! Not cool, not cool. Sure, my date was getting a little too excited. You can understand that. Coralee is just too much for some men." Cory's eyes were cast down. Lipstick-smeared mouth tight with hurt and shame. "He tried to mess up my face."

"Who did this to you?"

"I never kiss and tell. Don't remember his name anyway. Nice car, though. Black and gray Mustang. Mm, that V-8 engine growled like a big cat."

Mike sighed. "Cory, you don't have to do this. I've been talking to some of your friends. They want to help—"

"That's *Miss Coralee* to you! Listen here, Mr. Good Cop, I'm heading out to San Francisco. Pretty soon you won't have Coralee to kick around anymore."

Cory never made it to San Francisco. Never got the chance to join drag queens who left a "fairy farm" outside a small town in Iowa to form the Sisters of Perpetual Indulgence. Never got to raise hell and consciousness out there. Cory was found in the back room of a bar just outside Iowa City. There were rumors of a drug deal gone wrong or of a customer enraged when Coralee revealed that something extra down there.

Those were the obvious answers, and they were too easy. There had been drugs in Cory's system—no surprise. Cocaine and crack had been Cory's drugs of choice, not the quaalude found in the lab work. Cory wouldn't have taken it to come down either, not while out on the town. Cory had always wanted to keep the party going.

Had the guy who'd beat up Coralee come back for more? Black mustangs were popular cars. Mike could try to find out how many were in the county and who they were registered to. But this was a crossroad for drifters, dealers, and others who tried to fly under law enforcement's radar. Not every car had proper registration. College students with cars registered in other states came and went without drawing much attention.

Mike didn't think Cory's killer had discriminated on account of sexual orientation. The bludgeoning wasn't part of a violent gay bashing. It was a prelude to what the killer really got off on. The ligature mark on Cory's neck was like the one on Sam's. Same as on the other two men who'd been murdered over the past six years.

***

Ed had been listening, a pensive look on his face. He said, "So you didn't want to bring queer into the conversation? That's why you didn't talk about Cory to Duane?"

Mike shook his head. "I avoided talking about Cory because of all the cold cases from that time, it's the one that eats me up. Except for Sam, of course."

Ed nodded but said nothing.

"None of the police in Iowa City wanted to hear about the murder of a gay man, much less a transvestite. Despite the initial support the U gave to the Gay and Lesbian Alliance, people in power were backing away from it. Antigay prejudice kept rearing its ugly head."

"Like racism, antisemitism, or any ugliness, it's never far below the surface," Ed said. "It doesn't take much to peel off the thin veneer of civilization and reveal what's really under the skin."

"Nope. At first, I thought maybe that was the reason Cory had been killed. A hate crime. But there wasn't enough evidence to fit with that, and I couldn't see it as part of a pattern in the other cases. The other men killed weren't gay. And then I had the awful thought: what if the killer was? I sure as hell didn't want to throw that out there. I still don't. I haven't come out to anyone at work, all the same anything that draws attention to the gay community here makes me nervous."

"Do you really think that's a possibility? I never want to believe someone in our community could be responsible for murder, then or now. That wouldn't be good."

"No. As for Craig, his girlfriend was at the funeral, crying her eyes out. I haven't heard any talk that he went both ways. But it's something to consider given the sexual presentation of his body. Did anyone we know talk about close calls with freaks? Games that went too far?"

Ed looked at him thoughtfully. "Not that I was ever into that, but everyone knows I'm with you. Kinda limits the conversation. I can make a couple discreet calls, though."

"Thanks." Mike stretched and stood. "Thanks for letting me talk too. I think there's a connection. Ligature strangulation isn't as common as manual strangulation. I've talked to coroners here and in Iowa. I don't believe those murders were random." As he said that, he felt something nudge his memory. Mike closed his eyes, as if he could shut out everything but that vague, fleeting thought. But it was no good, it was gone.

"Vitale's murder doesn't sound random or opportunistic to me, Mike. It sounds more local and considering his occupation probably financially motivated. I think you need to take a step back and quit trying to find links between his murder and the ones in Iowa."

Mike furrowed his brow. "Maybe you're right. It could be he was killed because of something he did or something he knew. Maybe that something *was* about money, or someone he owed, big time."

Ed put his hands on Mike's shoulders and gave them a squeeze.

"Let's get out and enjoy the spring weather while we can. To hell with the dishes."

When they returned from their walk and a game of hoops, Mike felt more centered. He kept thinking of what Coralee had told him about her "date" and the car he'd been driving. A black Mustang Mach 1. No, it had been black and gray—Coralee had been very specific. Why did that description ring a bell?

He'd do the dishes, and maybe the thing that had been on the edge of his awareness would make an appearance.

Chapter Thirteen

Sheila dialed Mike after a typical Monday at Hummingbird, "If you and Ed are free, I'd like to buy you dinner. I'm too wired to go straight home, and a Jackson Hole burger sounds good."

"Great to hear from you but bad timing." Mike told her, "I'm buried in paperwork, but let me check with Ed. I told him I was working late, and he said he wasn't going to cook. I bet he'll be glad to meet you."

She was disappointed that Mike was too busy to meet her. She desperately wanted to know if all that paperwork was related to Craig's case. But this was an opportunity to see if Mike had shared information with Ed that he hadn't with her. She was curious about Ed too. They'd met years ago, but she couldn't say she really *knew* him.

"Getting to know you, getting to know all about you," a song from *The King and I*, ran through Sheila's brain. It was her favorite musical. She had a thing for the exotically bald Yul Brenner. Ed looked nothing like Yul. She realized with a pang that Ed looked a little like her brother. She studied the titles on the vintage mini juke box that graced their table. Nothing from Broadway musicals. Only golden oldies and a few eighties hits.

She regained her composure and smiled at Ed. She'd need extra cheese on her burger and maybe more fries. A large mirror flanked by dark woodwork and antlers proclaimed the restaurant to be "the original, Jackson Hole, Wyoming, home of the seven-ounce burger." Most of the dark wood tables and avocado green banquettes were full of hungry Manhattanites. She and Ed studied the menu as they sat among the vintage Coke signs and cowboy themed chotchkes that peppered the walls. A shadow box frame over their table held a photograph of John Wayne and a six-shooter.

She gave the tired looking waitress her order—to hell with dieting. Coke, the real thing—not the chemical aftertaste of the diet version tonight. Sheila sipped, savoring the cold sweet elixir. Between sips she tried to get Ed talking about his work in hopes that like a couple other lawyer she'd known, he'd keep right on talking and she could bring conversation around to the topic that really interested her.

"Are you working on any interesting arbitrations, Ed? Or do your cases go to trial?" What Sheila knew about labor law could fit on the head of a pin.

"Labor law is my true love. Better not tell Mike I said that." He winked. "If it wouldn't include a pay cut, I'd consider going federal and try for the National Labor Relations Board. Writing the decision after an arbitration is what's most satisfying for me. You get that about the writing."

Sheila rambled a bit about her own work and writing.

Their order came and conversation paused as the mouthwatering scent of fat burgers dripping melted cheese and plank cut fries filled the air. They chewed in happy silence broken by moans and exclamations. They compared the signature burger here to the Jucy Lucy at Matt's in Minneapolis and waxed nostalgic about their early years in the Twin Cities.

Finally, Ed looked across the table at Sheila. "Okay, Sheila." He smiled conspiratorially at her. "tell me why you called us. Sure, it's been a while, but I don't recall you ever inviting us out to dinner before. Spit it out, girl. It's not going to take me that much longer to finish this burger."

Sheila looked down at her own plate, empty except for streaks of cheesy grease, ketchup and one fry so burnt that even she found it inedible.

"Mike isn't sharing where he's at on the Vitale case. I want Craig's murder to be solved, obviously. It's even more important to me to know if he's found anything at all that leads back to Sam." She looked at him directly, and shrugged, "So sue me. How awful is it of me to ask you about that?"

"Sheila, never lose your inability to be subtle. Hate to disappoint you, but I don't have any new information about Craig's death or Sam's. If there was a break, Mike wouldn't hold out on you. You already know about those old cases in Iowa. The student from the university, a truck driver not far from Iowa City, a transvestite, and a couple more men along I-80. Mike said you wrote an article for the paper about the student. Nothing new there."

The transvestite is news to me.

"You win. No more talk about murder. Tell me a little more about the parts of writing a decision. Want to split a piece of cheesecake?" She wiggled her eyebrows, and he laughed.

"How can I say no to that?"

***

Sheila didn't turn on the television or open a book when she got home. She sat on her bed, listened to the sounds that made their way through her window. The sounds of traffic comforted her. It was the quiet that made her uneasy. She let her imagination take her places she didn't want to go. Was it a big deal that Mike never mentioned those other murdered men? Only the student, Jay. Why not the drag queen? That was a question with a capital *Q*. Mike had been like a second brother. Before Sam died, she considered Mike the better brother. But never mentioning the murder of a drag queen took some of the shine off "better."

She took out Marcus's business card. Ph.D. Forensic psychology, industrial psychology, and psychotherapy. She wanted to talk the case over with him, but Marcus only knew her as a would-be standup comic. And there was nothing funny about this. Sure, most comics had emotional wounds they tried to cover with laughs, but they hadn't played show-and-tell yet. She hadn't let him in on the trauma in her life—her connection with Craig Vitale—much less the decade-old wound of Sam's murder. What would he think of someone who hadn't been able to work through a ten-year-old loss, even if it was her brother's murder? *Why do I care what he thinks? Silly question. I care too much about what everyone thinks. Another chink in my armor.*

If she brought up Mike and the rest of the people from her small-town past, what did she expect Marcus to say? Would his opinion leave her feeling better or worse? *Only one way to find out.*

Finally, she had called him. After the initial riot of butterflies in her stomach, she found talking to him both energizing and relaxing. They had agreed to meet at an open mic the next day. She was willing to discuss his partners-in-comedy idea. She also wanted to get a better sense of him. Could she be a better comedian with him in the mix? Could he be an objective man she could talk to? And could his background in psychology help solve Craig's murder?

At the open mic, Marcus went up first. Sheila immediately saw it wasn't so much his material as him. He held the room. His jokes were a little too risqué for her taste, but he never crossed over the line into gross.

"There's going to be compromise with a capital C if we work together. Because the stuff that came out of your mouth will never come out of mine," Sheila said as she stirred milk and sugar into her coffee container. They were sitting on a ledge next to the comedy club. Marcus offered her half of his donut. She pushed it away. "I'm not so easily won over. Maybe an entire Boston crème."

Marcus was silent as he took another bite of the cinnamon sugared cake donut.

"You do yours, I do mine, but ours is what we agree on. Subjects we both want to write about, talk about, get laughs about. That's how I see it."

He licked the sugar off his thumb, slowly.

"Are you trying to distract me?"

"Of course. Is it working?"

"I'm still thinking. I'm considering all the angles of this. Let's meet the day after tomorrow. We both bring three ideas for bits. If we like how it goes, we'll get to work on a set for a showcase."

Marcus put out a sugar-free hand, "Agreed."

Chapter Fourteen

"How did Sheila seem last night?"

Mike tried to sound casual as he poured coffee for Ed and topped off his own. But he had been concerned as much as pleased that Sheila had suddenly asked them out to dinner. Sheila wasn't exactly a recluse, but after Sam's death she wasn't as outgoing as she had been. Loss and grief could do that to you. But after ten years? Billy might have a point about her needing to move on. Aside from work and comedy gigs, he had the impression that she was a solo act.

"Sheila and I had a nice dinner. She's smart, but she has no interrogation technique. It was clear she had an agenda for our dinner. Came right out and asked me if I knew anything about your current case and if there was anything that could tie it to Sam's murder. Said you'd been holding things back from her."

Mike sighed. "I suspected as much. Thanks for taking that one for me. I hope you didn't give her any new ammunition to ambush me with."

"No, I told her the truth. You haven't come up with any new leads, at least none you've shared with me. She did look a little surprised when I mentioned the other cases you'd investigated in Iowa. She seemed more wound up and I don't think it was the Coke she drank."

Mike paused midsip. He set his mug on the table with both hands. "What did you say about those cases?"

"I didn't think it was anything she wouldn't have known. There was the student from Iowa City—you said she wrote an article about his murder. Then there were a couple of other guys found along I-80, and the trans..." Ed's face fell as it dawned on him that Sheila might not have known about Cory. "Shit. I'm sorry, Mike. It never occurred to me that she didn't know about Cory."

"That's not your fault. That's on me. I'll talk to her. I need to think a couple things through first."

"After we'd gotten that out of the way we had a nice time. She seemed genuinely interested in my work and getting to know me," Ed said with a wistful smile. "You know, she really looks up to you. Don't let her independent act fool you, and don't be put off by her, uh, directness. She still needs you, and I think you need her."

Mike nodded and gave Ed's hand a squeeze. He saw Ed glance up at the sleek Canetti wall clock that hung above their table.

"Ed, do you have a few more minutes? I wanted to run something else by you."

"Sure. But if it has to do with Delmont or this case, maybe Billy would be a better person to check in with. I know you talked to him before that funeral, but have you had a chance to talk to him since? Seems to me he might know more about those cases in the past as well as the present one."

Chapter Fifteen

Sheila descended the stairs to her after-work destination, careful not to touch the wrought iron railing. God only knew what the shiny blobs that caught the late afternoon sunlight were. The Laugh Track Comedy Club was dark as a coal mine, and it took her eyes few minutes to adapt. She could make out the usual suspects: twelve T-shirt-and-jean-clad comic wannabes. Twelve angry men. Most likely all under thirty. She wasn't a genius at guessing ages. It was the same at every open mic. They all probably still lived at home and had empty pizza boxes and *Hustler* magazines under their beds.

I should talk. She gave a mental shrug acknowledging once again that her social life needed a life.

She signed up for a walk-in spot, paid for five minutes, ordered a Diet Coke, and looked around.

A guy wearing a Punisher T-shirt at the table behind her said to the Clash T-shirt guy, "Today's my birthday."

"Dude, how old are you?"

"Twenty-two," Punisher said.

"That was a good year. Twenty-five sucks," The Clash reflected.

No one asked her age or anything else. Not that she was much older than either of the T-shirt dudes, but she felt older. Even among these outsiders, she was an outsider. Comedy was still a guy's game.

Joan Rivers might be on the *Tonight Show*, but she was one of the exceptions. And she was no Joan Rivers. Tonight, Sheila was the only female in the room. The first three guys centered their whole set around masturbation.

Finally, the emcee called her name. On stage she felt the warmth of the spotlight on her face. She finished her five minutes and stepped down, thinking of the Zen koan: "What is the sound of one hand clapping?"

At least there was one person laughing—the emcee. "Not a bad set," he told her. "Sorry the house is empty."

The other comics had left. One by one, they shape-shifted out of The Laugh Track as soon as they finished their set. Nothing unusual. Some guys tried to make three open mics in one night. Their departure was nothing personal.

Literally the luck of the draw. At this open mic, you paid your five, the emcee put all the names in a fishbowl and drew them out. She'd been last... the "headliner."

She'd been hoping to see Marcus' name on the clip board or that by some chance he'd be in the audience. She'd found herself thinking of him. A lot. He intrigued her. And thinking about him kept her mind off other things.

The last time she ran into Marcus, they had a drink. That was when he told her about his day job.

"Despite an actual PhD, I reside in the adjunct circle of hell. I teach psychology at two colleges situated across town from each other. Assistant professor at one. So, you can dispense with the professor title, at least until I'm full time or a full professor."

Even without the title of professor, she'd been impressed. Her parents had always stressed the importance of education: "That's something no one can take away from you," her dad often said.

"My students wouldn't dare miss my lectures; I'm the biggest draw at the college," he'd said. She'd raised an eyebrow at that but kept from rolling her eyes.

She'd asked, "College lectures aside, how did you get your comedy chops?"

"There were breaks in my everyday schedule. I'd take a breather. I'd think about the ridiculous problems students and faculty members create and make them into bits. I had a few friends who were performing. Mostly music gigs. But now and then we'd all stop by one of the white-owned comedy clubs in Manhattan, like The Laugh Track. The lineup might include a black comedian—one, never two. I did a few of my bits for my friends. They laughed, but hell, they'd laugh at cockroaches crawling across a kitchen counter. I liked the idea of not having to answer or apologize to anyone for what I said. As we both know, laughs or no laughs are the only thing that counts."

She knew it, oh how well she knew it was the laughs that counted. Her delivery was better tonight. If only there'd been an audience. But it was still a thrill. Doing stand-up was still her creative outlet, her guilty pleasure. Every open mic still scared the hell out of her. She liked that about herself—she was scared, but she did it anyway. Like getting out of bed in the morning, wondering what new nightmare the day would bring. After Sam died, just getting out of bed had scared her.

She grabbed her bag and jacket and walked out of the darkened showroom into the brighter lights of the bar, past the pictures of the famous comics who'd performed there.

I'm so hungry, but I should go to the gym. While her fuel-starved brain tried to calculate how many calories she'd burned on stage, she had a eureka moment. If she walked up Third Avenue for twenty minutes before stopping for a slice of pizza, that would take care of her hunger without adding to her guilt about skipping the gym.

***

She was up to the door when she felt him. "Hey, Sheila. Sorry I missed your set."

"Just barely. I went up last."

"There's another open mic in half an hour at 32nd Street. If we hustle, we can get on the standby."

Suddenly, the accumulation of the day's frustration and exhaustion hit her full on. That gnawing inside. It wasn't only hunger, and she didn't have the energy to run from it now. She needed to talk to someone. Not Billy and not Mike. Maybe Marcus was the person she needed to talk to. *Take a chance.*

"I know this is unusual for me, but I don't think I've got it in me for another open mic."

He cocked his head as if he hadn't quite heard her correctly.

"Right now, I need a beer and pizza. And I need a consult with Marcus, the psychology professor."

He searched her eyes for a moment and nodded. "The professor is in. Hey, Marino's is a block away. You get a pitcher and a pizza, and I'll forgo my hourly fee."

"What a guy." Sheila meant to be a touch sarcastic, but the words sounded sincere. She needed to work on her delivery. "Deal."

Marino's was one of those old Manhattan standbys, a restaurant that had been in the same location for twenty-five years without ever being Zagat-rated. Marino's regulars were happy to order a pizza or spaghetti and meatballs and never venture toward the chicken scarpariello or veal marsala. Tables weren't on top of one another. That gave Sheila a small measure of comfort. Marcus ordered a fresh-garlic and pepperoni pizza and a pitcher of Italian beer.

The waiter always brought a basket of warm Italian bread, whatever the order. Sheila broke off a piece and played with the crust.

"Remember the night we met?"

Marcus nodded.

"One of my clients didn't show that day. He had a good excuse. He was dead. To be specific, he was murdered."

The waiter set down the pitcher like an exclamation point. Marcus poured for the two of them. "Tell me more."

"His name was Craig Vitale, and he was in finance. His death made all the papers."

"Sounds vaguely familiar."

The pizza arrived with the smell of fresh garlic stealing Sheila's attention. She slid a slice off the serving platter onto her plate, picked a piece of pepperoni off the slice, and popped it into her mouth.

"Craig's murder was more than a mention in all the papers. It was a big story, but it seems to have dwindled. Damn it, I never understand why they can't find the killer."

"It's not easy to catch a killer in New York City. Not that the police are inept. But there could be a million suspects here in the naked city. Like looking for a needle in a needlestack." Marcus took a sip of beer and continued. "I imagine that in a small town, where most people know or are related to almost everybody, it's easier. Not easy. Easier. This guy's murder must have come as a shock to you, Sheila. I came up hard. I've known people who were killed. Have you ever known anyone who was killed?"

She swallowed hard and cleared her throat.

"Right before he was to leave for college, my brother, Sam, was murdered."

Chapter Sixteen

Sheila dabbed her eyes with a napkin and waited while Marcus folded his slice and took a bite. She could feel his indecision, as if he wasn't sure where to take the conversation, but he started: "Like I said, I've seen my share of violence and even murder. Must admit, I didn't expect this from you, a white, Jewish girl coming out of a small Midwest town. I'm sorry for your loss. Want to talk about it?"

Sheila took a deep breath and shook her head. Her eyes glistened with unshed tears.

"How about we concentrate on Craig's murder, then? Okay if I ask you some questions?"

"Yes." Sheila took a sip of beer while Marcus took a long swallow from his glass.

"Was Craig married, or did he talk to you about his social life? He was in finance. Did he let on that he was in any kind of money bind?"

"Slow down, Marcus. Craig was a public relations client at my office. He wasn't married, at least not that I know of. We never discussed personal stuff. I can't be sure about girlfriends or boyfriends or any friends at all."

"Too bad, it's always the intimate partner," Marcus wiggled his eyebrows suggestively.

Sheila couldn't help feeling warmth spreading to her cheeks. She went on, "Craig said he was doing well, whatever that means, but he was always talking about expanding his income stream. Said he was more *entrepreneurial* than his partner wanted him to be."

Marcus raised an eyebrow at that last statement but didn't follow up on it.

"The first time you met Craig at your office, what were your thoughts about him?"

"First impression was negative. He showed up hungover and cranky. A thirty-something trust-fund brat. I gave him a cup of coffee, two Excedrin, and by the time he left, he was almost human. He apologized for not being at the 'top of his game.' He was slick, but almost too intense, obsessed with what he wanted to accomplish on his special project."

"And what was that project?"

"He wanted my help in writing an investor presentation for a new fund. He said he wanted it to be 'precisely vague.' I argued he had to be precise about his business model. I asked if he had seen that subway campaign where one exec says, 'Your business model is toast,' and the other exec says, 'At least toast has a business model.' He was not amused. I had a few concerns that this project wasn't too substantial. I have a copy of the little information he shared about this venture if you want to have a look."

"You know, I'm thinking of writing a book on the psychology of investing. Some insights from a study I was the primary investigator on. People don't realize how emotion can take control when they decide to buy their own stocks. It becomes too much like gambling. Like the song says: 'Gotta know when to hold 'em, know when to fold 'em.'"

"Marcus, you might be just the person I need." Sheila felt herself blush, but Marcus seemed nonplussed.

"Sure, I'll read it. If it was risky, that gave him more exposure."

"Exposure?"

"To rogue traders, con artists, and maybe someone with connections to organized crime. Of course, not having any knowledge of his personal relationships leaves us in the dark about the most likely perpetrator, someone close to him. And if he engaged in risky business in the office, he probably engaged in it in his personal life."

Sheila's breath caught at that suggestion.

They ate in thoughtful silence. Marcus broke it.

"Maybe this is a good time for me to let you into more of my history. Keep eating. You know I like to hear myself talk."

Sheila couldn't stop an eye roll.

"Before teaching, I was a prison psychologist upstate, not long after I got my PhD. The job had a perk: it paid off part of my grad-school loan if I stayed for two years. I had a fantasy that I'd write a seminal article at the end of my two years. But the work almost did me in. There was an incident, I misread an inmate. I insulted him, said I understood the scars on his wrist. Instant rage on his part.

I still remember every word of his rant: 'You don't understand shit, motherfucker. You got no right to be here. You're not tough enough. Somebody's gonna get you. You won't last.' I hadn't read him right. Jumped to a wrong conclusion. I apologized. He didn't back down, but he didn't ratchet it up, either. My supervisor said I handled the situation in an acceptable manner, but I didn't think so. The inmate calmed down, but I had felt a strong urge to beat him bloody. I gave my notice one week after the two years. I learned more than I wanted to know about the thoughts of killers. And that includes my own insight into the impulse to kill.

I never wrote the article. Came back to New York and started teaching. I've worked on industrial-psychology grants, the psychology of marketing studies, pet personalities, anything not related to those two years. Occasionally, I take on a patient for short-term therapy."

He took a deep breath as Sheila finished her beer. And then he looked into her eyes.

"Sheila, I'm not interested in being your therapist. But I like you and I know how to listen." He paused, waiting for her to respond. "I imagine that Craig's murder brings up some unfinished business about your brother's death. Do you feel a little more ready to tell me about him?"

Okay, okay, okay. Sheila closed her eyes.

"That whole year of my life was a blur. From the night the police chief came to our house to tell us Sam was... The first thing I really remember was Sam's funeral. It was the first funeral I'd ever been to. It was more than a week after Sam died. Between the police gathering whatever evidence and all our friends and relatives coming in from out of state, those extra days were needed, even though it went against Jewish tradition."

"Right, your people don't do the whole embalm and paint 'em and put 'em on display thing."

"Right. No open caskets. Just a shroud, a plain casket, the service, and burial."

She thought back to the funeral. Some people from Delmont who she thought would be there didn't come. Maybe they were afraid to set foot in a funeral that didn't take place in a church, maybe they didn't get why the Ross' couldn't hold a service in a church, or maybe they thought murder was contagious.

Snippets of funeral conversation came back to her: "Sheila, you people do believe in God and hell and the Devil, don't you?" That from one of the girls in her social studies class.

You people?

"One out of three," Sheila answered and never spoke to her again.

Marcus brought her back to the present: "Was his killer someone you knew?"

"That's the point, they never caught his killer. You're wrong about it being easier to find a murderer outside of New York. Not every small town gives up its secrets."

"It must have been very difficult for you and—"

"For everybody I knew. We all went a little crazy. I mean my friends and Sams's. Most of Sam's friends avoided me. My friends tried, at least they didn't desert me. But it was hard. We tried hanging out at new places, but there wasn't anywhere Sam hadn't been. Eventually things went back to the way they were before. That is, for everyone else. By the middle of August, no one talked about him much. At least, not around me. Everyone in our little group focused on what they were doing at the start of the school year, how they were excited about getting their learner's permits and Led Zeppelin's new album.

At first, I wouldn't cry around my parents, except one night when my mother made tuna-noodle casserole. Sam's favorite dish. I was pushing the peas around my plate, and my mother asked why I wasn't eating. 'Did you already forget, or is this meal a Freudian slip? Sam was the only one who ever asked you to cook this. Right, Dad?' My dad nearly choked. My mom looked like lightning had struck her. I admit, it was a lousy thing to say, but I couldn't help it.

We thought we had to be strong for each other, not let our feelings out. Around my friends, I tried to act like things were okay, but it wasn't a very convincing act. Sam wasn't just my big brother. He was my protector, my tormentor, and my mentor."

Sheila smiled and shook her head.

"He always pushed my buttons. He used to give me crap when I tried to tag along. One summer when we were little and still lived in St. Paul, we were playing in the yard, and he tried to convince me rabbit poop was chocolate-covered raisins. Luckily, I wasn't hungry enough. Back then I thought he hated me because I was in the way. But I think he wanted me to have my own friends and find my own way. I didn't always appreciate him. I was more than a little..."

"Jealous?" Marcus took her hand.

"Yes. We were like a rent-a-car commercial: he was Hertz, and I was Avis. Number two always has to try harder. Sometimes he made me so mad I could've strangled—" She gasped. It had just slipped out.

"Relax, fratricide is rare, so I'm not building your profile. Sibling rivalry, I'm sure you weren't immune to it."

"Not by a long shot. There were times when I was so angry at him. Angry at my parents for loving him more than me. You haven't told me where you are in your family lineup. But you don't know about a firstborn Jewish son. Automatic golden boy. My nickname for him was 'PS' for Perfect Son or Perfect Sam. To be honest, I did fantasize about what it would be like to be an only child getting all the attention and whatever I wanted. But I knew fantasy was all that was. After his death, I felt angry every day at everybody in that little 'American Gothic' town. It's both good for me and sad that so much has been diluted by time. I'm eternally grateful there's no Tractor Supply in Manhattan. One less reminder. But I still think of him, not every day like I used to, but I go a little crazy on his birthday and the anniversary of his murder."

"Not to pick at that psychic scab, but how far did they get with the investigation? You were old enough to hear gossip and read the newspaper and watch TV."

"That's just it, there was no gossip, nothing I ever heard, at least. Sam was popular. And he was a real straight arrow. Nope, there were no flies on Sam."

Marcus didn't challenge this statement. Sheila imagined he didn't want to push her.

"Well, I don't know about you, but it's been a full day. How about we talk about this more, another time. Can I give you a ride home? It's not out of my way."

She probably looked like she felt—at the end of her tether. She gratefully accepted his offer. They walked in silence the few blocks back to where his car was parked. She noted how clean the inside of the car was and let herself be comforted by the lingering masculine scent of his aftershave.

He walked her to the door where Anthony, the doorman had given them both a long look.

Marcus gave her a gentle pat on the back and a smile.

"Later, compadre," he said.

Sheila took the elevator to her tiny apartment trying not to think beyond the moment. She was more relaxed than she'd been all day. Thinking would only ruin it. Fortunately, the pizza and beer she had consumed with Marcus made her sleepy. She barely had time to slip into the oversized tee she slept in and plop onto her bed.

She totally missed the red message light blinking on her answering machine.

Chapter Seventeen

M ike stared at the phone on his desk. No message light blinking, no calls to return. He did have calls to make, and that was not energizing. Most people who answered a call from an officer of the law did so with reservation, distaste, and a touch of paranoia. Few were forthcoming with anything that proved worth the time the call took. Sometimes the only benefit was being able to cross a name or potential lead off the list and move on.

This case was killing them. Forget the critical forty-eight hours after the murder, they were way beyond that. He and Duane had been busting their asses to run down a handful of leads, and they had zilch. Two weeks had passed since Craig Vitale's funeral, and Mike felt pressure building. Not just from the top brass, he felt it inside.

He and Duane had interviewed everyone in Craig's immediate circle, from his parents to his girl of the month, Sarah Beal. Duane told him Sarah had seemed genuine and had burst into tears a couple times during the interview. She was twenty-something and pretty in a Heather Locklear sort of way. Mike thought he remembered her from the funeral. Sarah worked as a manicurist at the salon where Craig had his hair cut. In fact, she had been his manicurist. Craig had been enough of a metrosexual and narcissist to spring for a weekly shape-up and manicure. They'd only been dating a few months, but she thought they'd "really connected." As for Sarah's alibi, she'd been at a wedding shower for a coworker. The shower had been held in the party room of a midtown Caramba's. Wait staff remembered her because she'd paid for a round of aqua-blue margaritas.

Duane had asked her if Craig ever mentioned anyone he worked with. She told him that aside from "some old guy, his partner," the only other person he mentioned had been someone who "ran his numbers, like some human computer or something." Sarah thought she had seen her once when she and Craig were out for dinner. This woman had been giving them the "fisheye" from across the room, and Craig had stepped away from the table to talk to her. He hadn't introduced them, just told Sarah how he knew her. Sarah hadn't given her much thought as she "clearly wasn't Craig's type—too tall. Craig liked his women to have to look up at him."

The information Sarah provided had let them check off some boxes, but her mention of the tall woman at the restaurant would require more digging. And then there was the "old guy," Craig's partner, Sienna.

They had nothing from the doorman; of course, they hadn't checked him out yet. The guy said he'd only stepped away for a couple minutes, but it could have been ten or more. More than enough time for the killer to have entered through the back door that led out to the dumpster in the alley. It should have been locked, but the super admitted it was often wedged open.

Mike reread the crime-scene reports. It hadn't given them any prints, other than Craig's and Sarah's. No fibers or hairs, apart from Craig's and Sarah's. Except for a couple dog hairs. He noted that Craig didn't have a dog but guessed they were leftovers from a visit to his folks and the family dog.

Toxicology confirmed what they'd suspected, a common opioid dissolved in what appeared to be whiskey. There had been an open bottle of Glenlivet in Craig's kitchen. That would've gone down easily enough. Who would he have been drinking with other than Sarah? The killer tried to make it look like a sexual-bondage game. Had it been meant as an indignity or misdirection? It made Mike wonder about Sarah's alibi. She could have slipped away from the shower, done Craig, and returned. She'd sprung for those pitchers of margaritas. Had that been to keep her girlfriends too busy downing them to notice her absence?

Maybe Mike would have to talk to Sheila's new friend, Marcus, after all. This guy was a psychology professor. She wanted to involve him in her amateur-sleuth shenanigans. The idea did not sit well with Mike. Not that he didn't believe in the use of psychology in catching criminals, but he sure as hell didn't need any shrink looking too close at him. It had been less than a decade since psychiatrists stopped calling homosexuality a disease. But more to the point, it didn't make sense that this guy dropped out of the sky into Sheila's life one day, wanted to be her costar and best friend the next. Where in hell did this joker come from, anyway? Mike needed to see this guy's credentials. He'd have Duane run a background check.

Even if Marcus checked out, Mike's concern for Sheila made him leery of involving the two of them. He feared for her physical and emotional safety. He'd considered it luck that her past foray into investigative journalism involving a murder in Iowa hadn't gotten her hurt or killed. He remembered when an article she'd written on a case of his had put a scare into both of them after she'd received a threatening note. Nothing had come of it, and it had been an isolated incident. Still, it was a relief when she graduated from Iowa with her degree in journalism, then made a career move to advertising and public relations.

He lifted the receiver to call Billy. It bothered him that Billy knew Craig, but he had to admit that it was useful on more than one level. First, he'd ask him if he'd come up with a list of Craig's investors, past and present. See if any of them were in the crosshairs of any financial scandal investigations. If there was time, they could go over the well-worn tracks of their shared past in Delmont and Iowa City. Maybe seeing those years through Billy's eyes would give him another perspective.

Then he'd contact Craig's partner, the elusive Mr. Sienna. He'd talk to Sarah Beal again. It was worth bringing Craig's business buddy Kenneth Althorpe in too. None of those alibis were airtight.

Chapter Eighteen

Last night's beer woke Sheila's bladder and forced her from bed just before dawn. She caught the winking red light of her answering machine as she returned from the bathroom.

She could go back to bed without checking it, but she dreamily hoped it was Marcus. Calling to say goodnight? Good morning?

A female voice. Not Marcus. Damn. It was Jane. Would she like to meet for coffee this week? This was unexpected. Sure, she'd given Jane her card and there had been mention of coffee. She hadn't imagined Jane would call her. Sheila thought of the times she'd said the same thing to friends and acquaintances over the past several years. Regrettably few lunches, coffees, or nights out for drinks had resulted. So was that her fault?

Suzy and Renee, roommates when she had first moved to New York used to invite her out for drinks or to a concert and even fixed her up with someone from time to time. Despite some good times, she hadn't let them get too close. It had been a while since she'd talked to either of them. On the defense from her own inner critic, her response tended to be *phone lines work both ways.*

She sighed. No going back to sleep now, so she poured herself an orange juice and popped a frozen bagel into the toaster. Her inner defense continued: she was so busy. She'd built a career on being busy.

Hard work, long hours to facilitate the hop, skip, and jump career moves from one ad agency to the next provided her a reason to put social life on the back burner. She wasn't going to be promoted to work on the more prestigious corporate accounts if she lost that highly touted Midwest work ethic.

But everyone was busy. Competitively busy. Somehow other people seemed to manage to meet for lunch, for drinks, go to concerts. Other people had relationships. Was she truly busier than everyone else? So much so that she didn't have anything left for people or things outside work and her comedy. Or was it more like she was an emotional zombie? She had hung back from serious dating, too. She had so much survivor's guilt that she was stuck in a literal no-man's-land. Had she convinced herself she didn't deserve love?

She preferred to think she'd merely put parts of her life on hold. It was "ducks in a row" thinking. Each part in place before she could move on to the next. Sam's death had blown those ducks out of the water and the only way to set things right again was to solve Sam's murder. She felt it more urgently since Craig's death.

Sheila's conversation with Marcus had felt like flipping a light switch on. The dark, haunted place in her head wasn't quite so threatening, for now. Maybe she'd be able to look more closely and see, really see all the things that made her want to turn and run. Not just things in the past about Delmont and Sam. Things now. Why did she have such a visceral reaction when she learned about Craig? Her stomach roiled and her throat tightened. *The orange juice was talking back.*

Sheila took a deep breath, then another. She reminded herself that this was not about Sam. This was Manhattan, nineteen eighty-two, not Delmont, nineteen seventy-two. She took a bite of bagel, then dialed the number Jane had left. *Freezer burn. Yuck.* She tossed it.

"So, you're an early riser, too?" Jane said. "You can take the girl out of the Midwest and all that."

"Guess so. It was nice of you to call." Sheila was at a loss for further small talk with so little coffee in her. She said, "I've got time for coffee today if you do."

"I can meet you at nine, I've got an errand to run for work first. I'm in the financial district."

Sheila groaned inwardly. No time for the long hot shower she needed. "Chock Full O'Nuts on 34th Street?"

"Perfect. Quick and not too far. See you there."

***

Jane was waiting at the counter, an empty spot beside her, sipping her coffee when Sheila arrived. Sheila wasn't sure what a cup of coffee would do to her stomach. She got one anyway.

"Sheila, I'm glad you called me back. I was surprised to see you at that funeral. I didn't mean to just split afterwards. I wouldn't want you to think I was being rude." Jane arched a brow.

Sheila nodded. "It's okay." She thought of all the times back in high school she'd been rude to Jane. She thought of heir stilted relationship when Jane tutored her in math. They had a complicated past—not exactly friends, but not enemies. They seemed to keep running into each other. Maybe Jane had seen Sheila's proffered business card as an olive branch. Maybe Jane felt isolated, too. Maybe she'd seen the slick card embossed with art deco elements as a lifeline. Sheila warmed to Jane's new openness.

"So, tell me about life in the financial world. What's it like to work for Elliot Robinson?"

"Robinson is larger than life. Big guy, big belly. Wears a different pair of suspenders over a new Brooks Brothers shirt every day and it's a good thing because half his lunch ends up on the front of his shirt." Jane smirked. "But he's a smart man and he's always one step ahead of everybody else. I've followed his newsletter since college days. He's been a great mentor. Sure, he's quirky, but I've got him figured out. I know how to work his angles."

"Sounds like quite a character. It must be a fascinating job. I knew math was your thing, obviously, but were you always interested in working on Wall Street?"

"Sheila, you know how poor we were growing up." Jane's face was solemn. She shrugged. "Then again, maybe you didn't. Trust me, it sucked. All I knew was that I wasn't going to be poor once I got out of Delmont. I've always had a head for business. I started cleaning houses, anything to make money back in high school."

Sheila nodded. Jane hadn't tutored her in math out of the goodness of her heart, Sheila's parents had paid her. Generously.

"I had a plan. Of course, it changed a bit as I got older, but I always saw myself in a big city. Didn't you? I know you hated Delmont nearly as much as I did. You weren't from a dinky town. You were different. That's what Nancy saw in you." A distant look clouded Jane's face.

Nancy had been Jane's friend before she'd been Sheila's. Then the two of them had shut Jane out. Sheila flushed and looked away.

"It didn't always feel good to be different," Sheila said. "You're right, I couldn't wait to get out of Iowa. When I left, I felt I had nothing to lose." Sheila found her throat tightening and her eyes prick with the start of tears. *No. Don't cry.* She took a big gulp of coffee and stared into her cup. She looked up to find Jane watching her. She swirled her cup and set it down.

Jane said, "I'll never go back there."

There was a note of alliance in that statement. They'd more than broken the ice. Now Sheila had more questions for Jane. Not about back then, but about now.

"I keep thinking about Craig," Sheila said. "It's so strange that we both knew him."

"Not surprising that I knew him," Jane said. "We were in the same industry. But how'd you manage to snag his PR account? Isn't Hummingbird a small agency?"

"I wondered that, too. He told me that he sought out a small, trendier agency because he wanted to keep things quiet until he was ready to roll out this new project. I just happened to be available."

"Makes sense, I guess," Jane said.

"What doesn't make sense is that someone murdered him. Who would want to kill him?"

Jane shook her head. "It's a big city. Murder's an everyday occurrence. Not like. . ." she trailed off. "Who knows? With all the nut jobs running around in this city it might not have even been personal."

Sheila scoffed, "Not personal? From the newspaper articles I've read, it sounded pretty personal. It sounded like he knew his killer. He opened the door to him."

Jane shrugged. "Craig knew a lot of people. Between his parents and workplace, I imagine he moved in lots of circles." She hesitated, then said, "some weren't so nice."

"The first time I met him, he showed up to our appointment hungover. He admitted that much to me." Sheila sighed and drained her cup.

"He'd been to rehab multiple times. At least that was the talk around the water cooler at the firm we both started out at. Who knows what else he was mixed up in?"

"But this didn't sound like a drug deal gone wrong."

"Oh? Has Mike Sloan has been sharing information with you?"

Sheila gasped, "No!" When she saw a smile play across Jane's face, she recovered. "He's not sharing anything with me."

"Of course not. He's too professional for that. Like his old man. I suppose we'll just have to wait and let him do his job before we find out more. Let's hope he can catch this killer," Jane said. She glanced at her watch, "I'm sorry but I've got to go. She touched Sheila's arm and said, "Let me get the check. I'm glad we got together."

"Thanks, Jane. I'm glad we did, too. Next time it's on me. Let's not wait ten years."

Jane left the shop, but Sheila stayed at the counter. It hadn't been as awkward talking to Jane as she'd anticipated. Jane had been surprisingly easy to talk to. Or maybe Sheila was lonelier than she'd let herself know. It felt good to have someone here besides Billy and Mike who shared her Midwest perspective. Her appetite had returned. She was thinking of having the date nut bread with cream cheese.

She wiped the last crumbs of date nut bread from her mouth while she thought about her conversation last night with Marcus and her conversation just now with Jane. Marcus had asked Sheila if she knew anyone from Craig's past or his girlfriends. *It's always the intimate partner.*

Craig's murder might involve something from *his* past, but surely it involved his project. *Was there something about Craig's project that would make someone murder him?* If Mike and his partner Duane had turned up anything, they weren't letting the public know about it. She cursed their close-mouthed professionalism. She was determined to help. She couldn't stand by as a useless observer this time. There had to be more if she went over her work on his project. It was their only point of connection and her only real source. Wasn't it?

Mike had mentioned Craig's girlfriend, Sarah, who had been Craig's manicurist as well as love interest. Mike had let slip that she was at a salon in the financial district. *Salon Renee*. Sheila thought she might be able to get a little more out of her than Duane and Mike had. Woman to woman. It was worth a manicure appointment. She looked at her nails and sighed. It wouldn't be hard to convince Sarah that she had a nail emergency.

She wasn't cluing Mike in until after she'd met Sarah. She didn't want him smothering the first idea she'd had that might shed some light on who Craig Vitale had been. She might need to use her improv skills as well as her journalist skills to make Sarah divulge personal information beyond the condition of Craig's cuticles.

***

The salon Sarah worked in felt tony. It was furnished in sleek brass and smoked glass, with gray, beige, and teal chairs upholstered in an art deco print. An elegant chandelier lit the reception area. All the manicurists wore gray skirts with gray-and-beige tunics. Sarah's demeanor as a manicurist struck the right balance between professional and easy warmth.

"You aren't the neon-nail type. But hot pink with a hint of coral would suit you. It's one of the new spring colors." She suggested the perfect shade. Her manicure table was immaculate. In a soft voice, Sarah chatted her up making it easier for Sheila to ask a few questions in return. After a little weather-and fashion-related small talk, Sheila got down to business.

"Sarah, I asked for you because I heard you're one of the best." She waited while Sarah's smile widened, and a blush spread from her neck to her face. "And, not to upset you, but I worked with Craig Vitale. He's our connection."

Sarah put down her nail file. Her smile vanished, and the blush on her face deepened.

"I don't know what you want, but I don't think I care to answer. The little time I had with Craig was our time. We didn't talk about work or other people. Pretty sure he never mentioned you. Besides, I've already had a chat with two policemen."

"Detective Sloan and Detective Corrigan. I know them too."

"Am I supposed to say, 'good for you?' Why are you here asking questions? You're not from some trashy rag like the *Post* are you?" Sarah narrowed her eyes. "What are you after?"

"I'm sorry, Sarah. As someone recently pointed out to me, subtlety isn't my strong suit." She took a deep breath and plunged right in. "Ten years ago, my brother was murdered in our hometown, back in Iowa. Right after he graduated high school. The police never found his killer. Craig was killed the same way my brother was. There were other men murdered in the years between my brother's murder and Craig's. Men killed the same way." Sheila looked at Sarah. "No one was ever arrested. It's been haunting me for ten years. The feeling grows stronger every year that his murder goes unsolved. You might still be in shock, or maybe Craig didn't mean that much to you. I don't know. It's different to lose your own flesh and blood, I guess." She sighed and looked into Sarah's heavily mascaraed eyes. "Sarah, I'm just after anything you remember about Craig that would help. I want to find his killer as much as you do, maybe more."

Sarah's pretty mouth turned down, and her smooth brow creased as sadness replaced the tension in her face. She played with her gold-and-pearl nameplate necklace while she looked Sheila over.

"That's a terrible story. I'm sorry for you."

"Thanks." *How to make the most of this flicker of sympathy?* "That's a pretty necklace."

Sarah smiled, then lowered her head.

"A gift from Craig?"

"Yes. One thing about him, he liked to impress. This was to mark our first date. Can you imagine?"

Sarah picked up the nail file and began to work on Sheila's right hand.

"You can see why it's important to me to find who killed Craig, can't you?"

"Round or square shape?"

"Round. Sarah, you want Craig's murderer locked up forever, don't you? You understand I'm not being nosy for the hell of it."

Sarah gave a little shrug as she continued to shape Sheila's nails.

"Did Craig ever introduce you to any of his work buddies?"

"More like one of them introduced me to Craig. A couple of those men were customers here at the salon. Craig walks in with my twelve-fifteen appointment, and the guy takes Craig's hand, puts it on mine, says something like, 'Sarah, this is Craig. Craig, Sarah. Sarah, take him in *hand*, and see what you can do with him.' He laughed one of those sleazy laughs. The guy was a jerk. But Craig seemed different. Sure, he was handsome, but there was something sweet and soft about him. I liked him, and he liked me, right away."

"What was your twelve-fifteen's name?"

"Kenneth Althorpe."

Althorpe, Kenneth. Wonder if Mike has checked him out.

"Was he one of Craig's investors?"

"I have no idea. Craig seemed to know him from business, and I didn't ask. I was kind of relieved when Mr. Althorpe quit coming to the salon. All the facials and manicures in the world couldn't change him. I could shine up his outside, but he was no diamond in the rough. He was just a lump of...”

“Coal?”

“Something like that. The only thing he ever did for me was introduce me to Craig.”

“Is it too personal of me to ask if you’ve been to Craig’s place?”

Sarah glared at her and blew out a breath between pursed lips.

“Yes, it is, and yes, of course. Couldn’t very well bring him up to mine. Not with two roomies in a one-bedroom walk-up. Besides, he wanted to show me he’d made it. Like I said, Craig always liked to impress. It was a nice place too. Real elegant. Not a lot of stuff, but it was all quality. He spent a fortune on the furniture. Four thousand bucks for one chair, if you can believe it. He told me this old, corny joke: ‘What’s the best way to make a small fortune in the stock market? Start off with a big one.’ He said he was going to do the opposite.”

“How was he going to do that?”

“He talked about some secret investment strategy he had.”

“Did he mention what that was or any of his investors?”

“No. At first when we started dating, he told me all sorts of stuff. It didn’t mean anything to me, but he liked to talk, and I let him. But he got very secretive about things. Cancelled dates on me a couple times. Made me wonder if he was seeing someone else, you know?”

“Was he?”

She shook her head. “I don’t think so. I think my only competition was this project of his, but there was something. . .” She frowned, “Something was bothering him. He started drinking again. That really upset me. It made me think he’d started using stronger stuff again.”

“Had he?”

“No. Good whisky was his thing. Single malt. But I was keeping an eye on him, you know counting bottles, making sure he didn’t have drugs stashed around his apartment. One night, he caught me poking around in his desk drawer, and he freaked out. He never yelled at me or laid a hand on me, but I'd never seen him so uptight. I asked him what the big deal was. A girl's got to feel safe. See, I found a tape recorder inside the bottom drawer of his desk. He likes, I mean *liked*, a lot of sexy talk and sounds. I made him pinky swear that he'd never record us while we were getting it on. He promised it was only to keep two of his 'subordinates' in their place. You're welcome to that tidbit if it means anything to you. And I'm sure you're going to leave me an *extremely* generous tip, so thanks."

She rolled Sheila's chair to the dry bar and stuck her hands under the UV lamp.

***

The minute Sheila got back from her appointment with Sarah, she called Mike. "Mike, when I went to Sarah for a manicure, she opened up to me. Stop me if any of this is old news."

"What do mean she opened up to you? Why didn't you tell me you were going to see her? Sheila, I've told you—"

"She's at a great salon, and she comes highly recommended. Can't a girl get a manicure? Anyway, she told me Craig recorded most of his conversations. Maybe he recorded something someone didn't want recorded. She also mentioned the man who introduced them, Kenneth Althorpe. That business associate of Craig's. Sarah thought he was a real creep. I'd be glad to check him out. It won't be a big deal for me to follow up with what details I can get on the guy. He sounded like a scumbag, maybe even one of *those associates*."

"Sheila. I know who Althorpe is. He was the guy who found Craig dead. He was supposed to meet him, and Craig never showed. The guy was worried and went looking for him when he couldn't get ahold of him. We've talked to him already. Is this the hundredth or thousandth time I've told you to stay out of this? Knock it off. The bits of information you bring are not worth the risk. Not to the investigation or to you. Listen to me. Please."

Anger and hurt flared in her chest, and although she tried to tamp it down, she growled, "No, you need to listen to me. Sounds like you've got nothing."

Silence on the other end.

She calmed her breathing. She said tersely, "The least you could do is follow up on Althorpe. Craig's girlfriend is suspicious of him and if you dig a little deeper, I bet you find something. You're wrong about the information I've given you. There's something important there. Damn it, Mike, you need to quit treating me like Sam's little sister."

Chapter Nineteen

Mike stared dumbly at the receiver in his hand. He shook his head. *Sheila, Sheila. I understand Sam's frustration with you better and better.*

Duane looked up from his notepad, "What was that about?"

"Sheila. She just talked to Vitale's girlfriend. Now she's fixated on Althorpe."

"The guy that found the body."

"Yep. Sarah, the girlfriend, didn't like him."

"The girlfriend struck me as somebody who was not an especially great judge of character. Maybe she had history with him," Duane offered.

"Sounds like it. Okay, the guy wasn't prince charming. Maybe his rep as a real estate developer isn't squeaky clean. He's still got as good an alibi as Vitale's other business associate."

"Sienna."

"Right. Long as we're looking at business ties, let's see if Sienna had anything going with Althorpe. And anyone else the vic had business with."

"Did you get hold of the numbers person for Vitale's project?"

"Not yet. But I think I've got an idea of who to talk to next."

Chapter Twenty

Mike had tracked Jane Brown through DMV records. The address didn't ring any bells with him. It might be an older building that crouched between newer ones, towered over by monstrosities with their own zip codes. He thought it might not be too far from Craig's modern glass-and-concrete condo. Did that matter? Mike still didn't know half the people in his own building, much less the ones on the next block.

Jane owned a car and a nice one at that. She must be doing well—better than well. New Yorkers often wore their wealth on their backs, because most of them lived in apartments and had little space to devote to larger symbols of success. But the fashionably elegant clothes Jane had worn to the funeral were matched by her elegant, if ostentatious, Lincoln. Mike wondered where she kept the car and what that cost—nearly as much as her car payments or apartment rent, he'd guess.

He'd been thinking of the years when they both had lived in Delmont. She was two years younger than him. There'd been nothing to make her stand out in his memory, and by the time he was eleven he'd begun to suspect that he didn't feel the same way about girls that other guys did. She'd been nearly invisible to him. If he tried, he could recall seeing her from time to time at the grocery store or out walking. She'd always been alone.

No, that wasn't true. Mary had said that she used to talk to Jane and her little sister, Peggy, when she saw them. She used to see Nancy, Sheila's friend, at the Browns' house. Jane and Nancy had been close once. Mike knew some kids changed best friends like they changed T-shirts, and Nancy had always been outgoing and popular. But when did Nancy and Jane stop being friends? Probably not long after Jane's father had left them. Mrs. Brown had been well on her way to becoming an alcoholic even before that. A hell of a lot of loss for a kid to handle.

Mike could relate. He'd been seven when he'd lost his older brother. Ten-year-old Joseph Jr. had been on his way to ball practice when the car he was riding in was hit by a truck. Joe had lived a few agonizing days, then succumbed to massive internal injuries. Mike's parents had never gotten over the loss of their firstborn son. He'd never gotten over the loss of his big brother either. But they all had dealt with Joseph Jr.'s death in different ways. His mom's tender heart had become more tender, while his father's had grown callous in response to his pain.

He guessed that Jane's reaction to loss was more like his father's. That might account for her seeming lack of emotion after the Mahoneys' disappearances and after Sam's murder. She'd kept her head down and her nose to the grindstone. She had wanted to get out of Delmont as soon as she could—same as he, Sheila and Billy had. And they had all gotten out. But the years and miles they'd put between themselves, and their hometown hadn't been enough. Because he couldn't shake the feeling that a murderer had followed them all the way to Manhattan.

✱✱✱

He'd left two messages and was about to leave another when Jane picked up. Her voice was calm and pleasant.

"Jane, this is Mike Sloan. Have you got a minute?"

"Are you calling me in an official capacity, Detective?" She sounded light, teasing.

"I didn't have a chance to say more than hello when I saw you at the funeral. I was surprised to see you there. I hadn't realized you were in New York."

"I was just as surprised to see you. I'm happy to catch up on old times, but I confess I haven't been back to Delmont in years, pretty much since I graduated high school."

"I see." He paused for a moment. "Jane, you're right, I'm calling because you knew Craig Vitale. I understand you two worked in the financial sector, and I believe you said he'd gotten you your current job. Did I get that right?"

"Not exactly. I think what I said was that we had a mutual friend who indirectly introduced me to my current employer." Jane paused, waiting for his confirmation. Mike let her wait. She asked, "What is it that you wanted to talk to me about?"

"I was hoping you could tell me more about Craig. We're investigating his murder and talking to anyone who knew him, who might have seen him in the days or weeks before his death. Had you seen him recently?"

"I'd spoken to him the week he died, about business, nothing personal. We didn't have that sort of relationship."

"What sort of business matters did you discuss?"

"Craig had wanted me to crunch some numbers for him. Nothing too tough. Not for me anyway."

"Had he hired you to do that?"

"I wasn't his employee. You could call it contracted work."

"And did he pay you?"

"He hadn't." Jane paused, then scoffed. "I guess I can kiss that money good-bye. At least it wasn't a make-or-break job for me."

"Won't his estate pay you? Isn't that usually how it works?"

"I imagine that could take some time," she sighed. "Are we done? I was just going out."

"Sure, just one more thing. Where were you on April thirteenth?"

"At home, just putting the finishing touches on my tax returns. I sent them in the next morning. Got them postmarked at the post office, eight in the morning."

"Was anyone with you that night? Did you speak to anyone?"

"I spoke to the receptionist in our office early in the evening. I'd thought I'd left a folder on my desk."

"Did you go to the office to get it?"

"Turns out I didn't need to; I found it at home."

"And you didn't leave your apartment any other time that night."

"No."

"I'd like you to come down to the station sometime this week to make an official statement. The house is close to the Financial District. Or if that's not convenient I could stop by your office."

"I'll make time to come to you. I'll be in and out of the office since my boss is out of town. I can make time Thursday. I'm an early riser; is eight too early for you?"

"That'll work. I appreciate you coming in. See you then."

Jane said that she'd been in New York since she'd graduated from Iowa. That would have put her here in seventy-eight. She'd been in Iowa for part of the time he'd been back there. When she'd left for New York, he'd still been working active cases in Iowa. What had she been up to in the two years before he'd returned?

Chapter Twenty-One

Sheila was still doing a slow burn after her conversation with Mike. Infuriating to be talked down to and dismissed. If Mike wasn't going to act on what Sarah had revealed, she would figure out where to go with that information herself. But she needed a break from thinking about it. Her stand-up sideline offered a different kind of challenge, and it was just the right kind of distraction. So was Marcus.

She and Marcus had similar ideas for bits, and she started to feel more at ease. It seemed natural to work with him. She also had talked to the emcee. Yes, he knew Marcus from his open mic performances, and a couple of conversations. And yes, he thought Marcus was an 'ok guy.'

After she had a conversation with herself she concluded that this would be a comedy experiment. A journalistic endeavor, too. Even if their act went nowhere she might be able to write a piece about it and sell it, somewhere.

She hoped the material she and Marcus had come up with for their upcoming showcase would really gel. Was she deluding herself that they were good together onstage because she wanted it to be true?

The showcase they had a spot in was only weeks away and they hadn't rehearsed much.

Marcus showed up at her apartment with two containers of coffee and the large movie theater-size box of Junior Mints.

"As the saying goes, 'Candy is dandy,' and I need a hit of sugar and caffeine. How about you?" he asked as he poured mints into her open hand before she could protest.

The rest of that saying crossed her mind: *But liquor is quicker, and sex won't rot your teeth.* She said, "Good thing those aren't Raisinets."

Marcus smiled and said, "What would you say to us working on more than our next stand-up bit?"

"Obviously you have an idea. When you sound vague, you're usually hinting at something specific you have in mind." *I've got some things in mind too.*

There was so much she wanted to discuss with him that she didn't mind missing a chance to rehearse or catch an open mic. They settled in on her secondhand sofa, and she took a sip of coffee. She looked at him over her cup, letting herself sink into his warm brown eyes. So there was *that*. She surprised herself thinking, *Let's work on more than our stand-up. What would happen if I said it?*

Marcus said, "Could you handle it if we sort out some pieces of this murder puzzle?" He stirred a packet of sugar into his coffee.

That burst her warm bubble. But Marcus was right on time. She'd been stewing in frustration and anger at Mike for trying to keep her out of the investigation.

"Could I handle it? You don't get me. That's all I've been trying to do. But what about Mike? He's warned me off, right before you got here, in fact."

Marcus leaned in and gave her a conspiratorial look. "Mike may not agree, but the enlightened detectives I know will accept help from wherever they can get it. And that includes psychics, nosy neighbors, amateur sleuths, and psychologists. I've worked case studies on a variety of killers. What type of killer are we dealing with? I think we need to consider that."

Sheila raised her brows, her curiosity piqued. "Such as?"

Marcus continued with relish. "There are the visibly angry ones. Like growling junkyard dogs. They didn't bother me much. The ones who got to me were the quiet ones. Ready to tell you every detail of their acts in a monotone and with zero affect. Some of them never wanted publicity. The kill was enough. Especially if they could find a way to relive it."

Marcus was on his feet now, and Sheila felt his intensity as he almost acted out a scene for her.

"Then there were the ones who felt supercharged after the first death. Wanted the new thrill that only another death could bring. And then another. For some of those, it was the notoriety. A competition, a game. The one with the most kills wins. So, I ask you, what kind of killer was Craig's?"

Sheila shivered. "A successful one."

"Too true." Marcus nodded. Then he sat down next to her. "Sheila, I still have a 'rabbi' down at One Police Plaza, a lieutenant who looked out for me before and after my work upstate. He told me I had a crap start but that it was a detour. He urged me to be a criminal or forensic psychologist. Forensic psych is only about twenty years old, but he swears it's going to be important. If forensic psych were a stock, he said he'd buy it. I admit, although I want to help, I have something to prove, mostly to myself. I want to hone my forensic-psychology skills, get out and use them in the real world."

"You mean working on Craig's murder investigation?" Sheila was wary, not sure what part she wanted Marcus to play in all this. She was the one who wanted, *needed*, to be involved.

"Would you mind if I call Mike now? You can listen."

Her mouth had gone dry. She wanted to protest, but she didn't want to shut Marcus down. She took a sip of coffee and shrugged. She listened as he punched in Mike's number.

"Detective Sloan? This is Sheila's friend, Marcus."

Pause.

"No, Sheila's fine. Yes, I'm fine too. Thanks. Hey, Sheila might have mentioned, I've got some experience in forensic psychology, and I think my perspective might be useful. I've worked as a prison psychologist. My interest isn't only as a friend of Sheila's but as a professional. I'd like a chance to assist in any way I can."

There was a pause, then Marcus responded. There was another pause. Marcus looked animated but continued in an even tone. "Sheila and I have been talking about Craig Vitale's murder. She's told me it brings up memories of her brother's unsolved murder. She said there were other unsolved murders in Iowa that had some things in common with her brother's. Did the police department or another agency try to involve a forensic psychologist?"

A long pause while Marcus listened nodding his head.

"Right. Like I said, it's a field that's gaining momentum and I know resources are tight. That's why I'd like to offer my services, pro bono."

A brief exchange of pleasantries followed, and the conversation ended.

That was quick. Sheila thought Marcus sounded neutral enough. But she also thought Mike was stubborn enough not to give anyone from the outside, including Marcus, an inch.

Marcus returned to stirring his coffee.

"Mike said he was glad to hear from me, and sure, he'd welcome my professional input. He said he'd call me. End of conversation. Do you know if he's worked up a psychological profile?"

"If he has it's without any of my non-professional input," Sheila said.

Marcus raised an eyebrow and continued, "When there's not much physical evidence, motive counts even more. And motive derives from internal combustion. External events triggering internal pressures. You've drained your considerable brain to Mike. But dredge it all up one more time for me. Starting with Craig and working your way back to Sam."

Sheila tried not to react when Marcus said her brother's name. It was a prick of pain, and Marcus must have noticed. He turned his sympathetic-shrink look on her and was about to say something, but she cut him off.

"Marcus, the time to tippy-toe around my feelings is over. What's our first step?

"You said you weren't familiar with Craig's personal life, but of course, you were with Sam's. This might sound odd, but did you keep Sam's high school yearbook?"

"Sam's room has been frozen in time since the day he was killed. If you think it's important, I can ask my dad to express mail it." *Damn, it's been over a week since I spoke to them. Might as well kill two birds with one call.*

"It's a little thing but ask him. Your brother's personality is part of the profile. If I said Sam's outstanding personality trait was his willingness to help others, would you agree?"

"Yes."

"Admirable. But that also makes him a little naive."

Sheila bristled at that assessment. She wanted to object to Marcus calling Sam naive, but it was true.

"He was a good guy who thought everyone else was basically good too," she said.

"It's not always what you do but who you do it with. The company you keep. Is there anyone you remember Sam hanging with who was not a good choice?"

"Not exactly, but the night of his senior prom, he mixed it up with his date's ex-boyfriend. He also helped Mike with a few of their teammates. Mike was the better player, but Sam smoothed a few ruffled feathers. Not sure what precipitated it, but now that I see Mike more clearly, it makes sense."

Sheila was sure Marcus had read between the lines. *Change the subject before he says word one about Mike.*

"Sam had a part-time job at Tractor Supply. He never talked about it much, other than he could have used a few more hours and better pay. I'm trying to recall if he mentioned anyone who gave him a hard time at the job. I went back there with Mike a year after Sam's murder. Mike was home for the summer because his mom had been diagnosed with cancer. I made him take me back there to talk to Sam's manager to see if there'd been anyone at the store that day who had seemed suspicious or who Sam had trouble with."

"Take your time. Memories don't always come up on demand."

"Sam had a customer his boss remembered," Sheila said, her mind already back there.

***

She felt the blast of cool air and smelled the bags of lawn products heavy with pesticide, cedar chips, and wood as the automatic doors of Tractor Supply opened. Gene was back in customer service leaning against the counter, a can of Diet Pepsi in his hand. Gene Packer had been fiftyish, with a solid build still winning the fight against gravity. He greeted Mike with an outstretched hand and a smile, but his smile faded when he saw Sheila.

"Hi Mike, good to see you," he said. He nodded to Sheila. "Young lady, not a day goes by we don't think of your brother."

"Me too," she said.

"Gene, that's kind of why we're here," Mike said. "I can see the store's really busy today, but is there any way we can talk to you in private for a few minutes?"

Gene looked puzzled. "Sure. Let's go in the office. If someone needs me, they know where to look."

He sat down behind his desk, piled with stacks of invoices and notepaper.

"Pull up a couple of those deluxe folding chairs over there and tell me what's on your mind."

"Thanks," Mike said. "Sheila and I thought that maybe in the time that's passed you, or one of Sam's coworkers, might have remembered something. Do you remember Sam having trouble with anyone or anything out of the ordinary? Did he seem troubled or upset to you? I know my dad and Officer Piper have probably asked the same sort of questions, but I was hoping there'd be some little thing you thought wasn't important enough to tell them back then that stayed with you."

Gene turned his palms up on the desk, looking as if he were trying to read something on them.

"You know, I've gone over it in my mind so many times. It was an ordinary day. Sam worked in the farm-and-garden section restocking.

He had a few customers; one guy I remember sort of stood out. Tall, kind of overdressed. Nice shirt, khaki pants, expensive shoes. He bought some steel pipe, a shovel, and work gloves. Not your typical plumber type. No butt crack showing." Gene chuckled. "Something familiar about him, but he wasn't a regular. Sam waited on him. It's the only thing I can think of. I was looking at our inventory in that area this morning, and that's probably why it came to mind. Need to order more of that half-inch galvanized pipe."

"Is there any way you can tell us the guy's name or the company's name if he was working for someone?"

"Mike, that needs to come from your dad, or someone involved in the investigation. I don't want to make trouble for a customer. I'm not even sure I have the information. If it was a cash sale, there wouldn't be anything but a copy of the register tape. Tell you what, I'll look, and if I've got a name, I'll tell your dad."

Mike turned to Sheila and said, "Was there anything you wanted to ask?"

She shook her head. "Thanks, Mr. Packer."

"Sorry, honey. Everybody here liked Sam. We were all real tore up about what happened to him."

Chapter Twenty-Two

The remembered scene flashed by in an instant. Sheila looked at Marcus who'd been waiting patiently for her to speak. She shook her head. "His boss couldn't tell us much. One customer came to mind."

Marcus looked at her expectantly.

Sheila sighed. "The manager only remembered the guy because he was better dressed than their usual customer. But in the end, no. Probably another weekend gardener or homeowner trying to be handy. It was a cash transaction anyway. No trail to follow."

Marcus nodded, and they lapsed back into silence for a few minutes. Marcus shook the last Junior Mints from the box into his hand and held one out to Sheila. *Sweet of him.* She popped it into her mouth and let the chocolate coating dissolve while she tried to focus on something other than Marcus's hand.

"So, have we talked about who you and Sam knew from Delmont besides Mike? Billy was part of your group back then, right? Was he a friend to Sam or only to you?"

"Billy was friendly with Sam, but they weren't friends. Billy and Mike had more in common because their fathers were in law enforcement. Billy's father was the county prosecutor, and Mike's was the police chief. They saw a lot of each other back then. Billy was and still is trying to steer me away from the case. He told Mike that I had an unhealthy need to make Sam's murder a large part of my everyday life, even after ten years." Sheila felt herself flush with anger. "He has some nerve. Billy's lucky I still talk to him."

Sheila saw the frown on Marcus's face as he looked into her eyes. "Not everyone has attachment to each other the way your family has. Not everyone grows up with an emotional structure."

"Cut the shrink jargon, please. What's an emotional structure, in twenty-five words or less?"

"Maybe a safety net is a better way to put it. You felt safe enough within your family to say things to each other and more importantly to express feelings, both good and bad. Not everyone is so lucky."

"I never looked at it that way."

"You said there are so many days when thoughts about Sam run through your mind. Write them down. You don't have to make sense of it. When we get together, let's look at what you wrote. In the meantime, I might do a bit of research on my own."

Sheila felt like he was shutting her out, keeping her away from something he didn't want to reveal. Gently closing a door. And it left her feeling alone.

***

The left-out feeling didn't dissipate. Irritation joined it.

Of course, I can write down my thoughts. God knows I've had enough therapy, done enough journaling. More than that, I'll start my own psychological analysis of everyone I can remember from Delmont. Hell, I used to think they all thought alike.

Sheila remembered an entry in one of her journals from years ago:

Some places beg to be passed over. Not-too-big and not-too small towns where nothing much happens, and people like it that way. Delmont, Iowa, is such a place. Other towns might be swirling with change and rage over the Vietnam War and politics, but in Delmont it's all smiling faces and "quiet, please."

Obviously, that was wrong. Sam's murder proved it. But back then, everyone she knew put on a happy face. Nancy being the prime example. Now, in her mental rearview mirror, Sheila asked herself who wasn't as happy as advertised.

Janice had been totally smitten with Sam; prom night she looked like a she'd won a million bucks. But hadn't they ever fought? Sheila couldn't imagine *not* fighting with Sam. Janice's former boyfriend, Peter, had a quarrel with Sam. They had duked it out on prom night. Mike had come to the rescue, but Sam had come away with a black eye. Peter had probably looked worse. Peter always looked like a bad imitation of James Dean. He wasn't even a rebel; he was a surly guy without a discernable cause. She didn't have a clue as to why he was miserable other than Janice chose Sam over him.

But was Sam as in love with Janice as Janice was with him? Sheila remembered a conversation she'd had with Sam once. One of those rare times that she and her brother talked about what they saw for their futures. Of course, Sam had talked about med school and going on to become a doctor. He hadn't included Janice or getting married. He'd told her, "I've been happy enough here, but I'm not going to get stuck in Iowa. Not for anyone or anything. I know you want to get out and you will. Don't settle for just any guy along the way. Billy's okay, but you can do better." If Billy had heard that from Sam's mouth, what would he have had to say? Would he have been angry or just hurt?

Billy was smiling and easy going on the outside. But Sheila knew that was Billy's protective shell. He felt pressured by his father. Maybe even bullied by good old Bug Miller. He was no *perfect son* to his family. Not like Sam had been in theirs. Billy used to crack his knuckles whenever his father's name came up in conversation. Still did. Billy had known he'd better become a lawyer or else. Funnily, Billy had mentioned Craig trying to outdo his father, when Billy was clearly out to prove something to his own.

Mike always seemed happy when he and Sam were at basketball practice. Of course, that was Mike in his basketball-star persona. He'd put on a happy face back in Delmont, too. It couldn't have been easy for him. She hadn't understood how deep his attachment to Sam had been back then. Could it possibly been more than she'd let herself imagine even now? She wasn't going to let herself go there. She'd missed a lot, but everyone else had too. At that time in Delmont, would anyone have admitted that there might even be one homosexual in the whole town? Much less, the police chief's son, Mike Sloan, the all-around nice guy?

Then there was Jane. Divorce was commonplace these days, but back then it held a stigma. Especially in Delmont. Sheila remembered a conversation she and Nancy had about Jane. Nancy, Sheila's new best friend, had steered them to an empty table in the cafeteria. Sheila leaned over to Nancy and asked, "What's Jane like?"

"Who? Oh, Jane." Nancy shook her blond head. "She's different. A brainiac in math. We were friends in grade school up until her dad left, then she got weird. Her mom's got a drinking problem or something. It got worse after he left them. Her dad was as weird as she is."

"That's sad."

"I guess. I used to feel sorry for her. The Browns are poor. I mean Salvation Army-store poor. She acts like she's mad at everyone. Even when you try to be nice, she gets huffy and acts all superior. Weird, huh?"

Her recent conversation with Jane gave her some insight into what she and Nancy had perceived then as weird. Jane's abrasiveness might have been a reaction to trauma and neglect. *Who knows? Maybe I'd have reacted like that, too if my dad had left us.*

Mike had talked about Mary and Jack Mahoney, and to Sheila, they'd seemed like the all-American couple. Mary had looked like a wholesome, former Midwest beauty queen. On the other hand, Sheila's impression of Jack had been that of an ageing jock. One that wasn't ageing all that well either. Then they'd both disappeared. Her first glimmer of a realization that things in Delmont hadn't been what they seemed. Sheila concluded she'd had no clue about most of the people she thought she knew back then.

And what about herself? Had she adopted a "Delmont makes me miserable" persona so she didn't have to figure out what would really make her happy? *Happy?* Her mother used to quote Leo Rosten who said somewhere that the purpose of life was not to be happy but to do things that mattered. *Ten years and counting, finding Sam's killer still mattered.*

She still had some of her old reporter instincts, and she wasn't about to let this go. She had acquaintances from her days at the newspaper in Iowa City she could talk to. There was also a contact at the *Des Moines Register*. She could ask him to do some digging for her if she could only pin down who she wanted to start with.

Chapter Twenty-Three

M ike was on his second cup of coffee when he looked up to see her waiting. Jane was punctual. He'd been sneaking glances at her since she passed through the doors of the station house. She moved quietly and efficiently past the front desk as reception waved her through. Her gaze casually swept the room and came to rest on him. Today she wore her hair loose, and it framed her face. She'd grown into a pretty woman.

"Good morning. I appreciate your promptness," Mike said.

"Time's money," Jane replied.

Mike smiled and walked around his desk to pull out a chair for her. "Thanks again for coming in. Please, have a seat."

She sat and gracefully tucked her long legs under the chair.

"Can I get you a cup of coffee? It's not a gourmet blend, but if you're looking for a caffeine boost—"

"No, thank you." She reached into her purse. "Here's the post-office receipt for my taxes. I don't go through life expecting to need an alibi, so I don't have one. I was home alone."

"Oh, I don't expect you need one, this is just routine."

He kept in mind what his father had taught him about the art of a police interview and what he'd learned from experience as he leaned back in his chair, increasing the distance between them. He needed to make her comfortable and build a rapport. Poorly conducted interviews risked delivering unreliable information. Speak slowly. Then, give Jane plenty of time and his silence. Under her calm mask, he sensed someone tightly wound. He thought if he listened hard enough, he might be able to hear her tick. He took another sip of coffee and put his mug down with a little too much force so that it splashed on the desk.

"I'm a klutz. Sorry, hope I didn't get any on you," he said.

Jane scooted back. Her face registered surprise, then disgust.

"Let me grab a paper towel and clean this up, then we can get started."

As he walked away from the desk, he looked back at her. She gazed at the empty space before her. He'd hoped she would touch something on his desk, pick up the coffee cup or make a move to distance herself from the trickle of coffee that ran across the desk toward her. It was due to a slight slant in the floor. He'd learned the path liquid took on his desk the hard way because his workspace was usually a mess, and he really was a klutz. Sometimes it worked in his favor.

"Here we go," he said blotting the desk. He held out a clean paper towel, but she didn't take it.

"Missed me," she said. The corners of her mouth turned up slightly.

"So, you knew Craig pretty well. You two worked at the same place a while back, right? And then he got you the job you have now with—"

"Wait, Mike. I can call you Mike, can't I?"

"Of course, Jane."

"We did work for the same investment firm years ago, but I wouldn't say we knew each other well. As for my job with Elliot

Robinson, Craig had nothing to do with that, directly. I'd been following Robinson's newsletter, *Money Ahead*, since college. A mutual friend of Craig's and mine introduced me to Elliot. I found out his assistant was leaving and applied for the job."

She smiled and chuckled. Mike arched a brow, "Did I miss something?"

"No, I was just recalling my first day working for Elliot. He's a big man, and he's no neat freak. He told me flat out, 'Jane, think of me as the elephant in the circus: big, slow moving, and I make an awful mess. Your job is to walk behind and clean up after. But hell, without me, it's not much of a show.' He won me over with that, but he wasn't kidding."

Mike smiled. Nice to think that someone influential as Robinson had a self-deprecating sense of humor.

"But back to Craig Vitale. You hadn't worked with Craig on anything?" He waited a beat. "In the past, that is."

She looked up at the space over his head. "Well, of course, I may have worked with him in a tangential way when we were both at Dominick and Dickerman. We'd run into each other at the copier or coffee maker."

"But you hadn't seen him recently?"

She hesitated, then said, "Craig called me a couple months ago with some questions about an idea he had for an investment fund. He gave me an overview without specifics, but it sounded interesting."

"Was that *interesting* as in something that interested you personally? Did it sound like it could take off?"

Jane shrugged.

"What can you tell me about it?"

"Probably nothing you don't already know. I imagine you've been to his office, and he must have had notes for a presentation in his files.

I'm sure his partner, what's his name, Sierra? No, *Sienna*. I bet he's got a copy of it. Maybe you've even talked to him. Was he at the funeral? I'm not sure I'd know him if I saw him."

"He's been out of town, but we'll be talking to him soon. We did get permission to search his office. But would I know what I was looking for if I saw it?" Mike shrugged and sighed.

Jane's shoulders relaxed a little.

"Lots of numbers," she said with a soft, musical laugh. "It might not mean much to you unless it was in a finished form. Let's just say he was promising very high yields." She gave him a sales-pitch smile. "Do you have any investments, Mike?"

"What does Elliot Robinson recommend?"

"I'll sign you up for his newsletter. Despite his over-the-top persona, he gives very practical advice. If you don't mind my asking, how much do you have to invest?"

"Not much, apart from what's in the pension fund. Not on the NYPD's salary, not that I'm complaining. Pay here is better than Delmont."

Jane nodded. "Dull-mont." She wrinkled her nose as if she'd smelled a feed lot. "I haven't been back there since high school. Do your folks still live there?"

"They do. I doubt they'll ever leave, even after they retire. It's still home."

"And you, Mike? Is it still home to you?"

Her question caught him off guard. Mike stopped himself from answering. There was more than simple curiosity in her tone.

"My life is here, in New York. But my hometown will always hold memories."

"Memories, right. It must be hard for you to go there with the memory of Sam's murder. You never found his killer."

Mike blinked, trying to clear the sudden sadness and guilt. There was an edge in her voice; was it accusation? He took a deep breath and let it out.

"Sam's killer is still out there. But there's no statute of limitations on murder," he said.

Jane stiffened. Maybe she was surprised by the harshness in his voice. Mike saw a young, vulnerable Jane, the one he remembered from back in Delmont. He softened his tone.

"And you? What memories do you have?" he asked.

Now it was Jane's turn. She hesitated and again stared into that space above his head. It almost made him want to turn around to see if someone was behind him.

"Mostly bad. People there, especially kids…"

Her face registered a momentary sadness.

"But you had good neighbors, and you did well in school in spite of everything," he said.

Now she flushed and shifted in her seat. She recrossed her legs.

"I graduated summa cum laude if that's what you mean. Neighbors? If you're talking about the Mahoneys, well, I'll tell you something you probably didn't know about Mr. Mahoney, Jack."

Mike raised a brow and looked at Jane cautiously.

"I was only fourteen the first time he laid a hand on me."

Mike took a breath. He hadn't been prepared for this.

"It was winter. My mother had sent me out for cigarettes and groceries. Can you believe that?" Jane shook her head in disgust or anger. It looked like both to Mike.

"It was already getting dark, and it was cold. My feet were freezing. I could see the light on in the basement of the Mahoney house. I had a crush on him. I thought he was movie star handsome back then. He had that black curly hair and blue eyes with long lashes. Anyhow I was curious. I was a stupid kid. I heard a grinding noise, like metal against something. So, I crouched down by the window and I could see Jack sitting at a work bench. He'd been sharpening a knife. He was skinning a rabbit." Jane flushed. "It sort of hypnotized me, seeing the rabbit." She swallowed. "It looked naked, the body was pink and shiny. The feet were still covered in brown fur. There wasn't much blood, but it made me dizzy."

"Next thing I knew he was looking at me through the window. I wanted to run away but I felt like my feet were frozen to the spot. I thought I was in trouble for watching him. I knew it wasn't nice. But he opened that slanted cellar door and made me come in."

"He made you come in?"

"He put his hands on my shoulders and steered me in. Said I looked half frozen. I guess I was. It felt nice and warm inside. He said Mary was away visiting her mother and it was just us. "Just us *and the rabbits*," he said like it was some kind of joke. He took a piece of rabbit fur he'd dried and laid it on my collar. He touched my chest. Then he rubbed my cheek with the fur." She grimaced.

Mike waited for her to continue.

"Then I said I had to go. He let me out and I grabbed the grocery sack and ran. I ran across that frozen field all the way home."

"Was that the end of it? Did Jack try anything with you after that?"

"Yes. I don't really want to talk about it. It was so long ago."

"Jane if you ever want to talk about it to someone, if you don't feel comfortable telling a man, I know another officer, a woman. And there's a counseling center."

"Like I said it was a long time ago. I'm okay. But at least Mary, she was nice, wasn't she? I never told her. I never told anyone. I don't know why I told you."

Jane shifted in her chair, then shifted the conversation, "You liked Mary. Wasn't she, like, an older sister to you or something?" She shook her head, "Awful how she went missing. That must have been so hard for you."

Mike nodded. He felt his throat tighten. "We finally found her."

She nodded. "I read about that." She pressed her lips into a thin line. "In her own house." She looked at him with a challenge in her eyes. "But you never found Jack."

"No, we never did find Jack. Maybe he's another rabbit."

"Rabbit?" Jane blinked.

"What we call a guy who takes off, runs away. Police slang."

"Oh. I wonder where he is, don't you? You hear of people disappearing and then turning up in another town, living a whole new life."

"That does happen. I don't suppose you've heard from him?"

Jane's mouth twitched as if she were going to say something or spit, but she shook her head. Then she made a show of looking at her expensive watch.

"What else can I tell you? I knew Craig professionally. We didn't socialize. I heard he'd had some problems in the past—drugs, alcohol, that he'd gone to rehab. I'm not sure how long that lasted, his sobriety. He might have been clean for a while, but the last time I talked to him he wasn't sober." She narrowed her eyes, splayed her hands on the desk, leaning in toward Mike. "Don't mix alcohol and money. Despite the element of risk, the same goes for gambling. Addiction will derail any investment strategy. "Craig bragged about his investors and friends in high places." She scoffed. "With his past, he had more friends in low places. Maybe you should consider that."

"Jane, I don't suppose you ever met Craig's girlfriend, Sarah Beal?"

"Craig's girlfriend? I assumed he dated around. I don't recall meeting her, but as I said, Craig and I didn't socialize."

Mike opened his mouth, about to say something, but Jane looked down, dusted nothing from her hands, and pushed her chair back from the desk. She crossed her arms over her chest and raised her brows. She waited.

"Jane, I won't keep you. You've been a big help," he said.

"Have I?" She stood and hefted her bag onto her shoulder.

***

Jane hadn't given him anything more solid to go on than what Sheila had. He felt bad for her after what she had told him about her childhood. But she said she wanted to leave that alone. In truth, there wasn't much he could do.

He wasn't sure what to make of her claim that she hadn't been actively involved in Craig's project. If she'd been the woman Craig's girlfriend had seen when they were out, it didn't necessarily contradict that. But it made him wonder. Was Jane trying to distance herself from Craig because of his less-than-immaculate reputation? Billy might have more of the inside track on that. Mike had been playing phone tag with him all week. Billy was busy, but it was almost as if he was avoiding him.

Had Jane meant to upset him or put him off balance with her mention of Sam and Mary? She'd nearly succeeded. The heaviness of grief always took him by surprise. Then hearing about Jack had provoked a different sort of reaction in him and that had taken him off guard. He'd felt his fists ball up and an ember of anger heat his chest—something he'd thought had been extinguished long ago.

Mike had never had much use for Jack. Jack was always so full of himself, a big deal in high school. Mary had fallen in love with the handsome football hero. But the guy's ego was easily deflated as the footballs he used to stockpile and autograph for fans. He compensated with a tough-guy act that included bullying, including Mary, on occasion.

Jack had returned from Vietnam worse. PTSD, they called it these days. He'd seen it in the city's homeless veterans and civilians. Most of them were only a danger to themselves. But it sometimes came down to police intervention. He recalled his dad's stories about breaking up fights Jack had started at the biker bar just outside of Delmont. One of Jack's favorite haunts.

Jack had been a drunk and a drug user who had left his best days behind him in high school. With Jane's revelation, it was clear he'd sunk even lower. A predator, a pedophile. How long had that gone on? Poor Jane. Had he become a wife beater, even a killer? The thought that Mary might have died at Jack's hands haunted him. There'd been suspicion, but no evidence. Jane was right: they'd never found Jack.

Chapter Twenty-Four

J ane had mentioned Sienna, too. She must have known about him from her work with Robinson. Based on Vitale and Sienna's office address, they were in the same rarified financial territory as Robinson. At the very least, the same zip code.

He was about to call Billy again. The list of questions he had for him kept growing. Now he needed to pick his brain about Sienna. His phone rang. It was Billy, placating and apologetic that he hadn't come in to give Mike his statement. He suggested they meet for lunch.

"Good idea. I was about to call you again. I've left quite a few messages. I was beginning to think you were avoiding me. Makes a suspicious guy like me wonder what've you been up to," Mike said.

Billy gave a nervous laugh, "Sorry. It's been crazy time on Wall Street. More so than usual. I'm having trouble keeping up with new legislation: computerized trading links, deregulating insurance-company investing, not to mention the budget compromise. It's keeping us on our toes. I have a feeling we're in for a wild ride this month."

"It sounds like I've picked a bad time to ask this, but I need inside information about Vitale and Sienna Investments. I still haven't talked to Vitale's partner, but I'd like to get a feel for what sort of business they were doing. Their address is high rent, but that doesn't mean they were making it, right?"

"True. Mike, I'll see what I can find out. Could you be a little more specific about what you're after?"

"Would anyone have a motive for killing Craig because of his business practices or his partner's?"

"That's probably not something I can give a definitive answer on by lunchtime, but I'll do what I can."

"Thanks, Billy. I'll buy lunch."

"Which hot-dog stand?"

"Hey, you're worth more than that. Besides, there are a few other things I want to discuss. I'll get us a table at Pearl Diner."

"Big spender. You had me at 'I'll buy.'"

***

Pearl Diner was always bustling with the Financial District lunch crowd, so Mike arrived a little early and found a booth. The booth was at the end of the diner, past the counter seating, a little more conducive to the conversation he needed to have. He sat facing the door so he'd see Billy arrive. Billy walked in, and Mike caught his eye. Mike felt a pang of nostalgia for Smitty's, the diner in Delmont that had been their old hangout. Booths and a counter were pretty much where the resemblance between the Pearl Diner and Smitty's began and ended. Billy slid into the booth wearing an impeccably tailored suit. His haircut was sophisticated and not unlike Craig's. As Billy loosened his tie, Mike couldn't help noticing his nails. Jesus. Was he getting manicures now? Then Billy gave him his boyish grin, and it felt like home. For a minute.

They ordered, and the waitress filled their coffee cups. Mike had probably had more than he needed already, but the prospect of getting a good cup was hard to pass up. Billy poured two spoons of sugar from the glass sugar jar and a stream of milk from the small metal creamer into his coffee and stirred.

He bent his head toward Mike and said, "So, here's the thing: Craig Vitale is a known quantity, and as far as anyone knows he never had an original thought in his professional life. Not that the financial sector is known for innovation and creativity, but the only imagination Craig demonstrated was in padding his resume and exaggerating his investing success. Sheila was going to show me the package he had her working on, but I haven't seen it yet. Did she get it to you?"

"Not yet. I was sure we'd find a copy among the files in his office, but nothing's turned up. There's a chance his partner might know where he kept it or even have a copy. But he's been hard to find."

"Sienna? There's something about him, not a red flag, exactly, but..." Billy took a sip of coffee.

Mike waved him off. "Let's stick to Craig, for the moment. What about past ventures? Did Craig have any disappointed clients, anyone try to sue him?"

"He didn't have anything in arbitration that I know of. But who knows? Daddy was used to cleaning up his boy's messes."

The waitress set down their lunches, and Mike took a big bite of his Reuben, chewing while he thought. "Do you think Vitale Senior knew about his son's new investment fund?"

Billy popped a crinkle-cut fry into his mouth and shrugged. "Maybe. I'd bet Craig's pool of potential investors would have included some of his father's client list too."

"I think Duane and I will need to pay him a visit."

Billy nodded. "Meanwhile, I'll keep my eyes and ears open. But what I wanted to tell you is that Sienna's a cipher any further back than ten years ago when he began working with an independent stockbroker here. Did surprisingly well for himself, then made a couple more moves before he established his own office three years ago."

"Was that business under his name?"

"Yes, A. F. Sienna Investments."

"So, what are you thinking, Billy? Does that mean anything, that Sienna's from somewhere else, and we don't know where?"

"Lots of people here are from somewhere else, and they'll usually tell you about it—either why they miss it or why they're glad they got out. But I'm interested in Sienna's story because he's no spring chicken, and most guys don't pick up and go into investment banking—in the Big Apple, no less—on a wild hair during a midlife crisis."

Mike nodded. "Can't say I'd thought about it. Does he come from money?"

"Who knows? Not that I could find. So maybe he did it like Smith Barney." Billy did a terrible John Houseman imitation: "*He earned it.*"

"That actor guy's job is safe." Mike laughed. "But I see where you're going with this. Unless Sienna had some top-tier investors, he probably had some other help. Jane said that Craig had plenty of friends in low places. His partner might have too. Speaking of unknown quantities, there's Sheila's new friend, Marcus."

"Have you met the guy? What do you know about him?" Billy cracked his knuckles.

Billy's knuckle cracking usually accompanied stressful discussions. Mike remembered he used to crack his knuckles when he was around his father. Bringing up Marcus must have hit a nerve.

Mike kept his expression neutral, his tone light. "Haven't had the pleasure."

He shrugged and said "I've been thinking about Sheila and you and Delmont a lot lately. And Jane Brown."

Billy raised his eyebrows. "Elaborate, please."

"My brain works in weird ways, but it seems like quite a coincidence that four kids from Delmont, Iowa wound up in New York City."

"Maybe, but it's less weird than if four kids from New York wound up in Delmont," Billy said with a smile.

"As I was saying, four kids from Delmont wind up in New York City, a guy is murdered, and it turns out that the murder victim knew three of those same people."

"And that the fourth kid—you and your partner, Duane—caught the case."

"Right. Maybe there's no connection to Delmont, but can you see why I keep wondering if there is?"

Billy shook his head. "Sure. But, please, don't tell me you think Sheila, or I had anything to do with Craig's murder. And odd as Jane was back then, I wouldn't pick her for a killer. Especially not now. I mean, you saw her. She looks great, and she's done well for herself. Very well. She's Elliot Robinson's assistant. She writes his damned newsletter. Robinson might be quirky, but he doesn't hire psychos."

"Okay, let's say you're all in the clear. Was there anyone else from back then who might have turned up here who would qualify as a psycho?"

Billy chewed on his lower lip. "I doubt he's in New York, but when I think of a crazy asshole, I think of that guy Pete who was in your class. Janice's old boyfriend. Drove around in that shiny muscle car. He got into a fight with Sam and you at your prom. I heard all about it from Sheila. You put him in his place. What became of him?"

Mike tried not to react. Funny that Billy should mention Peter and that car.

"After his father gave him an alibi for the day Sam was murdered, he left Delmont. Went back to that military junior college in Missouri. Kemper, I think it was."

"Probably used those military connections, and now he's a vice president of some private-sector company. I suppose he married someone who looks like Janice, and they have a son as obnoxious as he was," Billy said.

"I'll see what we can turn up on him for old time's sake. Marriage records, arrests, and all," Mike said. "Do me a favor, and don't mention that to Sheila. I'm not sure she was ever convinced of Pete's innocence. She's on edge as it is, and I don't want to set her off."

Billy said, "Sheila's been obsessed with anything to do with her brother's death for way too long. Sometimes I get fed up with her. Sure, I know. Sam wasn't my brother, and I wasn't as close to him as you were." Billy paused and cleared his throat. Mike couldn't remember ever having seen him blush, but Billy's face reddened.

Billy brushed his nails on his lapel and continued, "I mean look at us, we've moved on. You made detective. I've worked hard to make it here. I keep my eye on the prize and I keep looking forward, not back."

Mike nodded. He wondered how much Billy had moved on and if he'd left part of himself in Delmont. Like him. The waitress refilled his coffee. "I'll take the check, please."

Billy smiled and said to Mike, "Damn, I should have saved room for pie. They make a killer chocolate silk."

Mike sighed. "You know who used to make the best pie, next to my mom? Mary."

Billy looked a little puzzled by this non-sequitur, "Mary Mahoney? Sorry, Mike. Damn shame about her."

"It was. Did your dad ever hear anything about her husband, Jack?"

"I haven't thought of him in years. Not that I knew him, although he was sort of legend among the football jocks. But you know, I wasn't in with the jocks. I tried to stay out of the way of anyone I thought might beat me up. I only knew what Dad told me, and the old man never had anything good to say about him." Billy gave his knuckles another crack.

"You don't think he could still be out there, do you?"

"Jack Mahoney? Where are you going with this? He's not on a most wanted list, is he? I never heard anything about him being involved in anything outside Delmont. Except for a few fights he started at bars in neighboring towns. Nothing that he'd spend more time in jail for than drunk and disorderly. Right?"

"He's always been a suspect in Mary's murder, but no one could prove it. Then there was..." He hesitated to discuss Jane's report of sexual abuse at Jack's hands. He didn't want to share that with Billy. Mike continued, "And he disappeared a month after she did." He took a sip of water and put his glass down carefully. "What are the odds he might have wound up here? In New York City."

"I'd say the odds would be astronomical."

"That's what I'd say too. Although I wish I knew what happened to him."

Mike picked up the check, and they made their way to the cashier.

"Do you have time to stop by the station and give a statement now?"

Billy glanced at his watch and blew out a breath. "Damn, I nearly forgot I've got a meeting back at the office in ten minutes."

Mike tried to hold Billy's gaze, but Billy was looking at his watch again.

"How about I come in first thing Monday morning?"

"Sure, no problem. I've got my afternoon work cut out for me anyway."

Billy plucked a toothpick from a shot glass on the counter. "Next time lunch is on me."

"Damn straight."

Mike clapped Billy on the back, and they parted company. He watched Billy hustle up the street, his hair barely moving in the spring breeze. Mike ran a hand through his own hair, devoid of hair product and in need of a cut. But he decided he's have to put that off. He also decided he could put off chasing down ghosts like Jack Mahoney and Peter Fritz. They'd waited this long; they could wait a little longer. He needed to talk to Alfred Sienna. Craig's senior partner had sidestepped Mike and Duane long enough.

Chapter Twenty-Five

Duane drove them to the office of Vitale and Sienna Investments, LLC without calling first. Mike hadn't wanted to give Sienna a chance to wriggle out of talking to them.

"Two o'clock," Duane said. "We might be too late on a Friday. Don't some of these guys take off early?"

Mike shrugged. "Market doesn't close until four, and it's no Wall Street holiday, but we'll see."

Sienna's office was on the seventy-fifth floor. The elevator they entered on the ground-floor lobby climbed without stopping until they reached the sky lobby on the forty-fourth floor.

"I think I'm gonna get a nosebleed," Duane cracked as they changed elevators.

The elevator arrived at their floor with a soft bump, and the doors slid open. Sunlight flooded the hallway, and Mike shaded his eyes against the glare as they made their way to the office at the end of the floor. The heavy glass doors were unlocked, so they entered. A chime sounded, announcing them, but no receptionist acknowledged their arrival. Mike scanned the sparely furnished space. He could see two desks: one in the front reception, one behind it, partially enclosed by a frosted-glass wall. In a corner opposite the second desk, an imposing wall of stainless-steel panels alternated with wood. It only comprised one wall, but the message was clear, and the door was closed.

Mike looked at Duane and lifted an eyebrow. Then he knocked on the door.

"Mr. Sienna? It's Detective Sloan. My partner, Detective Corrigan, and I have left you messages. We need your help with a matter regarding your partner, Craig Vitale."

The door opened, and a tall, well-dressed man ushered them in.

"Of course," he said. "Please, excuse me. I was listening to a letter I dictated; my headphones were on."

He pointed a long, manicured finger at a pair of Koss headphones sitting next to an Olympus mini-recorder machine. It looked like the one in Mike's drawer at the station house.

"Won't you sit down?" Sienna gestured to two leather and stainless-steel chairs in front of his desk. They were surprisingly comfortable.

"How can I help you? We didn't have an appointment, did we? Sherry didn't put you on my calendar." He reached into his shirt pocket and donned a pair of Gregory Peck spectacles. He looked down at his desk, scanning it. But they all knew there was no calendar and no appointment. He looked up at the two detectives and said, "I've been struggling since my partner's death. Awful thing."

Sienna's thin lips turned down at the corners, but the pale eyes behind the dark-framed glasses expressed no emotion.

"I'm trying to keep up here and take care of Craig's clients, as well as my own. This is an expansive time in our business. We—I mean, *I've* been swamped. I finally gave my receptionist an afternoon off."

Mike let Duane take the lead.

"Sorry for your loss. If we didn't think you might give us some important information, we wouldn't bother you, believe me." Duane raised a hand to fend off any protestations. "Thank you for being so forthcoming as to your whereabouts on the night of his death. We're verifying the information you gave us, nothing to worry about. Details, right?" Duane shook his head and sighed. Then he leaned closer to Sienna and said, "I'll get to the point, Mr. Sienna. Detective Sloan and I have some questions about a new investment fund Craig was working on. Were you familiar with it?"

"A new investment fund? Craig was an ambitious young man. He had lots of ideas." Sienna's mouth turned up in what might have been a bemused smile but just missed the effect. Those eyes. The spectacles couldn't hide the glint of calculation behind them.

"He would bounce ideas off me from time to time. He mentioned something he was working on, but he didn't get specific."

"So, you didn't see any of the presentation materials he put together?" Duane pressed.

"He must have been playing this close to his chest. Craig did say he needed to nail down some projections. Of course, he would have needed help with that, and he didn't come to me. Frankly, he didn't have the working knowledge of leveraged-investment strategy required for the kind of thing I imagine he was talking about. He didn't have the investors to fund that among his clientele either. He'd have to have been fishing in deeper waters."

Duane raised an eyebrow, and Mike gave him a questioning look.

"You never saw anything on paper about this new fund in the office, say, on his desk or in his files?" Duane asked.

"No. I've gone through his files; as I said, I've been trying to take care of Craig's clients, as well as my own. I'd have known it if I'd seen it, and I didn't see anything like that."

Sienna's face still wore the same expression, but his gaze slid in the direction of his dead partner's vacant desk. He steepled long, strong fingers and turned his gaze on Mike.

Mike said, "You wouldn't mind if we had a look around the office and, in his desk, again?"

"No, of course there's no problem with that." Sienna moved from behind his desk.

Duane nodded. "Thanks. Mike, I'd like to look in the back. Mr. Sienna we'll need to box up the contents of your partner's desk. Detective Sloan will take care of that."

"I meant to have Sherry box up his things. There should be an empty carton under his desk. Craig didn't keep many personal effects here. He liked a clean desk," Sienna said.

Mike followed Sienna to the desk. Sienna looked on distractedly as Mike pulled on gloves, opened each drawer, and examined the contents. Sienna glanced at his watch from time to time while Mike collected the mundane office detritus from each drawer in baggies and deposited the baggies in the box. The cache included a surprisingly small Hewlett-Packard calculator. It had buttons with symbols Mike couldn't identify. He guessed it was a model favored by financial professionals.

Then he turned to Sienna and said, "I think Craig had a very smart young woman working on the numbers for him. Did he ever mention a Miss Brown to you? Jane Brown?"

Sienna put on a thoughtful expression. Then he shook his head. "No. I don't recall him ever mentioning a Jane Brown. But as I said before, Craig didn't share detailed information about this so-called project with me."

They left the office with a box of Vitale's files and the labeled, bagged items from desk drawers. There was an Olympus microcassette recorder, very much like the one on Sienna's desk, among the things retrieved from the drawer, but the recorder held no cassette.

"Dammit, there's no tape. Looks like the thing that might have been useful is missing," Mike said. "Sheila said he liked to record conversations at home, and I bet he recorded them in the office too."

"Sheila told you that. And she knows this because…"

Mike groaned. "She got that from Sarah, Craig's girlfriend. Don't ask."

Duane shook his head. "How much you want to bet Sienna's got it? By now, if there was anything incriminating there, it's gone."

"Maybe. Let's keep a close eye on him. The Chicago hotel is faxing us the reservation and checkout information, but there are plenty of flights between Chicago and New York. He could have made it there and back again in time for a wake-up call from the front desk. He's still a suspect in my book, and I'd like to bring him in to the station for more questioning. We need to talk to Jane Brown again, and I want to pay a visit to Sarah Beale but not today. It's nearly six and it's Friday. For now, let's keep looking through these files. There's a motive for murder in there somewhere."

Chapter Twenty-Six

M onday rolled around too soon for Mike. He and Ed had planned to catch a movie Friday night, but they'd been too bushed. They'd wanted to see *Deathtrap* before it left the theatres. So, they wound up going to a late showing Sunday night, and meeting friends for drinks afterward. Mike made it to the station house minutes before Billy walked in.

Billy had two coffees in a cardboard tray from Caffe Regio in hand. He offered one to Mike, "I know better than to drink the stuff you've got here. You deserve better, too."

Mike reached for the cup and ushered Billy to his desk. They sat in silence for a moment, sipping the coffee. *You deserve better.* That tickled a memory, but it was a generic one, like the phrase. It could have applied to anyone. For a long time, he hadn't dared to believe it about himself.

A hint of shadow passed over Billy's bright face. He took a sip of his coffee, looked up at Mike and grinned. He sat forward in the chair Mike had positioned across his desk from his own. "So, what do you think?"

"I think you just made my day." Mike said after his first sip.

"I wouldn't be able to face most mornings without one of these."

They lifted their cups to each other and drank.

"Now, what can you tell me about your relationship with Craig Vitale?"

"Right to the point, eh?" Billy sighed and set his cup down. "Like I said, I didn't know him well. His reputation preceded him, though. All surface, flash, and big talk. Craig wanted everyone think he was smarter than his old man. Trouble was, he wasn't." Billy cracked his knuckles.

"Hard to live up to our fathers' reputations and expectations sometimes," Mike offered it as a statement rather than a question.

Billy nodded. "He let the pressure get to him. Not tough enough for Wall Street. Not these days. He had too many demons."

Mike cringed inwardly acknowledging his own. He would have tossed off a remark about people and glass houses, but he wanted Billy to keep talking. "Such as."

"His stints in rehab were common knowledge. But he had other addictions."

Mike raised an eyebrow.

"Gambling, for one. I think that's what got him in the deep shit."

"You think that's what got him killed."

Billy gave a single nod and scanned the right side of Mike's face. Mike rubbed his jaw. He'd missed a place shaving this morning.

Billy looked at his coffee cup, rolling the dregs around before tipping them into his mouth.

Mike said, "If he owed money why didn't he have Daddy settle his debts?"

Billy blew out a breath. "For some guys, it might have been a matter of pride. I don't think that was it. I think this was about who he owed."

"Was he afraid of his father or the people he owed?"

Billy shrugged.

"Who did he owe?"

Billy shook his head. "Can't say."

Can't or won't?

"C'mon Billy. You must know."

"Part of an ongoing investigation, Mike. Can't talk about it."

Mike wasn't sure he bought that but Billy had dug in his heels.

"When was the last time you saw Craig?"

Billy answered without hesitating, "Two weeks before he was killed. I ran into him at a charity fundraiser."

"Did you speak to him?"

"Just pleasantries. I had to schmooze some people. I was there for more than the canapes and the cause. Craig was busy doing the same, but he'd clearly fallen off the wagon. He was downing some expensive whiskey like it was apple juice. Getting sloppy and loud. His girlfriend, what's her name—Sarah. She was feeding him and dosing him with coffee trying to sober him up."

"So, he'd gone back to boozing and you think he was gambling again too."

"And that's not all. I was coming out of the restroom, and I heard them arguing. She sounded pissed off. She said, "Don't you dare tell me you've got a meeting. I know who you're meeting and that's not the kind of meeting you need. Call your sponsor." He teased her, "Jealous, baby?" Then she slapped him."

"Sarah thought he was meeting a woman?"

"That's how it sounded to me."

Mike had to be careful with this information. Hearsay. Mike was aware that Billy's habit of eavesdropping and gossiping went all the way back to their days in Delmont. Sometimes people divulged secrets about others to make themselves feel important or to deflect attention from themselves.

Mike nodded. "That's interesting, but back to your statement. So that was the last time you saw him."

"Right."

"Did you speak to him after that?"

"Our office was looking into some things. Transactions he might have had information on."

Billy looked down at his watch.

"So did you talk to him?"

"I wasn't the one handling that part of the investigation." Billy shrugged.

"Right," Mike said. He narrowed his eyes and looked at Billy, "So that's all you're gonna tell me?"

"You know how it is with an active investigation. I feel bad about Craig. Honestly, I wish I could give you more."

"I don't suppose you know which twelve step meetings he went to?"

"That would be a question for Sarah. Or maybe his family. But I hear there's a group that's been meeting in Greenwich Village forever."

Mike raised his eyebrows.

Billy held up both hands and gave his head a dismissive shake. "I hear things."

Billy had always been a straight arrow. Not much of a drinker and Mike doubted he'd experimented with anything stronger. But Mike remembered Billy grumbling about a time in college when he'd had to cash in his coin and his baseball card collections to pay off a gambling debt. He'd been terrified that his dad would find out and he'd never hear the end of it. After he'd been ripped a new one. Did Billy know about addiction and twelve step programs from personal experience? Had he seen Craig at a meeting? Gamblers Anonymous, maybe.

If that was true, he still didn't know what it meant. Billy had given him what he had and nothing more. But Mike had the feeling it wasn't everything he knew.

Chapter Twenty-Seven

Sarah kept popping into Mike's head. He wondered if anyone else had heard them argue or seen Sarah lash out at Craig. If what Billy had said was true, Sarah's reaction seemed out of character and out of place.

Had Sarah been more serious than Craig about their future together? She was obviously invested in his sobriety. She'd said so in her interview with Duane. But as disappointed as she must have been with Craig's latest slip, no matter how angry she'd been at him, Mike couldn't see her getting physical with him in a public place. He found it even harder to picture her drugging Craig, binding him, garroting him, and posing him; then removing any trace of incriminating evidence. Unless he'd badly misjudged Sarah, Mike doubted she was capable of that. The question remained: what had Craig done to provoke someone to murder?

If Craig had been playing around, who had he been with? Had another woman or a jealous husband confronted Craig and murdered him? Mike found it easier to picture an enraged husband or boyfriend as the perp than Sarah. Not that this was a typical crime of passion.

This was too neat. Almost practiced. His killer had planned his murder coldly, and methodically. Like a professional.

He needed to look at all Craig's connections: beginning with all his known business partners. They weren't done with Sienna, but Mike grudgingly admitted Sheila's insistence that Althorpe should be on their list wasn't wrong. Kenneth Althorpe was the guy Craig had stood up for dinner. Or so Althorpe had maintained. He was a commercial real estate developer who'd gotten lucky on a couple projects. That wasn't how Althorpe had put it. Regardless of how willing banks had become with deregulation to finance big and charge big, it was a gamble; for the developer and the bank. But Althorpe had been lucky, and now he evidently had enough loose change that he was willing to get involved with his buddy's new project. Mike wondered why he'd gambled on *this* project.

***

Kenneth Althorpe's office was not in a sleek high-rise like Craig's, but in an old, unapologetic eyesore among its gentrified neighbors. The space smelled of cigars and Old Spice. Mike had found Althorpe to be cooperative, if a little clipped over the phone. Now, behind the metal and Formica desk piled with job specs and bills, Althorpe looked beleaguered and distracted. He rested a jowly jaw on one big hand and scanned the paper landscape as he spoke.

"Craig's death has been a gut punch. The poor kid," He lifted his head and steadied it on his thick neck while he rubbed a hand over hooded eyes. "I met Craig through his old man. Carl Vitale helped me out. More than once. I tried to do the same for his son, but. . ."

Mike waited for Althorpe to continue, watching the man's face for revelation or evasion. He found neither.

"Craig was tough to mentor. He wanted it handed to him. Didn't want to sweat the details or do the hard work. He was what you'd call. . ."

"Entitled?"

"Yeah. He thought his partner, Sienna took him on because of his brilliant ideas. The only reason Sienna took him in was because of who he was. Carl Vitale's son. Everyone knows Carl, and everyone owes him. Sienna's no exception. Sienna might not have owed Carl, but like I said, he knows him. Don't let Sienna's tight lipped, tight ass act fool you. The old guy knows everybody's business, but not many people know his." Althorpe's mouth twisted. "Craig said that he did, though. Said he had the inside track when it came to his partner. Like he had some dirt on him or some deep, dark secret." Althorpe gave a sardonic grin. "Craig thought he knew people and could manipulate them. He was the one who usually got played. Look where it got him." Althorpe shook his head again and went quiet.

"You think someone was manipulating him?"

"Maybe, but Craig could get himself into trouble without any help. Craig wasn't the idea man he wanted people to think he was. But he fooled enough people. Knew how to talk the talk. He was bull headed, too. Once he got an idea in his head, you couldn't budge him."

"Think that got him into trouble?"

"Definitely. He hated deviations from his plans. Really threw him."

"Did that happen much?"

"In the financial world, hell yes. Especially these days. You've got to be on your toes, always thinking of worst-case scenarios because something always goes wrong. At least it does in real estate development. Gotta have plan B ready. Craig couldn't think that fast. The guy couldn't improvise."

"Improvise?"

"If an investor is about to pull the plug, you've got to be able to come up with a persuasive reason for them to stay in. Sometimes on the spot. But be careful because there are some people out there you cannot bull shit. Do not get caught by those people."

"Did Craig get caught?"

Althorpe looked at his hands. A deep line formed between his heavy eyebrows. His improvisation skills seemed to have deserted him. He shrugged. "I knew this fund of his was too good to be true. I wanted to see if he really had the goods the night we were going to meet. If not, I was outta there. I thought that was why he stood me up—couldn't come up with the numbers to convince me." He sighed.

"And you went looking for him to confront him."

Alford squirmed a bit. He tilted his head from side to side.

"You were angry. Was he afraid of you?"

"Craig? No way. I was like a big brother to him."

"Don't brothers sometimes mix it up, get physical?"

"I'd never lay a hand on him. Like I said, I owed his old man. I make good on my debts."

"What about Craig? Did he make good on his debts? What about gambling debts?"

Althorpe's fleshy face slackened. "Who told you he had gambling debts?"

"That's not important. I'm curious about Craig's gambling. It was one of his addictions, wasn't it?"

Althorpe let out a hollow, barking laugh.

"Addictions? Sounds like something his mother would say. Or his girlfriend."

"You know her, his girlfriend."

"Sarah Beal? Hell, I introduced him to her. He was so uptight; the guy needed a good lay. Great ass, that girl. I used to knock stuff off her manicure table just to see her bend over and pick it up. Great manicurist too. That's why I thought of her for Craig. His nails were a mess. Used to bite 'em down to the quick."

Althorpe looked at his own large hands again, "Anyway, they hit it off, so I quit seeing Sarah. But damn. The new girl just can't keep my cuticles conditioned like she could."

Mike had a hard time keeping his expression neutral. *This guy was a creep.*

"Back to Craig's bad habits."

"Craig liked to bet, and he liked to get high. Far as I know, booze was the only thing he still indulged in. Single malt whisky. The more expensive, the better. Don't ask me who his bookie was. The only thing he was gambling on was that fund of his."

Mike waited for more from Althorpe.

"Look, I've got people I need to get back to. I've got a business to run."

Mike would have liked to bring him to the station and let Duane have a go at him. But he said, "Sure. We'll be in touch."

Chapter Twenty-Eight

Mike hadn't liked Althorpe much the first time he'd met him. Today hadn't changed that. He was sure that despite his protestations, Althorpe could have hurt Craig. He just didn't think Althorpe would have chosen to murder Craig. And not in the way Craig had been murdered. He was willing to bet that Althorpe's business wasn't as good as he wanted everyone to think. Evidently neither was Craig's. Was it underfunded or was there something fundamentally wrong with Craig's investment project? A Ponzi scheme, as Billy would say.

Mike cursed his own lack of experience with investments. He hadn't come from money and never really hoped for more than job security and a decent pension. He and Ed could afford to live comfortably between their two incomes. Good enough for him.

He was talking it over with Duane back at the station when something from his conversation with Althorpe came back to him.

"Althorpe told me 'Craig's said he had the inside track on Sienna.'"

"What the hell had he meant by that?"

"Sounds to me like Craig knew something about our mysterious Alfred Sienna, something that nobody, not even my finance attorney friend Billy knew."

"Might have been brag and bullshit from Craig."

"Or Craig had known something about Sienna that got him killed."

"Or Althorpe's the one blowing smoke to take suspicion off himself."

"Would he have said anything to his girlfriend about his inside information?"

"Maybe. I guess we should talk to her again."

***

They got the call fifteen minutes before the end of their shift. Sarah Beale was in the ER at Bellevue. The admitting nurse found Duane's card in her wallet. Mike and Duane got there in time to hear her pronounced dead. Suspected overdose. Opioids. No one in the ER said it, but suicide or accidental overdose was the presumption. Still, they called it a suspicious death because of where she had been found.

"What the hell? Look, she was upset about Craig's death, but she didn't strike me as suicidal or even depressed. She was too busy hunting for a rich husband to do this," Duane said. "And I don't think she indulged in Craig's recreational stash. The one time I talked to her she told me she tried to keep Craig in line and away from drugs." Duane shook his head in disbelief. "She told me her idea of a party was some good champagne or a pitcher of margaritas. Another thing, why would she have tried to off herself at work?"

"You never know what's going on inside someone's head. Loss can sneak up on you. Maybe she hoped she'd be found or that someone would try to stop her. We need to get a look at the scene. Let's head over there," Mike said. "And let's wait for the toxicology report before we jump to any conclusions."

***

Yellow tape stretched across the threshold of Sarah's salon. They ducked under and entered. The crime unit was busy photographing the scene, and the responding officer was speaking quietly with the cleaning lady who had found Sarah. The aproned woman looked to be in her sixties. Her hand shook as she brought a half-empty bottle of Coke to her lips.

Sarah had been found on the floor in her own vomit, still alive. The cleaning lady had called an ambulance and Sarah had been taken away. She'd been instructed by the first responders not to touch anything, so remnants of vomit still speckled the floor and bottles of nail polish lay scattered nearby. A small empty pillbox sat next to a spiral-bound notebook on her worktable. The notebook was open.

Duane said as he looked over Mike's shoulder. "There's nothing in this little notebook except her appointments, and those ended at six tonight."

Mike bent closer to the notebook to examine it.

"There's a name penciled in."

Duane squinted and did a double take.

"Mike, that who I think it is?"

Mike lost his cool as he read the jotted name below the six o'clock name. *Sheila Ross.*

"Dammit. Sheila told me she had an appointment with Sarah yesterday, and I told her to knock it off," Mike said.

He watched the crime-unit guy bagging bottles of pink and red polish, scattered emery boards, and cotton balls—anything and everything that might be evidence. He sighed and said, "Duane, one of us has to talk to Sheila, and I think it should be you." His notepad and pen in hand, he clicked the pen as he scanned the room. "Something about this scene stinks."

Chapter Twenty-Nine

"Duane, how are you? Is Mike okay?" Sheila didn't quite grasp why Duane was on the other end of the line. She'd had so few conversations with him, her first thought was that something had happened to Mike.

"Mike's busy. Asked me to give you a call and see if you could help us a little more with Sarah Beale."

"I'm pretty sure I fed Mike her little *tidbits*, as Sarah called them. But what more did you want to ask?"

"How did she seem the last time you saw her?"

"You mean other than a glimpse of her at the funeral, the *only* time I saw her? She seemed surprisingly good. Must have chugged right past the denial, bargaining, and anger stages of grief and went full speed ahead into recovery." Sheila paused and noted that she still hadn't made it through that process for her brother. "She sounded like her future with Craig was planned out, all ready to pick out the wedding china, but a month after his murder she's adjusting to reality. Why? Has she done something to make you think different?"

"Yeah, it looks like she OD'd."

"What? No way. Duane, that's awful. Did they have to pump her stomach?"

"No. She's dead."

Sheila gasped. She was dumbstruck.

"Got to ask you this, Sheila. When was the last time you saw Sarah?"

"My manicure with her yesterday, Thursday afternoon at four o'clock. I called Mike when I got home and told him about it."

"Right." Duane paused, then asked, "Where were you last night between six and eight?"

Sheila's gut twisted.

"Wait, you want to know where *I* was? Duane, why would you even ask? I can't believe it; is this what I think it is? You're asking me if I have an alibi? This is crazy." Blood rushed to her face, and her head began to pound.

"Please, Sheila. Don't make this more difficult than it already is."

She wanted to scream into the phone, but she kept her voice under control. "I have a right to be upset. There's a killer out there, and you're wasting time questioning me. For your damn information, I was at work. My art director, Cyrus Wagner, was helping me finish up a storyboard for this new candy-bar promotion. We ordered in sandwiches. I didn't get home until after eight. Check it out. Damn it. Before I slam this phone down in your ear, you need to tell me exactly why you're calling me. Why in hell would I need an alibi?"

"Because your name was written in her appointment book. Right after her six o'clock appointment last night."

She could feel the blood drain from her face as nausea gripped her. Her throat was so tight she could barely protest. "No, I—I didn't, I couldn't. Why would she have written that? I didn't talk to her or see her after our appointment. You've got to believe me. Talk to Cy. I'll give you his number, and you can call him right now." It came out in a whispered rush. Then she was trying to catch her breath. "I need to talk to Mike. Duane, put Mike on the phone, or I'll come down there myself and talk to him."

"Sheila, Mike's busy talking to some of Sarah's coworkers. We're going to be busy for the next few days, but don't worry, Mike will call you, and I'll be in touch too. I'd like you to come back down to the station and make a formal statement in the next day or so. And Sheila, don't leave town."

Her initial shock at Duane's revelation and implied accusation turned to anger. *Don't leave town my ass! My name in the book doesn't mean I was in the salon. If anyone ought to know there's more than one way to look at this, it's them. Any of Sarah's clients could have come in after hours. Like Althorpe, the one who had brought Craig to the salon. Duane should be looking for him. Craig's business associate, and to use Sarah's word, creep.*

She'd have to start digging around herself. Better to ask for forgiveness than permission, especially when it involved Mike. When she talked to Duane again, she would tell him to refocus. And it would be Duane she talked to, not Mike. She'd bet Sarah had remembered something else. Something about Craig or one of his associates. *What if she meant to call me?*

Chapter Thirty

He felt rotten letting Duane make the call to Sheila, but he knew he couldn't pretend to be objective anymore. His need to protect her was too strong. Not that he really believed Sheila was capable of murdering Sarah. But he had to consider it—Sam, Craig, and now Sarah, she'd been connected to all three. Of course the same could be said of other people, himself included. But why was her name in Sarah's appointment book? It had been scrawled like an afterthought. Hard to tell if the writing was Sarah's or someone else's. Would it be worth it to try to get a handwriting analyst involved? There was probably too little there to bother. Just a name. Duane would have to call Sheila back to the station and question her the way he would anyone else. Anyone else who was a "person of interest."

The toxicology report was still at least a day away. Even from the little he'd gleaned from her coworkers and a few friends; Sarah seemed an unlikely suicide. Accidental overdose was even less likely. Sarah hadn't had anything stronger than Tylenol in her medicine cabinet at home. Her roommates hadn't either. Could whatever had been in the empty pillbox looked enough like innocent white pain-reliever tablets for Sarah to mistake them? Or could Sarah have found Craig's stash and secreted them away in her pillbox to keep them from him? Why not just flush them down the toilet? Unless she'd been planning to use them for something else. Could she have been the one to drop a few pills in his Scotch and play a game with him that went too far? Sheila said Sarah was planning a life with Craig. But Craig might not have been serious about planning one with her. Those other girls at his funeral. Sarah certainly hadn't seen herself as his girl of the month. How angry would she have been if she'd found out she were wrong? Then, after the heat of the moment, the reality of what she'd done would set in. Sheila said Sarah seemed to have gone through the grieving process relatively quickly. But that acceptance could have been an act. Sometimes people planning suicide exhibited serene and even cheerful behavior. Because they've planned an end to their suffering.

Thinking outside the box is one thing, but this is way outside.

Mike told himself Sarah might have been capable of poisoning Craig, but no way could he imagine her using a garrot. Even if they'd been playing some sex game it wouldn't have been with a wire around his neck. Maybe another silk tie, like the one his hands had been bound with. They would have recovered fibers, and none had been found in the deep depressions around Craig's neck.

Mike couldn't shake the feeling that the scene he and Duane had just come from wasn't a suicide. There had been something staged about it, especially Sarah's appointment book and that pillbox. He would have found it more believable if the book had been in a worktable drawer, the pillbox on the floor, along with the scattered manicure materials. He hadn't noticed a glass or a cup nearby. He'd have to check with the crime-scene guys. Surely, she would have had to wash down all those pills with something. Unless someone removed it from the scene—Sarah's killer. The questions remained. How did the pills get into Sarah? And why?

Mike clicked his pen in agitation, then pocketed it. "Who the hell needed Sarah dead?"

***

Two days later the report from the crime lab came in, minus any mention of a glass, cup, or soda can. No evidence of opioid residue had been found anywhere but in Sarah. Mike noted there had been no coffee maker at the salon where Sarah worked. According to her co-workers they usually brought their own from home or from a near-by shop. Yet, there'd been no thermos or other container identified as having belonged to Sarah anywhere in the salon. Maybe the killer had brought along the coffee, soft drink, or whatever liquid they had slipped the pills into and taken it away afterward. Death on delivery.

Mike looked at the coffee cup in his own hand and shuddered. Awful as the house coffee was, it wasn't deadly.

Duane had taken crime-lab guys to search Sarah's place and found nothing. Only a few cards from Craig, a dried rose in a bud vase, and a couple issues of *Bride* magazine. There'd been nothing found at the scene but Sheila's name in the appointment book to make her a suspect.

***

Mike decided to pay a visit to Sheila at her office. She'd made her formal statement to Duane at the station, and her alibi had been verified by her coworker. Not that he'd really believed, even for a minute that she could have killed Sarah. But understandably, she'd been avoiding Mike. Not returning his messages. He wanted to see for himself how she looked, take her emotional temperature, and see if she had any plans for more sleuthing that he could shut down.

Hummingbird's office was bright and filled with framed artwork from some of their recent advertising campaigns. The receptionist had a dazzling smile, and she turned it full force on Mike as he approached the desk. "Is Sheila Ross in?"

"Oh, are you a new client?" She dropped her eyes to the desk as she flipped through a large appointment book. "I don't see anything in the book for her, but she is in. Who shall I say is waiting?"

"We didn't have anything scheduled. Please let her know Mike Sloan is here to see her."

Danielle turned to her phone and rang Sheila's extension. "Sorry to bother you, Sheila, but a Mike Sloan is here. Should I send him through?"

The receptionist's eyes grew wide, and she blushed. She said, "Of course. Right away. Sorry, he didn't say."

"Please, let me take you through, *Detective*." She rose and motioned for him to follow her. A hallway hung with framed advertising-campaign awards opened to a large space flooded with light from windows on an entire wall. It was an open plan with dividers forming a mauve-and-teal maze.

Sheila's office was really a cubicle—no door, just a desk, worktable, and a couple raspberry-colored office chairs. Sheila was standing next to an easel that held a poster of a candy bar and some indecipherable columns of print.

"Mike, if you're here in an official capacity, I hope you've got something to tell me, because Duane already grilled me, and I've got nothing to say to you."

"Good to see you too," Mike said. "I do have something to tell you. We're not much further along on either Craig's or Sarah's murder. We don't have physical evidence linking you to either death, and your coworker confirmed that he was here with you when Sarah overdosed."

Sheila stood with arms crossed over her chest. She tapped her foot and scrunched up her face. "Well, that's a relief, I guess. Is that it? A phone call would have sufficed."

"You haven't been returning my calls. Besides, I wanted to apologize and ask you for help."

"What? Could you repeat that? I don't think I heard you correctly. Not the sorry part, but you could repeat that too; the part about needing my help."

"Okay, I guess I deserve that, but I have a proposition for you. I could use your journalist skills and connections to research something. Duane and I keep hitting a wall when we look for anything on Alfred Sienna before nineteen sixty-eight. Billy hasn't found anything, and he's got enough on his plate right now. I know you're busy too. But can you look through newspaper morgues for anything on Sienna going back to, say, twenty years before that?"

"That would be the late forties. How old is he?"

"He's sixty, so he would have been in his twenties then. Billy seems to think we should be able to find something on him, but there's nada. Sienna's an unknown quantity. Some parts of his alibi aren't solid for the night of Craig's murder either. Seems he left the hotel for several unaccounted-for hours. No one saw him return, but he did answer a wake-up call the next morning. And he has no alibi for the evening of Sarah's overdose."

"Aren't you at least calling it *murder* instead of *overdose*?"

"Suspicious death is the best we can do for now. So will you help me out or not?"

"Are you kidding? Of course, I will. If you haven't followed up on Althorpe, I plan to check on him as well. I can call a friend at the *Des*

Moines Register too. He's a friend of my uncle Iz. He's old, got to be close to Sienna's age."

Mike sighed when she mentioned Althorpe. "I remember your uncle, hope he's okay."

Sheila looked uncomfortable, then said, "Yeah, he's okay. I should call him. Thanks, Mike. I need to do this, you know?"

"Yeah, Sheila. I know."

Chapter Thirty-One

After graduation, she'd been at the *Citizen* doing investigative reporting. She'd written one article about the unsolved murders in Iowa City and another piece about the questionable sanitation and food safety in the kitchens of a few popular Iowa City restaurants. Then she'd been relegated to writing about momentum indicators for corn and other commodity-futures reports. She was battling her way back to real news while sending out resumes to bigger-city papers. One late July afternoon, her editor said: "Sheila, let's go into James's office to talk." She took her pen and notebook. *Not good. Don is never so polite. What pops into his head comes out of his mouth right at his desk so the entire staff can hear.*

"Advertising revenue is down, so junior staff has to take it on the chin. It's either you and Jill from the art department or Larry in the business section. And he's got a wife and four kids. Pick up your paycheck on the second floor. See Mrs. Miller." She shook his hand when he offered it, even though she wanted to hit him in the nuts with her notebook.

"Always be a lady, and leave on good terms," her father had once said. "You don't want a bad reference."

A bad reference had not been her biggest worry at that moment. She went back to her rented room, uncapped her emergency supply of Ripple Red, and drank straight from the bottle. In a slightly altered state, she flopped down on her bed and closed her eyes. *I've got to get out of here, out of Iowa.* Only one place came to mind: New York.

Her parents had freaked out when she told them over the phone that she had lost her job, wasn't coming back to Delmont, and was moving to New York. They couldn't tell her that New York was too dangerous. There was no guarantee of safety, wherever you lived.

"I'll send you a check to help you get started," her father said after her mother clicked off the bedroom extension. "And an open plane ticket to come home for a visit."

Sheila had no doubt she'd made the right decision. *Thank you, universe.* No way in hell she could stay in Iowa City, much less go back to Delmont. It hurt to be there without Sam.

Sam had predicted she'd never come back to live in Delmont after college, and she hadn't. It had been a couple years since she'd even been home for a visit. But at least she still had some connections at the newspaper and her uncle's friend. She'd start there. The *Des Moines Register* had wide national, as well as regional, reporting. She had a hunch that wherever Sienna had spent his early years, it hadn't been in Iowa City.

***

It felt bittersweet catching up with her uncle's journalist friend. She did miss reporting. She missed the hunt for the story and crafting more than advertising slogans. But she'd never go back to the Midwest, and any newspaper job she'd be able to get in New York City wasn't one she wanted. Her uncle's friend had given her a few good leads on Sienna. The thing was, the Sienna she found was a Francis Sienna.

The article appeared in the *Moline Daily Dispatch*; the year was nineteen forty-eight. Francis Sienna had been murdered. A gang-style execution. Survived by his common-law wife. There was no mention of children. His name appeared with a photograph of him and a woman. The photo was from earlier, happier days, no doubt. The woman was sitting on his lap, all dressed up. Something about her face made Sheila look closer. She wasn't exactly pretty but striking. She had a straight nose, piercing, light eyes, and a mysterious half smile.

Francis Sienna was all wolfish good looks. He was dressed up too. He looked like an extra from *The Godfather*, right down to the fedora and dark, wide lapel suit. Sienna had been known as Frankie "Fishhooks." Sheila didn't want to think of how he'd gotten that nickname. There were a couple other articles, from the *Chicago American*, a sensationalistic newspaper of that era. The articles were lurid accounts of murders in Illinois and Iowa. They'd been suspected 'hits' carried out in multiple towns. Victims had been garroted. That got Sheila's attention. One known associate who had fallen out with Sienna, had been bludgeoned and garroted. He had been last seen leaving a bar he frequented. A waitress later came forward to say that she'd seen a tall, well-dressed man who fit Frankie Sienna's description leave the bar shortly after him. There had been no arrests. As for Frankie, he'd come to a bad end. Given his profession, no surprise. But Sheila wondered what had happened to the woman.

The next mention she found was for Alfred Sienna in the *Rock Island Register Star*, dated nineteen sixty-six. He had been listed as the seller of a property in Rock Island and another in Moline among the real-estate transactions. Moline and Rock Island, Illinois, were two of the "Quad Cities." The other two being Davenport and Bettendorf, Iowa. Aside from their proximity to Chicago, their historical ties earned them an honorable mention in the story of organized crime.

From what Mike had told her, Alfred Sienna still had business in Chicago. But what interested Sheila was the business he'd had in Rock Island and his possible association to the "made man" from Moline.

She'd see what else she could dig up on the Siennas. She'd love to find out about Francis's common-law wife too. There was something about the pair that played on the edge of her awareness. A bit of a memory. Something she'd seen or heard or maybe just a feeling. She'd name this feeling *Spooky*. Whatever it was, it would have to wait. Cy wanted her to take a final look at the artwork for the candy-bar campaign again. Something about the colors.

***

Sheila tore the yellow-and-red wrapper from a sample "healthy" candy bar their client had distributed to the office and broke off a piece. It wasn't quite candy. There was some texture thing going on. She popped the chunk into her mouth. The taste, while it wasn't bad enough to keep Sheila from finishing it, wasn't good enough to make her want another one. Fit Bar was the name they were going with. *Fit for consumption? If you didn't have to pay for one, sure.*

She wiped her hands and stared at the paste-up of the ad Cy had left for her to review. He'd left her a note with a couple Pantone color samples: *Which brown do you like for this—burnt sienna or burnt umber? Think chocolate.* Okay. She hadn't even known there were so many names for brown. Sepia, mahogany, raw sienna, burnt sienna, burnt umber, and on and on. She stared at the printed color swatches, trying to decide which one looked more chocolatey when something else occurred to her.

Brown, Sienna. Sienna was another name for brown. Alfred Sienna... Alvin Brown? Alfred Sienna was in Illinois in nineteen sixty-six. Alvin Brown left his family in Delmont in nineteen sixty-five. Alvin Brown—poof. Never heard from again. One year later, one state away, Alfred Sienna sells a home to an Elizabeth Brown. *I need to find a photo of Elizabeth Brown.*

Then Sienna goes on to Chicago. Does he look up some of his father's *family*? Did the son of Frankie Fishhooks receive a warm welcome? Maybe they made a place for him in the family business. Alfred Sienna had to have been doing something besides selling real estate in the years before he arrived in New York. Whatever it was, he finally managed get to New York City and make it big in the world of high finance. What kind of influence and money did that take? She had to call Mike and run it by him. Did it relate to the murders? She felt something like a story tickling her brain, and she needed to know.

What about Jane? Had she ever tried to track down her father? Did she know he might be here, living as Alfred Sienna? That would be mind-blowing. No way could Sheila ask her. Besides, she still had no real proof that Alvin Brown was Alfred Sienna. But she was dying to know if one of the things that had brought Jane to New York had been looking up her father.

Chapter Thirty-Two

When Sheila called him, he could hear her barely contained excitement.

"Mike, you're not gonna believe this. Alfred Sienna is Alvin Brown."

"What? You mean Al Brown from Delmont."

"That one."

Mike frowned. When he'd asked Sheila to see what she could find about Alfred Sienna before nineteen sixty-eight, he hadn't expected that she'd end up finding "old Al Brown."

"And you know this because? You can't come out with a statement like that. What evidence did you find? Was there a paper trail, photos? Public notices of legal name changes or 'now doing business as' notices?"

"Not exactly. I found articles in a couple of the Quad Cities local papers. My friend at the *Des Moines Register* found the first one, about a Francis Sienna. Also known as 'Frankie Fishhooks.' Great name, huh? It was an obituary that appeared in the Moline paper and the *Register* in nineteen forty-eight. It only listed a common-law wife as a survivor, but what if she had a son? Maybe she didn't want him mentioned in the paper. After all, Francis wasn't exactly a pillar of the community."

"That's all you've got? How do you know Alfred is this guy's son or stepson or if they're even related? And what's that got to do with Alvin Brown?"

"Hold on, I'm getting to that. The next article I came across was from the *Rock Island Register Star*, nineteen sixty-six. Alfred Sienna was listed as the seller of a couple properties in Rock Island and Moline. That's the first mention of Alfred Sienna that me or my friend at the *Register* could find. And guess who took off from Delmont in nineteen sixty-five? Alvin Brown. But here's an interesting tidbit, the buyer of the house in Moline was listed as Elizabeth Brown. So maybe good old Alvin left one family in Delmont and set up housekeeping in Moline with another."

Mike tried to assemble these bits of information into something more than speculation or possible defamation of character. He didn't want to upset Sheila, but he couldn't see what this had to do with any of the murders they were investigating.

"Let's say your theory is correct. I don't see how that's a motive for murder. Bigamy may be illegal in most states, running out on your family makes you an asshole, but it doesn't make you a big-time criminal. And it's unlikely that it makes you a murderer."

"But Mike, don't you think it's suspicious that Francis Sienna was a gangster and definitely a killer, and Alfred Sienna, who he has to be related to, has some connected business associates?"

"Wrong. Alfred Sienna doesn't have to be related to Francis Sienna. Not unless you've found a birth certificate proving it. *Connected*," Mike scoffed. "Who told you that?"

"Billy did. Well, not in so many words."

"Sheila, Billy has no business making statements like that." Mike was silent for a few moments. He was irritated with Billy's latest grab for Sheila's attention. He lowered his voice and said, "Did you find any marriage licenses for Sienna or Brown? I need something more than what you've told me."

"Wait, there's a photograph of Francis Sienna and a woman. It's from the newspaper article. There's something about her, I don't know. You need to look at it."

"A photo? Do you have it with you?"

"I made a copy from the microfiche. It's not great, but I've got it with me. I'm at my office."

"If you're going to be there for another hour, I'll come by."

***

The timelines and identities were too hazy. They'd need more than a grainy photo to confirm anything. Meanwhile, she needed to keep quiet about what she'd found.

"Whatever you do, don't mention this to Jane Brown. Please, Sheila. Whether or not you're right about the guy's identity, it's got to be an emotionally charged subject for Jane. She's been through enough."

"Hmm?"

"Never mind." He hadn't meant to give Sheila another tangent to go off on.

"Okay," Sheila paused a beat, then said, "Guess I was getting a little ahead of myself. I mean, I never met Jane's father, so I wouldn't know what he looked like," Sheila admitted. "It's just the woman in the photo, she reminds me of Jane. But who knows. Craig's funeral was the first time I'd seen Jane since our Iowa City days. We've gotten together since then, but I don't know." She blew out air. "Mention this to Jane? You must think I'm an idiot."

"No, I don't think you're an idiot. What I do think is that your curiosity and tendency to talk, especially when you're nervous, gets you into trouble."

Chapter Thirty-Three

Mike filled his partner in on Sheila's discovery, and Duane agreed they had questions for Sienna that would be better posed at the station than the comfort of his own office.

"I don't believe that the guy doesn't know more about his dead partner's pet project," Duane said. "He's hinky. Any evidence of mob connections?"

"I was hoping Billy would be able to give me something more than innuendo, but he hasn't. Or maybe he can't for other reasons. If Sienna's a player in a case that has the Feds' big thumbprints on it, he may not be ours for long. If he's our killer, I don't want him making a deal and vanishing into WITSEC," Mike said. "But aside from his possible pedigree, his relationship to Francis Sienna, I don't have anything to identify him as an associate."

"There's gotta be something we can find out from Quad Cities law enforcement."

"I've got a police chief in Davenport name of Griener. Still waiting to hear from him."

"Why does the trail keep leading back to flyover country?"

"Hey, you're talking about my stomping grounds. But I wish I knew. Other than the history there that began with prohibition and that it's in the middle of the country..." Mike shrugged.

"Could be because I've lived in New York City all my life, but I think there's something eerie about wide-open spaces," Duane said.

Mike imagined he was only half joking.

***

Sienna looked unruffled as he sat in the interrogation room across from Duane and Mike. He'd agreed to come down to the station. He hadn't seemed especially surprised.

"I've told you everything I know, detectives."

"We just have a few more questions," Duane said. "Can I get you a cup of coffee?"

Sienna shook his head and put up a hand in front of him, then made a "come on" motion.

"What was your occupation before you began working as an investment broker? Specifically, before you came to New York," Mike asked.

Sienna cocked his head and searched Mike's face, then Duane's.

"I worked in investments. Venture capital, some real estate."

"Ah, real estate. Where was that, specifically?"

"Illinois. I spent most of my time in Chicago, but I did buy and sell some residential properties in the Quad Cities. Real estate is always a good hedge. How is this pertinent to Craig's death?"

"We'll get to that. My partner and I wondered how you knew Vitale—Senior, that is. You didn't graduate with a fancy business degree; you don't come from money—or do you?"

"Hard work, Detective. That and luck. I pulled myself up by my bootstraps, like most men of my generation. I didn't have the luxury of going for a so-called 'fancy business degree.'" An edge crept into his Sienna's voice. Mike wanted to poke that soft spot.

"So, your *family*, they didn't have a successful business you could go into?"

Sienna blinked at the word *family*. He shook his head. "I started small, worked hard, and made smart investments. I came to New York at the suggestion of the head of a company I'd turned around. He'd given Carl Vitale my name. He was gracious enough to give me some business. We worked on a couple deals together, and through word of mouth, my business here expanded."

"Did Vitale fund your fancy office? Is that why you took Craig in?"

"Hardly," he scoffed. "All this is the result of another deal I put together." Sienna's eyes slid to the clock on the wall and then back to Mike. "Detective, I was happy to give Craig a chance to prove himself. I felt I owed it to his father." Sienna sagged a little in his chair, looking every bit his age. "Poor Carl, he's devastated. And Laura, so hard on her. A mother's bond with a son is special." He bent his head and rubbed his temples. The first indication Mike had seen of any emotion, but perhaps it was only fatigue.

"Do you think any potential competitors had it in for him?"

"Competitors?" Sienna glanced from Mike to Duane and back again. "Business is all about competition. But this isn't the Wild West. There are better ways to take business away from competitors, believe me. I'm sorry, but speaking of business, I have an important call with a client in half an hour. Are we done here?"

"Just a couple more things. Did you sell a house in Moline, Illinois, to Elizabeth Brown in nineteen sixty-six?"

Sienna's lips parted. He closed his mouth and swallowed. "Yes. I'm not sure of the exact year, but I recall that sale. Why is that important?"

"It was the only sale you had in Moline that spring. That must have been a tough year financially if that was your only sale."

"Real estate was a sideline at the time. I was more involved in diversified investments. I spent more time in Chicago than the quad cities, but I kept my real estate licenses active."

"What was your relationship to the Brown woman whose home you sold?"

"Mrs. Brown was my real-estate client, obviously. Why do you ask?"

Mike pulled the photograph of Francis Sienna and the woman from a folder on the desk and pushed it toward Sienna. "Is this Mrs. Brown?"

He blinked and bent closer to look at the photo, mouth a thin line. "That's an interesting photo, Detective. But I couldn't say if that's a likeness of the Mrs. Brown I knew." He continued to stare at the photo. "It looks quite old."

"Clipping from an old newspaper. It was with an obituary."

Sienna looked up, wariness on his face.

"The obituary was dated nineteen forty-eight. It was Francis Sienna's," Mike said. "Did you know Francis Sienna?'

"No."

"He was the common-law husband of your client, Mrs. Brown. I'm surprised that you didn't at least know of him."

"My clients don't usually give me details of their intimate past. If he died in nineteen forty-eight, I would have been twenty-two. That was a very long time ago. He certainly wasn't in my peer group."

"Not a relative?"

"Sienna is a common name, Detective. We weren't related."

"It's not such a common name in the Midwest. That seems like quite a coincidence, considering you both had business and lived in the Quad Cities."

Sienna raised his eyebrows. He looked at his watch, then back at Mike.

Mike waited for him to speak, but Sienna was a patient man. He continued to look at Mike and Duane without speaking.

After minutes had passed, he asked, "Detectives, exactly what am I under scrutiny for? I want to help you find Craig's killer, but if this is how you go about it, the odds are against you."

Duane stroked the stubble on his chin, turned to Mike, and shrugged. Mike sighed.

"We're simply taking a close look at all of Craig Vitale's business associates. That's all, for now. Thank you, Mr. Sienna. We'll be in touch. And for now, let us know if you plan to travel. We'd prefer that you not leave town."

Mike and Duane watched Sienna's tall, wraith-like form glide out of the station.

"Slippery," Duane said.

"We were getting close; that photo had meaning to him. He's got his mother's eyes. Do you think she's still alive?"

Chapter Thirty-Four

It was far too beautiful a Saturday morning to stay inside. Sheila and Marcus were scheduled to rehearse, but that was later. Sheila was up for something that had nothing to do with comedy. There were plenty of choices.

She thought back to when she had first arrived. The move to New York had its bumps. When she had arrived in New York she'd felt like Dorothy in Oz. Everything was bigger, brighter, and overwhelming. Including the smells. Every day was garbage day in Manhattan. The Big Apple smelled a little rotten, especially in summer. With hot-dog and pretzel carts, cigarette and pot smoke, the dog poop some owners never scooped, and all those unwashed bodies, it was olfactory overload. Sheila loved it. She'd smelled enough freshly mowed grass and hay back in Iowa to last a lifetime.

She also noticed a language barrier. Her first time in a New York deli she asked for a sweet roll and coffee. The counterman educated her: "*Sweet* roll? What would I want with a *sweet* roll? Would I put ham and mustard on it? You mean a *Danish*, kiddo. Cherry or cheese is all I got. Where you from?"

"Delmont, Iowa."

"Iowa, that's like Nevada? Out west."

"Midwest."

"Like I said, out west."

Still have to work that into my five minutes.

Nests-R-Us had found her a studio apartment. The whole place didn't feel much bigger than her bedroom at home. The two windows looked out at the walls of surrounding buildings. Her next-door neighbors were about her age. Suzy worked as a sales associate at a radio station and Renee as a personal shopper at Saks Fifth Avenue. They assured her she'd never be home enough to care about the view.

She also learned time was important. New Yorkers weren't so much rude, as they were in a hurry. Everyone's lives were ruled by the train or subway schedule, running to catch one or the other, navigating from uptown to downtown and everywhere. Sheila's first time in the subway was intimidating. Steam shooting up to the street from the trains below didn't make her feel like Marilyn Monroe in *The Seven Year Itch*. No billowing skirt as she stood over the sidewalk vent; hers was stuck her body with sweat. Not a great look, but evidently it caught someone's attention.

"Your first time on the subway?" a large man had asked. "Stand in front of me, and I'll get you on." Sheila planted herself in front of him, and he pushed her in. She felt him still behind her as the doors closed. Then, she felt something hard pushing into her back. She moved to grab a pole in the middle of the car. At the next stop, she noted the guy's open fly. As she exited, she'd glared at the creep, too shaken to think of a scathing remark, too angry to say anything. She cursed him as she walked the extra ten blocks to her intended stop.

"Lesson learned," she'd told Suzy.

Renee had chimed in: "Men. Some days I think they're all pigs."

"No," Suzy had said, "I think they're more like rabbits. Hopping from one female bunny to another. Shooting their little dab of white stuff to make more rabbits. Isn't that what that infantile Playboy Club is all about?"

They'd shared a laugh. But her subway experience was too disgusting a memory to work into her set.

Marcus had said: "You look so innocent. The audience would love to hear a few dirty words from you."

She'd shaken her head, "Nope."

Those were easy laughs. I prefer to do everything the hard way.

The geographic cure had given her a change of scene, an escape from those little town blues. But the magnificent skyline and brisk pace of life here hadn't been as life-changing as she'd imagined. It was hard, she was still doing things the hard way.

Is that how I keep myself from moving on? Insisting on doing things the hard way? I want to change, but I'm not sure how to get unstuck.

She wasn't the only one on hold. Billy didn't have a woman in his life. That thought provided some comfort, company in misery. Was Billy a ducks-in-a-row person too? Maybe lawyers were like that. Was she a "duck" in Billy's life? Sam had thought Billy wasn't right for her. He'd witnessed their on again, off again friendship and he'd even gone as far as to weigh in on Billy as "boyfriend material." He'd told her simply, "You can do better, sis. If you let Billy tie you down now, you'll get stuck here. That's not what you want. You deserve better." At the time she hadn't been sure what to make of Sam's statement. But deep down, she must have known he was right.

Billy asked her to their senior prom just two short years after Sam's death. Back then she looked for things to take her out of her bedroom, away from her parents and the sadness that had settled like dust in every room of the house. Looking back, she saw how dismissive she had been of Billy.

Prom night he had showed up with a red-rose wrist corsage for her. He hadn't worn one of those rented powder-blue tuxes. No "Nerd Prom" from *Saturday Night Live*. He sported a dark suit with a red shirt and white tie. Snazzy. Sheila wore the dress her mother had chosen, an empire waist, high-necked thing in navy-blue-dotted Swiss with white lace trim. Not sexy. She vaguely remembered kissing Billy hello on the cheek and goodnight somewhere near his earlobe. Helen Gurley Brown would beat her with a vibrator. Sheila would need a calculator to add up how many times she'd blown off Billy. *No, Helen. Not that way.* Her lack of response was a thing she could never make up for. She hadn't even tried.

Too hurtful to think about. Next.

At the funeral, Jane's clothing and demeanor said she enjoyed a better lifestyle in New York than in Delmont or Iowa City. What role had Craig played in Jane's life? She hadn't seemed emotionally affected by his death. Jane was something of a mystery to Sheila. Jane had transformed herself in New York. A chic butterfly who had emerged from a shabby cocoon. But Sheila had a hunch that there was nothing fragile or ephemeral about Jane, despite her looks.

Mike ran a close second to Jane when it came to hiding things. He had chosen a career in law enforcement over all the other things he might have become. Despite being gay. He had to be struggling to fit his personal life into the NYPD mold. He'd made detective—no small thing for a man under thirty. Then there was his relationship with Ed. Did Mike's work partner, Duane, ever wonder about Mike's "roommate?"

Sheila had kept herself in the dark for a long time before acknowledging that Mike was gay. Must have been a dose of Delmont denial. Mike chose the hard way too. Not that being gay was a choice, but his career was. When he finally came out to Sheila, he'd told her, "Leave it to me to pick a career that will keep me in the closet, even in New York City." She felt for him. Not everyone had Charlie H. Cochran's courage. Maybe things were changing. *If only.*

Sheila played the "If" game with herself. If Sam had lived, would he be married to Janice and be chief of staff at some hospital? If Sam had lived, would Mike have moved to any city Sam called home? If Sam had lived, who the hell would she be?

Survivors' guilt. Is that why, even though the four of us made it out of Delmont, we're all stuck in one way or another?

***

Enough. Time to get out of her head and out of her apartment. She pulled out her list of major New York attractions. She'd crossed out the ones she'd seen. No red line over the one that piqued her interest in architecture: the Cloisters.

The subway took her uptown to Washington Heights, the northernmost neighborhood in Manhattan. The Cloisters, a museum built to include parts of a European castle, was a way to relive medieval times through architecture, sculpture, and decorative arts—nearly far enough to escape her messed up modern life. Sheila walked into where the "Hunt for the Unicorn" tapestry was housed and allowed herself to feel enveloped by the floor-to-ceiling tapestries. The brochure she grasped in her hand said that visiting the Cloisters was like traveling through time. The space calmed her until a voice behind her unsettled her.

"We meet again," Jane said.

"Jane." Sheila heard the note of surprise and irritation in her voice. She tried to recover. "Guess you caught me zoned out. This is so peaceful, isn't it? These beautiful tapestries and the architecture—kind of inspiring."

"I guess. Someone I'm interviewing for *Money Ahead* is into this place. Thought I better check it out. I think I've seen enough for one afternoon. I'd say let's grab a cup of coffee now, but I need to finish prepping for that interview. I'm running up against a deadline."

Jane glided away as silently as she had appeared, but Sheila spent a bit longer walking in and out of the rooms, watching the sunlight coming in through the high windows.

The beauty of the art was undeniable, the architecture transporting. Like being back in the Middle Ages—good times. Not. It left her with feelings of heaviness and sadness. Impending doom. It failed to inspire the same awe that her Christian friends claimed to experience. Did being Jewish lessen her appreciation of icons and other Christian themes? *Or am I just uncultured?*

Sheila got *that feeling*, the not quite nausea, as she passed another tapestry and walked out into the sunshine. She forced herself to try to identify the cause every time she was swung by: *I have a bad feeling.* The shrink she'd seen in college during a recurring bout of the anxiety and depression she experienced after Sam's murder had tried to get her to be specific and not just lump "the bad feelings" together. He told her to "put a name to your feelings."

"Dopey, Sleepy, and Grumpy?"

"Sheila, I was talking about anger, grief, and shame. Your sense of humor carries you through a lot," he'd said gently. "It's a defense, and here, in therapy, it stops you from doing the work."

Maybe a shrink would call it 'projecting,' but today it seemed Jane and the feeling were connected.

As she walked from the subway back to her apartment, it came to her.

Sam, sticking his head into her room, saying to Jane: "We meet again." It seemed odd, out of character then. Now, hearing Jane say those words felt stranger still. After all those years, she wondered, where would Sam and Jane have run into each other? Sam, as usual, hadn't felt the need to explain anything to her at the time.

Jane had seemed flustered that long ago afternoon. Spooked, like a deer in headlights. Maybe that was how it felt to her to be *seen* by someone older, popular, and male. Had she had a crush on Sam?

Sheila needed to make time to have another coffee with Jane. She wanted to ask Jane about her memories of Sam and the Mahoneys, and all the sad, strange things that had started in that spring ten years ago. Because to Sheila, that had been when their lives in Delmont had begun to unravel. She wanted to talk about it even if it brought up unhappy memories of Delmont for them both. Maybe her own unhappy memories of that time weren't so much worse than Jane's.

Chapter Thirty-Five

S he'd fixed herself a cup of tea in the calm of her apartment, and she was still on edge. She shrugged it off. She was on her way to meet Marcus, maybe it was nervous excitement. She focused on her destination and their comedy routine.

Later, after rehearsal, Marcus insisted on sharing paella with her in a cozy Spanish restaurant where he spoke Spanish to every waitress who seemed to recognize him and wanted to flirt.

"You're bilingual?" Sheila was impressed.

"Makes sense to be able to converse since I live in Spanish Harlem. Or East Harlem, if you like. It was the cheapest, easiest place to live when I came back from my upstate job. Parking's not a bitch either. And now, I'm only twenty short blocks from you."

"So, you wanted to show off for me?"

"No. Well, maybe a little. Rehearsal went fine, but you looked a little out of it before and right after we came off stage. Thought this food and, of course, more time with me would do you good." He smiled at her, but there was real concern in his eyes.

"I'm fine," she said. But she saw from the way he looked at her that Marcus wasn't buying it. "No, I'm not fine." She took a deep breath. "I went to the Cloisters this afternoon. It was still on my places-to-see list. Born and bred New Yorkers like you probably don't have a list."

"Oh, I've got a list all right, a list of places to avoid," he said with a wink.

Sheila forced a smile. *How the hell did he manage to be so upbeat?* For a moment, she thought better of whining about this latest upset. In the end, her anxiety won out, and she blurted: "While I was weaving in and out of the tapestries, I saw Jane."

Marcus's eyebrows shot up. "*Delmont* Jane?"

"Yep, that Jane." Sheila's mouth tightened. She wanted to tell Marcus what she'd found out about Jane's father. *Nope.* She shook her head and continued. "Jane said something today that reminded me of the first time she was at our house to tutor me in math. Thinking of it today gave me a creepy, déjà vu feeling. I told you we were up in my room and Sam had peeked in. Now I remember he said, 'We meet again,' when he saw Jane. It sounds silly, innocent enough. cliché, really. Sam never told me why he said it or where they had met in the first place. Jane had been so flustered by it. She'd practically run from my room."

Marcus shrugged. "Not surprising that Jane and Sam had run into each other, you all went to the same high school. I'm no expert on the behavior of teenage girls, but they're an unpredictable demographic. It is a bit unexpected that you ran into her here in the city." He smiled. "But not all that unusual either. I see my students and co-workers around town in the least likely places all the time. It can be a little disconcerting." He took her hand and gave it a gentle squeeze. "I'd say don't give it any more thought. But I know you will. Please save a few moments to think about our set: we're doing it in six days. For real."

There was that little spark between them again. She felt warmed by it and she wanted it to last.

***

Sheila sat in front of the roll-top desk in her bedroom, digesting the paella and *ruminating*, as one of her English Lit teachers had liked to call it. Odd how people who were peripheral at one point in your life suddenly reappear front and center. Repeatedly. Jane, for instance. She tried to remember details of her first awareness of Jane in high school.

Jane had been staring at her. Lots of kids had stared at her—she was the new girl. She and Jane hadn't exactly hit it off, and she'd never been sure why. Maybe it had something to do with her friendship with Nancy, the most popular girl in their class. Nancy had told Sheila that she'd been friends with Jane when they were little. Then Sheila had moved to town and had suddenly become best friends with Nancy. It had been so awkward when her parents had paid Jane to tutor her in math.

Then they both ended up at the University of Iowa—okay, not surprising. Most of the kids from Delmont ended up there or at Iowa State. Weird thing was that she never expected to see Jane after college, not after she escaped from Iowa. In Manhattan, of all places. Given her math genius it made sense that Jane would be in finance, even if it was only at an investment newsletter. Jane still projected that aloof, loner air. Sheila hadn't seen her interact with anyone else at the funeral. What did Jane do for fun, besides popping up at the Cloisters?

She remembered Jane playing cards back in their college days. She'd see her sitting with other card players at the student union. Was it bridge, pitch, or poker that she had played? Sheila never had an interest in card games. There'd been some campus poker games back then. Sheila knew nothing about poker or gambling here aside from the time an account exec in the office bitched about shuttling a special client back and forth between an Atlantic City casino and a game in a bank vault in Manhattan. Was that legal? Mike had talked about illegal games in some of the seedier parts of the city. She didn't picture Jane involved in that, but she'd read about some invitation-only private games. Sheila could almost see the now-elegant Jane at a table with high rollers. Jane with her machine-like computation and recall would be able to hold her own there.

Jane seemed all cool rationality, but she had some quirks—that hand-washing thing back in high school. An obsessive compulsive disorder or something else? Sheila had read somewhere that gamblers were a superstitious lot. Did Jane carry a four-leaf clover, lucky penny, or rabbit-foot in her purse? That thought made her grimace—damned rabbit-foot again.

Marcus had pressed her about the "Delmonts," as he referred to them, like a music group from the sixties. How well did they know each other back in Iowa? She and Sam had been the newcomers. Nancy, Mike, Billy, and Jane had been born there. Mike had known Sam best. And who had spent the most time with Sam? Mike. But something made her hesitate to bring all this up with Mike and Billy. And Jane? That was a nonstarter. Especially given what her digging in the newspapers had turned up. She'd let Mike ask Jane the hard questions. She'd keep most of her speculations to herself. The rest she could share with Marcus. There were other things she'd like to share with Marcus. That thought made her smile.

Chapter Thirty-Six

S howtime. It was a "bringer show": to qualify for stage time, they had to have seven friends who were willing to pay the cover charge and two-drink minimum. Danielle and Kevin came, along with Billy and Mike. Ed sent his apologies, but he had a dinner meeting. Marcus had his friend Joe and Joe's fiancée, Faith, and two women Marcus didn't introduce her to. They both looked hungrily at Marcus and ignored each other.

Sheila kept playing with the hem of her "little black dress" as she and Marcus sat in the small, crowded greenroom of the club with the other comics waiting their turn. They couldn't hear each comic's set, only boisterous laughter from time to time—or worse, when it sounded too quiet out in the big room.

"We're different enough to win this," Sheila said more to herself than to Marcus.

"Why? Because I'm black and you're not?"

"No, Marcus. It's because, who else has jokes about academia and Sigmund Freud?"

"Different can be a plus or minus. This is our first venture outside the safe nest of our open mics. We're like little chicks breaking out of our shell. Let's hope we don't get hit crossing the road."

"I'm nervous enough without imagining us getting run over by somebody else's punchline."

"Try creative visualization, Sheila. See us up there, smiling, remembering the precise order of every word, not stepping on our laugh lines, getting laughs without listening for them, then coming off the stage to thunderous applause."

With that, he closed his eyes and didn't open them until the emcee tapped him on the shoulder: "You two are up after that guy in the baseball jacket. How do you want to be introduced?" Sheila left that bit of showbiz to Marcus.

Marcus held her hand, and they bounded up on stage to get the energy going. Their five minutes was a combination of Freud 101 and dating in New York. They were halfway through their set when one of the mics died. Marcus finessed it, putting his arm around her, pulling her in next to him with only the working mic between them.

"Quite the threesome, and please remember, sometimes a mic is only volume." He slid Sheila's hand up and down the mic, suggestively. The audience laughed, and Sheila found herself relaxing with the warmth of his arm encircling her.

They went to the pub across the street for hamburgers with their friends after the show. Of course, their friends told them they were great. Kevin was laying it on thick, "When you make it big, we'll put a plaque on the wall of your cubicle at Hummingbird. I'll say I knew you when you were a humble copywriter."

"Thanks. We'll get an honest opinion on Monday when we hear from the booker," Sheila told Kevin.

"The booker isn't the be-all, end-all," Marcus countered. "You and I are going to do this again and again."

His two female friends pretended they didn't hear that.

Billy and Sheila parted ways after they left the restaurant. "We'll definitely hang out Monday night," he apologized. "I have to finish a brief for first thing Monday morning."

"No apologies needed. By the time I get home, my adrenaline rush will have evaporated, and I'll be ready for the pillow show."

***

She walked into her building lobby and noticed Anthony wasn't at his doorman post. *Probably on a break.* This time on a Saturday night was in between the peak hours of residents going out for the evening and coming back. Sheila enjoyed life in a doorman building. The extra money spent in tips was worth the convenience of having someone bring up your packages, hail a taxi, and most important, announce any visitors.

She took out her key as she stepped off the elevator and walked toward her apartment. Before she could get the key in the lock, the door opened. She stepped back and shivered. She never forgot to lock her door. Her New Yorker's sixth sense overtook her curiosity, and she didn't go inside.

She rode back down to the lobby. Still no Anthony. She went to the mailroom, but he wasn't there either. She left her building, walked down to the corner, crossed the street to a pay phone, deposited a dime, and without thinking dialed Marcus.

"Are you alone?" It suddenly occurred to her he might be with one of the two women.

"What's wrong?"

She told him.

"Stay in the lobby. I'll get there as fast as I can."

Sheila was sitting on a lobby bench talking to Anthony when Marcus arrived. She made the introductions. Anthony swore to Marcus he only took a few minutes longer than his scheduled break.

"Anthony, we're not looking to get you into any trouble. How about the three of us go upstairs?"

Marcus noticed there was no double lock. He shook his head at Sheila. "Any credit card will crack this."

"Hey, don't blame me. I found this apartment after I got my second job and a big raise. I always felt safe. The doormen."

Anthony hung his head.

The living room/dining area looked neat enough with nothing seemingly out of place.

Anthony looked at Marcus and back to Sheila. "Miss, you sure you locked it? It don't look like nothing's missing."

Sheila reddened. "I locked it."

They walked into the bedroom, and Sheila saw her jewelry box sitting on top of the dresser.

"That's not where it was when I left for the club. I don't own much jewelry. The only things I keep in here are emergency cash, some gold and silver earrings, and a couple of pins. I'm wearing my pearls." She grabbed a tissue to open the lid of the box.

"Goodbye to whatever was there."

"I'll head down to the lobby and call the police," Anthony volunteered.

"Should I even bother with a police report?" Sheila asked.

"Yes," Marcus insisted.

Half an hour later, two police officers showed up, but they weren't optimistic.

"Not to discourage you, miss, but we've been to two other buildings in the area tonight. One, the owners came home and found the place cleaned out: silverware, china, jewelry, and clothes, and the second guy had a big stamp and coin collection. These may be inside jobs."

Anthony wasn't there to look insulted.

Marcus called a twenty-four-hour locksmith before the police left. He stayed while the Segal lock and chain lock were installed.

"Got any alcohol? I think we both could use something stronger than tea."

Sheila slid back a bottom cabinet door. "Ta-da, help yourself."

There were bottles of Tanqueray, Johnny Walker Red, Smirnoff, Chianti, and Amaretto.

"I'm really not a big drinker," she said as she pulled out the Amaretto.

"Of course not. Otherwise, these bottles wouldn't be full."

He sat quiet with his arm around her as they sipped their liqueur and watched the last few minutes of *Saturday Night Live*.

"Marcus, go home. I'm okay. Billy had a lot of work to do. I'll fill him and Mike in tomorrow."

"I'm not asking you to think about this now. In the morning, look around, see if anything else was taken. This doesn't look like your run-of-the-mill apartment robbery. Right? So be careful, you're important to me."

Marcus was looking at her with concern in his eyes. She gave a shiver and nodded. As she stepped to the door with him, he said, "Now lock both those locks. And put the chain on. Do it for me, Sheila."

A wisecrack was on her lips, but she let it die there. "Thanks," she said.

Sheila was scared. She admitted it to herself. She remembered back to college and reading *Nineteen-Eighty-four*. Forget the propaganda and Big Brother. What scared her were the rats. Brilliant move, Sheila.

New York City had more rats than people. One night she had watched in fascination, as two rats crossed the subway tracks and came up onto the platform while she waited for her train. They scurried down to a corner where a bag of chips lay split open and began to feast. This was worse than rats.

Sheila was beyond tired, but she couldn't sleep. She turned on every light in the apartment. She sat down at the roll-top desk, still her favorite piece of furniture. She opened the top where she kept her typewriter. If she wrote about this, she might get some distance and be able to sleep. But before she could type the first word, it was as if she stepped outside herself and back in time. High school.

Chapter Thirty-Seven

Sheila opened the scarred wood top of her desk. A crumpled tissue sat on her math book. She poked at it. There was something hard stuck in it. She opened it and let out a gasp. *A rabbit-foot.* Not the bright-colored, fluffy kind you buy on a keychain for luck. This one was stained with something brownish red. *Ugh. Dried blood.*

Sheila folded the tissue back over it and held it between her thumb and forefinger. Her face tightened, and she turned away. Billy was watching her. She leaned over to Billy's desk and dropped the thing in his lap.

"Keep your paw off my desk."

Billy unwrapped the tissue. His nose wrinkled in disgust, and his face reddened. Kids around them started to snicker. One girl, silent and expressionless, just stared. Sheila sat, cartridge pen and blue-lined paper in front of her. Her hand might start shaking if she picked up the pen to write.

It was a stupid prank, a creepy one.

Did Billy just want to mess with her? It was the stupid kind of thing Sam might have done a couple years earlier. If he hadn't put it there, who had? And why? What had she done to anyone? What was it, some small-town initiation? Maybe it was her wild hair and freckles. Kids had picked on her before, but that was back in grade school. Or was it because she and Sam were Jewish? When they had first moved to Delmont from St. Paul, she'd heard a whisper: "That brother and sister; they're Jews."

Depressing Delmont. How did they land here? *Of all the gin joints.*

Her father said it was a promotion, but Sheila didn't believe him. Yes, their Tudor-style house in Delmont was about the same size as their Tudor Revival back in Minnesota. And it did have a back porch and a yard full of pink peony bushes. But their old house was on a broader street with a grander feel. The name of their new street: East Ninth. Numbered streets were so mundane. So small town.

She realized most people in the town felt they missed nothing by not living in a big city. Nancy said her neighbor across the street let her use her grand piano, which was always tuned, for practice. "Come in anytime it suits you," her neighbor had told her. A kind gesture wasn't anything to put the town in a AAA tour guide. All in all, Delmont was a Wonder Bread hellhole with too many wooden homes, wooden heads, and a church on every other corner. As she complained in her daily writing: *winter only makes it worse. When we lived in the Twin Cities, Minneapolis had a winter carnival. Delmont has snowdrifts and yellow snow.*

"Tell us how you really feel, Sheila," her brother had said during one of her soliloquies on Delmont's shortcomings. "You need to give this town a chance, sis. 'Try it, you'll like it,'" he riffed off the Alka Seltzer commercial. Easy for him. But wasn't everything? He was a smart jock. A team player. No one would put anything awful in his desk or locker.

She took a deep breath and sat up straight. Nobody was going to ruin her day. She picked up her pen and started writing. Her hand didn't shake. And the next period was library—she loved library.

Didn't every aspiring writer? *And dammit, I'm going to be a writer. Someday. Oh well, it's lunchtime, and I'm starving.*

Nancy, Sheila's new best friend, steered them to an empty table in the cafeteria. Sheila leaned over to Nancy and asked, "What's Jane like?"

"Who? Oh, Jane." Nancy shook her blond head. "She's different. A brainiac in math. We were friends up until third grade, then she got weird. Jane's dad left, and her mom's got a drinking problem or something. Her dad was as weird as she is."

"She sounds sad."

"I guess. I used to feel sorry for her. The Browns are poor. I mean Salvation Army-store poor. She acts like she's mad at everyone, but if you try to be nice, she acts all superior. Weird, huh?"

Sheila nodded. She understood feeling like an outsider too.

"Oh jeez, here she comes," Nancy whispered.

Jane was approaching their table. She was headed for the empty seat across from Sheila.

"Sorry, Jane, that seat's saved," Nancy said.

Ashamed of her relief as Jane pivoted away, Sheila looked down at her tuna salad. *If Nancy weren't my friend, it would be "Sorry, Sheila, that seat's saved."*

Sheila had been pleasantly surprised when they'd moved to Delmont that the most popular girl in her class had wanted to be her friend. It had been the only pleasant surprise about the town. Nancy had bopped up to her on her second day and said, "I want to get to know you, new girl. You're different. You're smart and funny—you crack me up. And by the way, your older brother is hot!" Then she'd giggled and winked at Sheila.

Sheila crunched on a carrot stick. She was so hungry. She was always hungry. Sheila wolfed the rest of her lunch and wished she had eaten the piece of toast earlier in the morning. She skipped breakfast to lose the fat that refused to be banished from her middle. *Why can't I have a flat stomach like Nancy?* Sheila looked longingly at Nancy's half-eaten Twinkie.

They walked into the girl's restroom. Jane stood at the sink splashing water on her face and washing her hands. No one spoke. Nancy shared a critical glance with Sheila. They each dashed for a stall and closed their doors. They waited until they heard the water stop running and Jane's footsteps on the cold tile floor.

Chapter Thirty-Eight

The vividness of the memory took her by surprise every time. With it, a flash of shame at her teenage self, so insecure and easily led. Shame, too, at being so callous to someone who could just as easily have been a target for pranks. The way she and Nancy snubbed Jane back then. It made Jane's candid conversations with her even more gracious. Remorse pricked her.

Okay, let it go. Let the past go and be in the "now." Breathe. She took a deep breath through her nose and slowly let it out, then another. Her gaze was soon drawn to the notepads and papers she kept on the desk, and she felt the hairs on her arms stand. The stack of papers had been messed with. She never locked the desk because who'd look in there? She kept the desktop down to make the room look more presentable when she wasn't writing.

What would anyone hope to find in my desk? My desk. She shuddered. *A stranger rifling through my papers, touching my things. It's almost like being touched by a stranger.* Tonight required letting herself fully acknowledge her fear and settle into serious thought. *And seriously, why did I call Marcus ahead of Billy or anyone else? Because Marcus is used to life's little, ugly moments? Or because he makes it bearable to get through mine?*

She sat in her rocking chair next to the window, rocking to soothe herself, feeling Marcus's words: "Be careful, you're important to me." Finally, she fell asleep.

Marcus called the next morning.

"Before you hear it from Anthony, I admit I sat in your lobby for another half hour, then waited outside for a few. I was afraid a cop would come along and hassle me or ticket me for loitering. And not that I'm cutting cops any slack, but them not being more concerned about your unwanted visitor doesn't surprise me. Not that I think I could have prevented last night's incident. But I haven't followed the threads of your story and seen the whole cloth. You knew Craig, worked with him on this high-finance, high-risk project. And Jane from your town had at least a tangential relationship to Craig. Then, we throw in your friend Billy, who had more than a passing interest in Craig's business."

"What the hell are you insinuating, Marcus?" Sheila was almost squeaking.

"Not insinuating anything. Not mentioning Billy for any reason other than it makes sense. I'll gloss over the fact he doesn't want me as part of this investigation or anything that involves you."

"Don't even go there."

"Fine, you chew on that. I'm not done thinking this through. Mike is one of the two detectives heading up the investigation. You never stop telling me how your brother's murder has colored every area of your life for the last decade. But you refuse to consider anyone you know might have committed the murder. And you don't want to admit your refusal might make you a target."

"What?"

"You act like you're safe because you're surrounded by Billy and Kevin and Mike... they might not be enough. Here's a number for you: more than eighteen hundred murders in New York City last year. Enough to make Mike one busy detective. And speaking of Mike and Billy, what's with the mass exodus of people from your hometown? Delmont's population must be close to single digits by now."

Sheila refused to dissolve into tears, mainly because Marcus was making her so angry, she could spit. "Marcus, give it a rest. You might be right about me. Over the years, I've procrastinated, not only about writing but about taking a bag of bricks out of my emotional walls. But I swear you're wrong about Billy."

After she defended Billy to Marcus, Sheila thought back to university days when she'd been ready to swear her friendship with Billy had reached its expiration date. It was after she'd spent half an hour on the phone with Nancy being consoled over her breakup with Russell. Her college boyfriend had revealed himself for who he really was, a schmuck.

"Good riddance!" Nancy had said.

One week before college graduation, as they sat in his car, Russell had broken up with her. Technically, she was the one who had told him to go to hell, but that was after he confessed he'd gotten a girl pregnant.

It's not like we'd sworn our undying love, but still...

"Russell. How *could* you?"

"Sheila. I did it for us. I was practicing. For when you finally gave it up to me. Guys have needs."

"What a bunch of crap."

She'd opened her purse, taken out the pack of Trojans she'd been saving for when she'd decided to "give it up," and slapped them across his face. "Happy Father's Day."

Billy had called her an hour after she'd hung up with Nancy.

"Sheila, let's go out for pizza."

"I look like crap, Billy. Don't think I have the energy to get dressed up and go out."

"No problem—I deliver. I'll bring beer or your favorite cheap wine and pizza. My treat."

"Billy, you're a true friend. Make that a bottle of Lancer's, and I may be able to drag myself into the shower. I'll still look terrible when you get here, but at least I won't smell bad."

"Who could ask for more? I'll be at your place about eight with wine, pizza, and consolation."

"Just bring the wine and pizza."

Billy arrived fifteen minutes early.

"You came early!"

"Who told you?" He laughed and handed her the bottle of wine.

The pizza was hot, and the wine went down easy. So easy, that before she knew it, they were on top of each other on the avocado green Naugahyde sofa. Her T-shirt was up around her neck, halfway off, and his jeans were unzipped.

"No, Billy, I can't. We can't. We've known each other so long we're practically like sister and... you know what I mean. I don't want to ruin our friendship." *I've probably already ruined it,* she thought as she pulled her shirt down and her pants up. Billy sighed and shook his head. He stood and zipped his jeans. He sat back down, slumped on the sofa.

He put his hands on his knees and looked at her. "Sheila, I always thought someday things would be different. I've felt this way about you for as long as I've known you. I get that you don't feel that way about me, but why'd you string me along? You're a cock teaser." He said it with more than a trace of bitterness. "I better go." Billy picked up his keys, the wine bottle, and slammed the door behind him.

Sheila looked at the leftover pizza in its grease-and tomato sauce-stained box. The cheese and toppings had congealed in an unappetizing lump on the crust. She ate it anyway. *What have I done?* She reached for her glass and drained the last quarter inch of wine from it.

She was nauseous. *Great. Tomorrow I'll be hungover, bloated, and depressed.* She had thought of calling Billy, but what would she have said? What *could* she have said? And now, though she thought Billy had forgiven her for the assault on his ego, had he truly forgotten?

Chapter Thirty-Nine

M ike sat, hands cupping his forehead and swore softly. Sheila had waited until the morning to tell him about last night's break-in at her apartment. Her voice on the phone was steady as she assured him she was fine, that she had called Marcus and the police.

In that order.

She hadn't called him or Billy until this morning. And it was nearly noon. At least he hadn't heard about it from Billy. Mike wondered if she and Billy were on the outs again. No detective skills needed to know how Billy felt about Sheila. He'd been crazy about her ever since she'd moved to Delmont. Everyone knew it. But even then, Billy had been relegated to the friend zone. Mike knew how that felt. But Billy had never been able to accept it.

Billy also had a talent for pushing her buttons. Most often about her brother's death. Mike understood Sheila's loss, but Billy had no frame of reference for that. Some of the friction between Sheila and Billy was caused by his insistence that she needed to quit grieving and move on. It didn't work that way.

But why hadn't Sheila called him? He had listened to her talk about how Marcus had rushed over when she'd called and went to look around the apartment with Anthony, the doorman. He'd felt he had to pose a question or two to her about it.

"Sheila, I guess it was good that Marcus was there for you, but I wish you would have called me first. Or nine-one-one."

"Mike, I acted on impulse, and I felt better after Marcus got over here. I appreciate the sentiment, but it was late, and I'm sure Ed wanted to spend time with you."

"Ed would have understood. It's damn important to me to make sure you're okay. I guess that's what counts, that you are okay. But how well do you really know Marcus?"

"What's that supposed to mean? How well do I know anyone? You included. Do you know how obnoxious you sound? In fact, if anyone but you asked that question, I'd say they were prejudiced. Marcus and I have something good or something that *could* be good—our comedy act, okay? Not that it's any of your business." Sheila's anger was coming through.

"Sheila, you misunderstood me. If you think I sounded biased asking about Marcus, that wasn't my intent. If he was white, I'd be asking you the same thing. You told me you two met the day after Craig was murdered. That's less than a month ago, which is not much time to figure out someone or their motives."

"I'm a decent judge of character, and I'm not going to apologize for or justify who I choose to spend my time with, not to you or Billy or anyone." She exhaled. "Let's move on, as Billy would say." Sheila sounded tired and stressed.

Mike asked if anything had been stolen, and her answer was defensive and vague.

"I'm sure someone messed with the papers and notes in my desk. It's an old roll-top desk, and I always leave it rolled down."

"Was it locked?'

"Why the hell would I lock my desk in my own apartment?"

"It's a valid question. But if there were valuable documents or personal items, I'd lock it. We're not in Delmont." Mike was sorry he'd said that. "Look, of course you weren't expecting a burglary, but times are tough, and that sort of crime is up. Drawers get rummaged through or dumped out when the perp is looking for valuables. Sometimes they're not so tidy. Sometimes burglars can be malicious. Everything is fair game to a crook—closets, mattresses, medicine cabinets—"

"Stop!" Sheila broke in, her voice shaky. She sighed. "I get it. It sounds like an ordinary break-in to you. But not to me. I'm not sure anything of value was stolen, but it feels awful. I felt safe in this apartment. Now, I don't know. It makes my skin crawl thinking about it. They took my emergency cash and jewelry, not that I had much. They left my typewriter."

Mike nearly laughed at the thought of a burglar running down the sidewalk with Sheila's manual typewriter. But he controlled himself; dark humor aside, there was nothing funny about this. Poor Sheila, traumatized by Craig's and Sarah's deaths, now this.

"No keys, checks, credit cards, or passport missing?"

"The only credit card I have is from Lord and Taylor, and it's maxed out. I've got it in my purse. But something is missing. I don't know what, but I can feel it. Do you think this has anything to do with Craig or Sarah?"

Her question took him aback. It hadn't immediately occurred to him that this was related to Craig's murder. It seemed unlikely. Sheila didn't live in Craig's neighborhood, and there had been several burglaries in hers. But now he had to consider Sheila's question: could it have had anything to do with Craig Vitale? With Sarah? He didn't think it had to do with her looking up Sienna. Nobody knew about that.

"Did you keep a copy of your work on Craig's project or any copies of the newspaper microfiche in your apartment?"

"No, I either kept it in my locked file in my desk at work or in my messenger bag. I gave you what I had on Sienna." Sheila paused. "Wait. I had some notes about the project in my desk. I need to think about what else was there."

Mike hesitated before he spoke. "While we're on the subject of notes, you remember the threatening note you received when you did that story on Jay Walker's murder?"

"Seriously? Not like I'd forget that, Mike."

"Do you still have a copy of it?"

"I do, although I have no idea why. Not sure where it is either. What does that have to do with what's going on now?"

"Probably nothing. I'm looking back at that case, and you know, I thought of it. I think the original is in the file back in Iowa, along with the rest of the evidence we collected. On the shelves in the evidence room where we keep things from the cold cases. I'm having some of it sent to me here, but if I could look at your copy, I'd appreciate it."

"Okay. I'll find it."

"Meanwhile, be careful."

"I get that a lot lately."

Chapter Forty

Sheila's attitude had Mike on edge. Waiting for the materials from the cold cases he'd investigated while he was back in Iowa in nineteen-seventy-six had him nearly as amped up now as he had been then. It felt like a replay of that winter.

Mike had called to give Sheila the heads-up. Everyone in Iowa City was talking about it as if it had happened on campus. He told her that she might hear some things that would upset her, things that might remind her of Sam's murder. That was one reason he was sticking around town. The department was putting him up in one of the dorms for a week.

Sheila said she hadn't known the dead student—she wasn't even sure she'd seen him on campus. She asked him, "When can we get together and talk?"

"I'm meeting with the victim's family today."

Mike winced as he heard himself: *the victim's family. That sounded so cold.*

Sheila was silent.

"How about we meet for dinner tomorrow night? On me. Ask Billy to come along too."

"We don't see each other much lately."

"Why not?"

"He thinks I should be over Sam's murder. He wants me to forget about it and get on with my life. How am I supposed to do that, Mike? I'm not you."

Mike took in a breath and let out a sigh.

"Sheila, I'm not over Sam. Not any more than you are. Let's have dinner tomorrow night. Just you and me. I'll pick you up in my cruiser." His voice was suddenly playful. "Everyone will think you're a narc."

"Wow, who can refuse an offer like that?"

Mike and Sheila ate burgers at George's. He was in his *civies.* He ordered a Hamm's, a solid Midwest brew. Seated in the dark-wooden booth, he looked around at the restaurant's late-art deco style. The symmetry and clean lines made it feel solid and safe. Their coats hung on brass hooks on the supporting pillars, giving them the illusion of privacy. She pointed a french fry at him.

"Are you going to tell me about the way this case is like Sam's, or do I have to beg?"

"I'll tell you what I can."

"That sounds familiar. I may have been Sam's baby sister, but I'm no baby."

She wasn't going to make any of this easy. But why should she? She deserved him to be straight with her.

"His parents are devastated, of course. They were on vacation when it happened. They had no idea what his plans were on the evening he was killed. He left his apartment after classes.

His suitemates said he was going to see a friend up in Davenport. He was driving with another student. They didn't know who."

Sheila put down the fry that was halfway to her mouth. She raised her brows.

"They thought it was someone he played cards with at the student union. Apparently, a bunch of them sit around and play cards there. He didn't come home that night. They expected him back late. Blamed the weather. He wasn't back the next day. Or the day after that. They reported him missing. He wasn't the sort of guy to ditch classes. He was smart, a good student. Kind of a nerd. About a week later, someone spotted a car down in a culvert off the highway just beyond a bridge. He was in it, dead. No wallet. Blunt-force trauma to the head. Asphyxiation. Might have drowned. Hard to tell if he was unconscious when he went into the water." Mike shrugged. "It could have happened when the car went off the road into the culvert."

She gave him a hard look.

He returned her gaze. "Confidentially, Sheila, and when I say *confidentially*, I mean it. It looks like murder. Like Sam's murder. There's another one under investigation too. Out past Coralville. A couple months ago. As for this one, we've got no murder weapons, no suspects. Combed the car. Nothing."

Sheila had stubbed the French fry into her plate like a cigarette.

"Mike," she said after a while. "I'm going to write a story about this for the school paper."

"You can't use the information I just told you. When I said confidential, I meant it. If you can write a story for your paper on the information that's already been released and give it a more personal angle, okay. But let me see it before you turn it in. Promise me."

Chapter Forty-One

Back in college, she had fantasized she could help Mike. Write a story, and the killer would come on over to the student union and meet her in the school-newspaper office.

Back then. Mike had been in Delmont exactly when she needed him in Iowa City to talk to. She'd written the story about Jay Walker. Mike had given her the okay to turn it in. It appeared in the school paper, and the response had been surprising. People had been calling the *Daily Iowan* with tips. She needed to put them in touch with Mike. Was she fooling herself again to think that they finally could get somewhere in this case?

Think positive, for a change. This could be the break they needed to find the killer. Sam's killer. She'd bet this semester's tuition; the same person was responsible for her brother's murder.

She started with what she knew about Jay. Wealthy. Math nerd. Played cards in the student union. Maybe played for money. Came back and flashed a big wad of bills at his roommate one weekend. Roommate told her Jay had this chip on his nightstand. Not exactly a poker chip. What did he call it? It said *DEALER* on it. His roommate had laughed at him.

"You're a drug dealer now? Way to go, Jay," he'd said.

"No, imbecile. It's from a poker game. As in *dealer button*. I won big that night."

That's what it was. It was called a button. To show whose turn it was to deal. Jay's roommate wasn't into poker or card games. That was the only thing he remembered about that weekend—that and the money. Jay had seemed a little nervous for the next couple weeks. Then he was back to his nerdy normal. Jay drove up to a game in Davenport in December before break. That was the last time anyone saw him.

A week after the story appeared, Sheila came back from her last class, opened the door and soon as she turned on the light, she saw the paper on the floor. The article she wrote about the murder was taped to a sheet of typing paper. In block letters: STOP BITCH OR YOU'RE NEXT.

Sheila had felt gooseflesh on her arms and stood rooted to the spot. She'd waited, listening to the dull tick of her desk clock a full minute before she stooped to pick up the paper, barely pinching it between the nails of her thumb and forefinger. As if contact with her skin would burn her.

"Another satisfied reader." She'd said it aloud, trying for bravado. A lame joke at her own expense to a non-existent audience, while a shudder ran through her. Her hand shook as she folded the paper in half and stuck it at the bottom of her desk drawer. She had to tell Mike. But she'd hesitated. She'd bet his response would be a version of 'What did I tell you? Leave this to the police and mind your own business.'

***

She'd been right about Mike's response to the note, of course. After she'd told him, Mike had kept her as far away from his investigation as he could. Along with any information the investigation into those murders in Iowa had yielded. Never mind that the cases remained unsolved. Nothing had come of the story in the *Daily Iowan*.

What story could she write now? It wasn't as if she was working for any rag that would print her conjectures about present day murders. Especially not cases under active investigation. But if she could, how would she do it? How to bait a trap to lure an animal—the one who had killed Craig and Sarah? And maybe Sam. It was a stupid thought. It sounded naïve, even to her. Excusable back then, but not now. All she'd had to show for her story then had been that nasty note. Now, she had even less: some random newspaper articles and a bad copy of a photograph that Mike didn't think counted for anything.

Chapter Forty-Two

All they had were phantoms and the shadowy photo of a gang-ster. Mike was still trying to find something solid on Alfred Sienna. Mike and Duane had been waiting for an "aha" moment in this case. Something that would click for one of the people who had known Craig, something to provide more than a solid lead, actual evidence.

Mike found himself thinking back to the threatening note Sheila had received after she'd written that article about the student's murder in Davenport. Mike had tried to walk the narrow line between giving Sheila enough information to keep her safe and not too much—he'd been afraid of what could happen.

He was afraid for her now too. She hadn't even known the student who had been a victim back then. How much more dangerous was it that she knew the two current victims? Not to mention the latest revelation about someone he still considered a suspect. He needed to have a face-to-face with Sheila. Was she holding back something? There could still be something she wasn't telling him, or even Duane. But he and Duane had been holding out on her, too.

Mike hadn't given Sheila an update on the conversation Billy had overheard between Sarah and Craig. Or his conversations with Al-thorpe. Althorpe hadn't confirmed Billy's implications that Craig had gambling debts and maybe another woman. But he'd given them a reason to think Craig was in trouble with his investors. Mike wondered if that had been a play by Althorpe to shift suspicion away from himself. If anything, his close ties to Sarah made him a suspect in her death as well as Craig's.

Duane had convinced Althorpe to come in for another interview. As the three of them sat in the oppressive interview room, Althorpe had sweated profusely but produced an alibi for the time Sarah was murdered. He'd also given Mike and Duane the distinct impression that Sienna had something to hide. Althorpe claimed not to know what it was. Mike assumed that if Althorpe had worked with Carl Vitale, he would know what other work Sienna had done for him. Beyond conventional investments. The kind of work that smooths the way for projects that have hit a slowdown. Usually, that involved a human resource problem. But Craig wouldn't have wanted to expose anything that put his old man in a bad light. No, the information Craig had on Sienna wouldn't have involved his own father directly. But was it something about Sienna's past, before he came to New York?

Something Althorpe had said resonated with Mike at the time. Mike could use the perspective of someone with more knowledge of the human mind. Maybe it was time to set up that meeting with Sheila's friend Marcus.

Chapter Forty-Three

Sheila flashed on an image from a dream she'd had before she'd left home for school. She and her mom had talked about it on a long drive to Des Moines. They'd gone to do some shopping and to visit Uncle Irv. It had been a quiet ride. Her mom, usually animated and talkative, was concentrating on her driving. Sheila had been writing in her journal for the first half hour. As she wrote, things bubbled to the surface of her consciousness—things she needed to talk to her mom about.

"Mom, we haven't talked much about Sam this summer."

"No, I guess we haven't. Doesn't mean we're not thinking of him, darling."

"He's always on my mind, Mom. I think I hear him in his room sometimes. Not like a ghost, exactly, but..."

"I feel his presence too. I'll be dusting in his room, and something of his I had put away in one place seems to have reappeared in another. He was always playing little tricks like that on me." She was smiling, even though Sheila could see her eyes glisten.

"Mom, I had a dream last night about Sam. He was holding these two big plastic Tractor Supply bags. He held them out to me and said, 'Take 'em, they're yours now.' I took them, and as I opened up the first bag, he walked away. He just vanished. I looked in the bag, and it was full of paper, like when you ship a package. I took the paper out, and there was just a deck of cards in one bag. There was a rabbit-foot in the other. What do you think that means?"

Her mother took her eyes off the road for a moment to look at her, then went back to the long, flat expanse of highway before them. The road became hillier as they neared Des Moines.

Finally, her mother said, "I'm no interpreter of dreams, Sheila, but I think it means that you loved your brother very much, and you want to keep his memory alive."

"But what about the deck of cards and the rabbit-foot, what do you think that means? That rabbit-foot creeps me out. Mom, I never told you this, but back in my first year here, someone left a rabbit-foot in my desk. It wasn't a purple cute one on a keychain. It was brown and matted with blood. I never told anyone about it, and I never found out who left it there."

Her mother gasped and shook her head. "This dream, Sheila. I think it means that Sam wants you to find something good, something lucky in life, even among the bad things that happen. Even the things that scare you. That's what I think."

"You mean, like everything, even Sam's death, happens for a reason?" Sheila spat.

"No, dear. I don't think everything happens for a reason. After the holocaust, I heard people say, 'There is no justice and no judge.' My uncle told me that saying, *leit din, v'leit dayan,* came from a Talmudic story. In it a young boy performed a good deed, and he died because of doing it. My uncle said that when something so unfair happens, no matter how terrible, we were to say *Blessed is the True Judge, Dayan ha Emet.* I'll never understand how something so terrible could have happened to my boy, to your brother. But I still believe. I believe in acts of kindness and love. We try to balance the scales. We can't let the evil in the world outweigh the good. That's what I think your dream means. Sam was giving you a gift of love."

Sheila hadn't known whether to cry or scream at her mom. *A gift?* She took a deep breath and let it out slowly. *A deck of cards and a rabbit-foot. Sounds like the kind of gift Sam would give me.* "Thanks, Mom. I'll try to think of it that way."

But that had been a lie. To herself she'd thought, *There will be justice. And I'll be the judge.*

Chapter Forty-Four

Sometimes Sheila felt her life was divided into *then:* before Sam's murder, and *now:* everything after that. *At least now contained Marcus.* That had seemed easy too. In the beginning. Writing comedy. Their five minutes on stage. Easy to work together. Easy to be together for rehearsals. He made it fun, and there'd been so little fun in her life for years. More than fun, he was super smart, good looking, sexy, and not afraid to ask questions that went deeper than her favorite show or song. No one else had been able to draw her out about the tough stuff the way he did. And he got five points for not caring about the Yankees.

Where was it going? Where did she want it to go? Sheila didn't know, but she did want it to keep going. Did she have the guts to follow her heart? Was the hesitation because they would be an interracial couple? *Hell, yes.* When they walked down the street together, she could feel the stares. And this was New York City.

Imagine bringing Marcus back to Delmont, to my parents' house.

Would her mother be quivering over what the neighbors would think? Would her father pull him in for a hug like he did with Mike or keep his arm stiffly at his side?

For that matter, what would his family think of her? Marcus alluded to a cousin who had married a white man, and his aunt and uncle were extremely upset. "Why on earth would she marry the oppressor?" they'd asked Marcus.

Nancy would probably make some racist remark like: "Is it true what they say about black guys?"

Nancy, at this moment I have no idea. The weird thing is how I think of Marcus. Obviously, he's not white. I can't begin to know what it's like for him to be a black man in this country. But mainly, he's Marcus. He's a sensitive, funny, sexy man, and I think I'm in love with him. If Sam were alive, would he say, "He's a good guy," or would he tell me "You can do better." Like that time he caught me making out with Billy. Or would he ask, "What the hell do you think you're doing?" She wanted to think that if Sam were alive, he'd say, "I trust you to make a good decision for yourself."

It was the "couple" part that made her put her head between her knees so she wouldn't faint. What would be left of her if she opened herself to Marcus and lost him? Sam was enough loss. It had taken her all this time. She wasn't sure she had the strength for a relationship with Marcus, even though she longed for one.

That's all for tonight's episode of To Love or Not to Love. *Tune in again, Sheila.*

Sheila started a letter to her parents. Too many long-distance phone calls threw her budget out of whack. She remembered the letters she composed when she first moved to New York telling her mother and father about the little things that were so *New York*. You could get a delicious bagel at a hole-in-the-wall coffee shop; you might see a famous actress as you passed Saks Fifth Avenue, or you could get a cheap seat at a great Broadway show if you stood in line at TKTS. Wherever you turned, there were people who dressed, looked, and spoke differently. She'd kept it light and entertaining. Was this going to be an honest letter?

Dear Mom and Dad,

Sorry I haven't called or written much in the past couple months. I've been busy: after doing a comedy set with my black, almost-boyfriend, my apartment was broken into. Nothing much was taken—that I know of. Work is going well. One of my new accounts is a healthy candy bar—perfect, right? Except the 'Fit Bar' tastes like cardboard. I got to work on a new financial fund campaign with a young, eligible bachelor. You might have heard of him, Craig Vitale. He was murdered. Then his girlfriend was murdered, and I was a suspect for about two days.

Maybe: *I saw Mike and Billy, and even Jane recently.* Editing required—leave out: *at the murdered guy's funeral.*

No, this had to be another version of "work is fine." She couldn't bear to give her parents any more reasons for worry.

Sheila tried to start a letter to Nancy. *Dear Nancy.* She put down the pen. Time and distance had eroded their friendship over the past years. Whose distance? Had it been physical distance or emotional? It had been both. They were in different stages in their lives. Sheila was sure as soon as she got married and pregnant, they could pick up their friendship the way they used to pick up their attempts at knitting scarves. It would still be fun, but there would be a lot of dropped stitches and a few holes.

She snapped her fingers in front of her face and blinked, surprised to find herself blinking away tears. *Focus on now.* How could any of the people in her high school circle be related to the threatening note she'd received back then? What did it matter? The note had nothing to do with the rabbit-foot prank back in high school. Both belonged in the *then* category. Thinking about them, disturbing though they might be, wouldn't do her any good *now.*

What she needed now was to find connections to Craig's project. There had to be something hidden in the fat folders and padded prose. She needed to cut through the crap and focus on all the details she could find. If this were a news article, she'd need facts for every connection. Problem was, she didn't have any.

Chapter Forty-Five

Mike hadn't expected Marcus to have such presence. He looked professorial in his shirt, tie, and seersucker suit. The aviator glasses were his nod to cool. Like Linc Hayes, the hip undercover detective in *Mod Squad*, minus the afro. Marcus was handsome, and the whole was greater than the sum of his parts. Mike could understand Sheila's attraction to him.

He introduced himself to Marcus, "Thanks for coming in, Marcus. I appreciate your help in this investigation," Mike said. "I know it's out of concern, because of your friendship with Sheila. I know she's shared information about the Vitale murder and how it brought back memories of her brother's murder ten years ago." Mike pressed his lips into a thin line. "I didn't appreciate that she'd told you, but I think I understand." He cocked his head and said, "So you don't discount Sheila's feeling that there's a connection to her brother's murder. As a professional, not just as a friend."

"Correct. But my experience in police work is limited. Likewise, my experience in murder cases. I can only go as far as my work as a psychologist and concern for Sheila will take me."

"So where do you think you can help?"

"I have some ideas, some from previous work experiences."

Mike remembered Marcus mentioning that he had worked as a prison psychologist. Mike had been impressed when he'd heard the name of the prison.

Marcus continued. "From what Sheila told me about your lives together in Delmont and here in New York City, I see some threads, some strong connections."

Marcus sat back, resting his hands on his knees. He was calm, cool, and collected. Mike sensed an intentional deference in Marcus, a reluctance to assume the lead. He was a successful black man living in a white man's world—he had to take the temperature of the room before he engaged. He wasn't going to challenge the status quo here. Living in a straight world, Mike often had to fight that reluctance within himself.

Mike wanted to draw him out, so he asked what he thought was a straightforward question. "What exact services did you perform working with prisoners, and how do you think what you did could help us here?"

"Forensic science is still new and a broad topic," Marcus began. "It's the research and application of psychological knowledge in the legal system. I administered tests to see which prisoners might fit back into society more easily. Also, ran a few group-therapy sessions. And since I've been back outside prison walls, I've become intrigued by ink analysis and..."

"Determining if documents contain more than one kind of ink, indicating forgery, or that a document was signed at an earlier or later date than indicated. Not sure how that would help us."

"I'm interested in using psychology to build criminal profiles. It's a newer part of the FBI. Local and state police forces are getting used to asking them for help. I'd like to sharpen my skills in that area. Mike, are you familiar with the Behavioral Analysis Unit down at Quantico?"

"Yes, and I see possible benefits in their ways of looking at a crime." Mike took a breath and looked Marcus in the eye. "Sheila said you spent a lot of time delving into Sam's personality. Why?"

"I'm not trying to blame the victim or besmirch Sam's memory. I'm just trying to understand who he was. What about him might have made someone angry, frustrated, or frightened enough to kill him? From what I've learned about Sam, one of his strongest traits was his desire to help. That kind of interest in others, even altruism, can be misinterpreted as being nosy or controlling. He might have helped the wrong person. Someone who saw Sam's attempt to help as interference or threatening behavior. Sam might have gotten in someone's way."

Mike nodded and Marcus continued.

"As different as the two victims were, the same principles apply. Nothing Craig did seems motivated by a desire to help others. His interest seemed to have been in helping himself. Ego, compulsion, and ambition. Someone might have felt thwarted by Craig's ambition. The killer might have felt Craig threatened his own success either directly or indirectly.

What interests me is that three of you: Sheila, Billy, and Jane—all from Delmont, now here in the city—seem to have known both victims. And that you caught the case. That's one hell of a coincidence considering the span of time and distance between the two murders."

Marcus looked at Mike pointedly and continued. "What I'm offering is: share your information with me, and I'll work up a profile of the killer. Then you can use your professional judgement as to whether you think the killer could be the same for both Sam and Craig."

Marcus looked at his watch.

Mike wanted to hear more from Marcus. He wanted to know more about his experience as a prison psychologist. He wasn't sure how accurate a profile Marcus could create or if it would even be useful, but he said, "Thanks, Marcus. You've given me a lot to think about. I'll be in touch.

Marcus was right about Sam. Mike sat alone in the interview room trawling through memories. He cast his mind back to a morning in his hometown ten years ago. Sam had been determined to help find the Mahoneys. Sam had barely known Mary and Jack, yet there he was.

As chief of police, Mike's father had been desperate enough to try to appease the town letting them be involved in a search of the perimeter of the Mahoney's property after his men and the county forensics people had finished. Mike remembered Sam scouring the field, finding that class ring, and wanting to relay information to Mike's father about something he'd seen, in case it would help the investigation. The scene from that day in 1972 was vivid in Mike's mind now.

***

The sun was just rising as he arrived at the empty field. The yard of the big yellow house, still in shadow, was festooned in yellow crime-scene tape. A squad car was parked in the driveway, its interior dark, its occupant leaning back in the front seat.

Probably slept here all night, poor Piper.

Mike's dad arrived in a patrol car, and Mike drove his mother's sedan. His dad organized the half dozen men who had come to help with the search. They spread out abreast of each other and walked slowly across the field. About ten paces from where they began, Sam saw something.

At first, it seemed like a trick of the light, the morning sun striking a circle of metal, a ring. It was dirty, but it had a red, dome-shaped stone in the heavy setting. Sam stood still and motioned to Mike and his dad. As he bent down, not touching it, Mike could see it clearly. A class ring attached to a broken gold chain. His dad had shrugged. It might or might not be significant. He called to the photographer who leaned in and took a shot of it. Then his dad used a baggie to pick it up, sealing the ring and chain inside.

They continued their stroll to the other side of the field. Only one thing was sighted, an undisturbed wire snare for catching rabbits. It was empty. Their search was repeated all around the perimeter of the house. When they finished, the sun was high overhead, the sky a bright blue.

"Thanks. That's enough for today." Chief Joe Sloan spent a few minutes clapping backs and shaking hands. Then he called out, "Sam, Mike, get on over here."

They sat on the stoop of the farmhouse. Mike took sodas out of a cooler in the shade of the overhang and passed one to his dad and one to Sam. Joe popped the top off his Fresca.

"Sam, I think you might have found a lead today. But maybe I'm being optimistic. Mike told me there was someone you thought I should talk to. Want to tell me about it? Mike, why don't you head home and check on your mom. See if she made anything for lunch. If she did, bring some back for me."

Mike fiddled with his shoes, trying to appear as if he wasn't listening. But he heard.

"Sam, what can you tell me?"

"Probably nothing, but I was wondering if you've talked to the next-door neighbors," Sam had said, "you know, the Browns. I was sort of concerned, with them living right next door and all. Do you think they're in danger?"

"I told them they need to keep their doors and windows locked. I think I scared them. They seem shaken. Any reason you were concerned?"

"Jane," Sam started, then he paused. "I gave her a ride home about two weeks ago, and when I dropped her off, I saw her cross the field and go into the Mahoneys' cellar. I thought maybe Jane saw or heard something while she was there that could end up being important."

Mike's dad had said, "That's good thinking, Sam. Jane didn't volunteer any information but, like I said, she seemed shaken up. She comes across as quiet, but a good kid. She might not realize something she saw or heard could be important. I'll talk to her again."

***

Even now, Mike was sure Jane knew more than she had told him. He thought about what she had said about Jack Mahoney. It was possible that he was alive and had assumed a new identity, not unlike Sienna, and even that he had come to New York. But what possible motive could someone like Jack have to kill Craig? Or Sam, for that matter? Mike had been sure that Jack had murdered Mary, but he had never been able to think past that. Surely if Sam had information about Mary's murder, he would have told someone. He would have said something to Mike, wouldn't he?

As for Jane, he wondered how Jack's alleged abuse of her had shaped the woman she was now. Back in Delmont she had seemed mistrustful, closed off, and awkward. Angry? That was understandable. Now, ten years later her transformation into a confident, successful woman was remarkable. Beyond that, she'd cooperated fully with the investigation. He didn't see what she had to gain from Craig's death, and he couldn't imagine her killing him. Not like that. Jane could have had opportunity, but did she have anything approaching a strong enough motive? He couldn't grasp it. Yet there was something that kept tickling his brain. Maybe it was a connection she and Craig had to someone. Like Sienna. If so, could Sienna have been connected to murders ten years ago as well as now?

He remembered a detail from the interview with Sam's boss at Tractor Supply; a well-dressed customer who had looked familiar. Familiar, but somehow out of place.

Chapter Forty-Six

S heila felt a lingering unease every time she left her apartment. A
sense of being followed, but when she looked back—no one. She
felt almost as jittery inside her apartment. Only an hour after she'd
settled in for the evening, she heard someone try to insert a key into
her front door. She'd shouted: "Hey! Who is it?"

"Sorry for the bother; it's Anthony. I got off on the wrong floor. A
delivery for the Rosens."

She tried to calm herself. Fear kept fogging her brain. Other emotions found their way in, threatening to overwhelm her. Marcus's
fault. He'd forced her to dive into the memories, and each dive sent
bubbles to the surface. Bubbles making big ripples. Prime example:
the rabbit-foot, with dark dried blood staining its crumpled Kleenex
nest. Since the break-in that awful image popped up without warning,
like when she was on the verge of sleep. *Why?* It all came down to a
feeling. Still trying to make sense of seemingly unrelated incidents that
felt connected.

Dust off the old journalist skills, again.

She told herself: start with people who were there in Delmont
and are still around me now. That narrowed it down to Mike, Billy,
and Jane. Had the prankster had been one of them? Back then, she'd
thought Billy had been responsible, but the shock and distress on his

face when she'd confronted him about it the morning it happened had seemed so genuine.

It was the only incident like that she could remember. Disgusting, to be sure, but a break-in qualified as more than a disgusting prank. From there to murder? A journey of a thousand miles—and they were a thousand miles from where it had happened. *Let the rabbit-foot hop away for a moment.*

When she thought past Sam to the other murders, she slammed up against the possibility that the same killer had murdered at least four other men in Iowa. Mike had told her about two unsolved murders that had taken place near Iowa City when she was in college. Then there was the student found near Davenport. The one she'd done the story on. The story that delivered the note underneath her door. That was no prank, it was a warning. Both Mike and Marcus had talked about opportunity and motive. Had the killer started in Delmont, with Sam, and moved east taking opportunity when and where he saw it? But what about motive?

Revenge. How did that word enter her brain? Weren't all killers just batshit crazy? Like Son of Sam. Berkowitz took orders from a dog. No rhyme or reason. But this felt different.

She could imagine Craig being the target of revenge. The more she learned about Craig and his addiction-riddled past, the more that made sense. Maybe he'd run into someone who wasn't interested in him making amends.

When she brought Sam back into the equation, how could it be revenge? Revenge for what? Marcus had asked her if there was anyone Sam overshadowed in school athletics or beat out in academics. Someone jealous of his achievement. Had he kept a student off the debate team by being better? Doubtful. Had he said something hurtful to someone? *Besides me? Doubtful.*

Marcus had alluded to Sam's personality and asked her to think about who had been around Sam, who had wanted more from him than he gave. Or misinterpreted all that he gave as something more. Sure, Sam had been wild about Janice, but he'd hinted to Sheila that he was in no hurry to marry. Had he thought that he could do better? Maybe Janice realized that high school sweethearts didn't outlast the test of distances and time, or had she been sure Sam was *the one*? Sheila supposed jealousy could drive someone to a breaking point. But she couldn't seriously picture Janice jealous or angry enough to kill Sam.

But what if those feelings of jealousy and rage had been tangled up with fear of being exposed? Who had a secret that Sam had known about? Although she hadn't known it at the time, that could've been Mike. Sheila shook her head to erase that thought. Marcus had let that go too. Or had he?

Had Sam known something that could hurt someone? Again, in hindsight, that might have been Mike. But she didn't think Mike had come out to her brother. Sam had fixed Mike up with a date for their prom, and Mike had kept going out with her. What was her name? She'd been Janice's cousin. It didn't matter. No way Sam would have outed Mike, even if he had known. Besides, Mike had been bound for Syracuse that fall. Delmont, with its small-town opinions, had already been in his rearview mirror. The only thing she had to finally agree on with Marcus was that then and now, the killer was much closer than she'd let herself imagine.

Chapter Forty-Seven

Her next showcase was at a club in Yonkers. Sheila had received a phone call the day before from someone at the club telling her that she'd won a second spot after qualifying with her May showcase with Marcus in Manhattan. It surprised her, because she had expected a letter rather than a phone call, and she hadn't expected an offer of a solo spot. Not one to look a gift horse in the mouth, she took it. Deep down she wanted to get her solo routine shaped up. Marcus was great, but she feared she was using him as a crutch, in more ways than comedy. She doubted the viability of their act too. Not that they weren't good together. The feedback after their May showcase was positive.

"You didn't get the month-long comic residency," the club's booker had said, "but you and Marcus did win a Wednesday-night spot in the middle of the lineup, which is damn good for a start. You'll go up right after Sonny Hanover. He was on the *Tonight Show* last year. The spot's after the Fourth of July. Your writing was sharp: the Freud stuff was laugh line after laugh line. Next week you'll get my letter with your exact date and time."

"When you get the letter, we'll set up a rehearsal schedule," was all Marcus had said.

"You mean, we don't need to get together before I get the letter?"

They both seemed to avoid commitment. Not just in their act either.

"Is that what you think I said?"

Answer my question with a question. Shrinky and damn frustrating.

She'd sighed and said, "I'm not sure what I think you said. Color me confused."

"You're not confused, only reluctant to say what you want."

"So, you think you've got me all figured out."

"Don't I?"

She could feel the color spread across her cheeks. She wanted him to know her. How would that happen if she didn't stop being afraid?

***

Sheila couldn't bear the thought of the maze-like subway-bus combo ride to her showcase.

"Take my car," Billy had offered. "We'll ride home together after your show."

"What if you have to work late and miss the show?"

"Always the worrier. Not gonna happen. But if I do, you can drop the car off to me the next morning. We'll go out for breakfast. Either way, I get to spend a little extra time with you."

"Oooh. Your ulterior motives are showing. Is that a pen in your brief, or are you just excited to see me?"

"That almost works. But I wouldn't use it yet. Need to touch it up a bit."

"That sounds like fun."

They had fallen back into their pattern of flirting.

Sheila drove Billy's dependable Chevette to the Yonkers Comedy Club. It had been a while since she'd driven and it made her anxious to be driving someone else's car. She'd parked it with extra care, away from the others in a space at the far end of the lot. One or two other cars also parked at that end were much nicer than Billy's. Big, dark, and shiny. Lincolns or Caddies? Those town cars looked too much alike to her to differentiate. Besides, who cared? Those conspicuous consumption symbols were not her style, not that she'd ever have the money for one.

As she approached the door, a wave of insecurity hit, and she nearly turned around and started for the car. *I can do this.* She pushed the door open and stepped through. Inside the club, she looked for the booker as her eyes adjusted to the dim lights. A pale, older guy with a sad mustache and oversized horn-rimmed glasses stood by a podium with a clipboard in hand. He looked up at her.

"Sheila Ross, I have a spot tonight, but I don't know where I am in the lineup." She put on her most winning smile. The booker looked at her as if she'd just given him a line, and it bombed.

"Shirley, I don't know where you are in the lineup either. Nice pearls."

Sheila felt herself flush. "I'm sorry, there must be a mistake. I got a call yesterday..."

"Look, that's a new one on me. But I'll bite. You're cute, and we've got an empty slot. So, Shelley, it's your lucky day. You're on right before the headliner."

"It's Sheila, Sheila Ross. And thanks."

She bought a cup of tea and snagged a lemon slice from the bar to warm up her throat. She found a quiet corner to sip and to practice her visualization. It wasn't working tonight. She was one big fuzzball of tension. Other comedians were lining up. She took another sip of tea. Suddenly, it was her turn.

Kevin and a couple other friends from work, Bonnie and Lou, were in the audience. But Billy was nowhere to be seen. He must have had to stay late at work. She felt a little let down. She wanted to run a couple financial questions by him. Some troubling thoughts. Some bad feelings. She needed him to talk her down from that mental ledge. She had tried calling him at work. No answer.

"Sheila, that was great! You're really hitting your stride. Keep at it." Kevin was one of her biggest fans, bless him.

"You were almost going too fast. Slow down for some of your lines. Let us catch up to you," Bonnie said.

But she couldn't slow down tonight. Nerves had pushed the words out of her so fast, she'd felt like she was hyperventilating.

"Why don't we all go have a drink, and you can unwind."

"Thanks, Lou, but I'm really beat. I appreciate you all coming, and even more, laughing and clapping." She reached into her purse. "Here's some real, live cash. Go buy a round on me. I'll see you at the office tomorrow."

She didn't want to be rude, but she couldn't get away fast enough. She needed to be where she could unwind, but that place wasn't a bar. She had to get home. At first, the highway seemed busy for that time of night. Then the cars ahead of her thinned out and seemed to disappear. She could see headlights behind her, but they too were far off. She kept looking for exit signs to give her an indication of when she could turn off. Sheila wasn't sure how, but suddenly she found herself on an unlit, deserted stretch of road. *Great. I missed it.*

She had slowed a bit when she saw the headlights of a car closer in her rearview mirror. She gave a small sigh of relief. But her relief was quickly replaced by panic. The car behind her was driving fast, too fast. Was it going to pass her? It wasn't slowing. It was speeding up, aimed for her rear bumper. Sheila laid on her horn, but the big, dark car closed in, pushing her off the road. She swerved to avoid full impact.

No, not Billy's car! Shit. No.

She skidded into the guardrail, spinning. She rose in her seat a little from the impact even with the seat belt on. Her head banged against something as she braced herself against the steering wheel with both arms. She felt lightheaded, she was going to pass out. But she didn't. Sheila sat motionless, not wanting to believe what had just happened.

Her head ached, and her whole body felt like it was draped in a lead apron. Bits of the trauma kept penetrating her brain fog. She could see the headlights of the car overtaking her as she drove. She remembered swerving, the front passenger side of the Chevette scraping the guardrails, spinning around to face in the opposite direction. The car that hit her had slowed, then sped away.

She had bumped her head. Hard. She felt a trickle of warm, sticky blood in her scalp begin to ooze onto her forehead. Her shoulders hurt from bracing herself. But she was okay. *I'm okay, but I'm so tired.* She knew she should try to stay awake, but she closed her eyes. She drifted in and out. When she startled awake she glimpsed the dashboard clock. It was late, so late. *I'm okay. I'm okay.* She said it out loud, but it came out as a raspy whisper.

She tried to start Billy's car. Trusty, little thing, it rattled and made some new sounds, but it started. Scraping, whining, and the rattling—that was her teeth chattering. *That can't be good.* She sat for a few more minutes before she righted the car and inched back onto the dark highway.

She hadn't gone far when she saw it. Finally, a sign. *Of course. Now I find the damned exit.* Her hands shaking on the steering wheel as she

made it to the off-ramp. A Shell station was a block away. She called
Marcus and told him where she thought she was.

Billy's car, but I dialed Marcus.

"Please, your bathroom key."

The station attendant handed it over. She felt him look her up and
down, but he didn't say a word. She sat on the toilet seat with her head
between her knees. She shut out the pain. Fog rolled over her. Then
someone was knocking on the door. She turned the doorknob. The
attendant and Marcus were looking at her, eyes full of concern.

Marcus drove her to the nearest ER and called the police, then Billy.
Billy wanted to take a cab to the hospital. She felt bad, but she knew
she'd feel worse with Billy there. She felt terrible about the damage to
his car. How would she be able to make it up to him?

"How can you even want to see me after I got into an accident with
your car?"

"Sheila, the only thing that matters is that you're okay. You are okay,
aren't you? I'm coming over there. I'll sit with you."

"Billy, I'm okay. I really am. Marcus is here right now."

"Marcus is there? Why?"

Ignore that. "There's no reason for both of you to be losing sleep.
I'll call you tomorrow morning, and we can deal with the insurance
adjuster together. I'll buy breakfast."

Maybe she should have stayed overnight at the hospital. The ER
nurse had wanted her to, but she insisted on sleeping in her own bed.
Marcus drove her back to her apartment, giving her worried sideways
glances. He stayed the night, sitting propped with pillows, watching
her. She woke once to his soft snoring and felt the comforter from the
end of the bed. He had unfolded it and covered them with it. She fell
back asleep. No bad dreams. Only the sleep of exhaustion.

She heard the rattle of the spoon in a mug. Her nightstand clock said 7:00 a.m. He was standing by the side of the bed, coffee in hand.

"Go back to sleep. You need to take the day off," Marcus said in a tone she hadn't heard before.

"Hey, I'm okay. Just a little shaken up."

"Hear me out. Not to shake you up more, but I'm experiencing a bit of paranoia. After our show, I felt shadowed. I asked myself who in hell would be interested in following me. I didn't see any white guys driving around in a truck with a shotgun rack. I hadn't noticed anyone dressed in white sheets in the audience either. I didn't say anything about it, but maybe I should have. If someone had been following me last week, it might be the person who tried to hurt you."

Sheila gasped. She was already freaked, and now, on top of it, she was feeling guilty. She didn't want to put anyone else in danger. *Especially not Marcus.* She opened her mouth to protest or apologize, but nothing came out.

Marcus put a hand on her shoulder. "Look, I can take care of myself. But do us both a favor: don't go to work today."

Sheila gave an involuntary shiver. "I'll call and let Danielle know I won't be in."

"You need to see a doctor."

"I will, I will." She winced.

"If your headache doesn't disappear in another hour, promise me you'll go back to the ER." Marcus set down his coffee mug and put his arm around her. "You're important to me, so treat yourself accordingly."

Sheila sagged at the loss of his body's warmth as he left her side, walked to the front door, and closed it.

"Sure," she said. Her reaction to Marcus's touch was more than she could handle.

The warm shower helped. So did the Constant Comment tea and dry toast. Her stomach settled, and a bit of energy restored, she steeled herself and called Billy.

"You need to stay home," he told her, sounding like an imitation of his dad. "I'm dealing with the car and the insurance adjuster. Spoke to them already. It'll be a few days before they can get me a loaner, but mine's drivable, even though it looks like crap. I want to talk to Mike too. Are you alone or...?"

"Alone and doing fine."

"Are you sure you'll be okay alone? I never thought I'd say these words to you, Sheila, but I've got a bad feeling about this."

That makes two of us.

"I'm okay, Billy. Really. I'm so sorry about your car and all this weirdness. I think maybe I'm some kind of jinx."

"Sheila, anyone can be in the wrong place at the wrong time."

Chapter Forty-Eight

It took another day before Sheila felt well enough to go back to Hummingbird. She only left her apartment long enough to stop at the bookstore and grocery. She spent a large part of her mental-health day eating through a pint of Häagen-Dazs Rum Raisin and reading *Red Dragon* by Thomas Harris. The work of fiction produced real fear. Such a cunning, crazy man. In the mystery, the killer had an everyday job that allowed him to meticulously choose each family of victims. Why had her family been singled out? What had Sam done to be chosen? Did his killer and Craig's have an unremarkable job that let him blend in with people around him? That would be easier in Manhattan, but not in Delmont. None of it made sense to her.

The next morning, she *needed* to go back to work to take her mind off the fact that someone had tried to run her off the road. She made her way to the subway.

Sheila usually forced herself to pay attention to her surroundings, but today she barely registered the sights and sounds that enveloped her as she pushed through the crowded subway car. She must have looked as bad as she felt, because a young man stood up and offered her his seat. She wedged herself into the gap between two older women and muttered "Thanks."

She was aware of a familiar scent. One of the women smelled of Estee Lauder, the perfume her mother used to wear. Her eyes filled with tears at that remembered comfort. She suddenly wanted to be back home sitting on the sofa with her mom.

Okay, crybaby, keep it together. She'd call Mike from work and discuss the next steps. She'd given him only as much information as he needed to help her file the police report. That car seemed to come out of nowhere. Must have been going well over the speed limit. It was a boat of a car. Maybe an Oldsmobile, Lincoln, or Cadillac. Dark color, late model. The driver hit her and didn't stop, just slowed, moved to the left lane, and sped away.

***

At work, she took a break from visualizing dancing candy bars, thought back to what Jane had said about her missing papers, and called Mike—again.

"When did you speak to Jane? Never mind. If you two had a chat, did Jane share any details of her project with you? What did she tell you?"

"Nothing."

"Then, for the moment, drop it. If you discover something more concrete, I'm ready to listen. Jane does seem to have had more to do with Craig and his project than she first let on. So does his partner, Sienna. But we're still chasing down those tie-ins."

"What exactly is involved in the chasing and why can't I help? Isn't there anything I can research—"

"Please, Sheila, don't test your faith in me now."

Her irritation and restlessness peaked as Mike ended their call. She tried to work through her agitation, but she was spinning her wheels.

Faith, shmaith. Screw it. You and Duane keep chasing your tails. I'm screwing my courage to the sticking point.

***

Sheila went up to the East Seventy-Eighth Street Library branch after work. Where to begin in the microfiche? She went looking in the *Des Moines Register* for any item about the Iowa I-80 murders, from 1972 on. Sheila scrolled through article after article with a measure of disbelief at how many unsolved murders there were. The number of cases that fit the same pattern as that of her brother were few. But they were there, in black and white. The method and locations—ligature strangulation, deserted roads, less traveled parts of highways—were there. But the murders that matched most closely seemed to have stopped about four years earlier. Did that mean the killer had landed in prison for some lesser crime? What if Sam's killer was dead? No. Sheila didn't believe that. Maybe the killer had moved on to New York City. What better place to commit murder and hide in plain sight amidst all the random violence. Just as Craig's killer was doing. Why not Sam's killer?

Hadn't they all moved here? Billy, Mike, Jane, and herself included.

Sheila couldn't picture Billy hurting anyone. But wasn't that exactly what the neighbors and co-workers of serial killers always said: "He was a nice guy, a quiet guy; never bothered anyone."

Mike walked around every day with a gun strapped to his body, but killing outside the line of duty? Sure, she knew that Mike wasn't the perfect big brother surrogate she had wanted him to be, that he was only human. That was what made her doubt he was capable of murder, his vulnerability.

Then there was Jane. Would Jane have had a reason to kill either Sam or Craig? Sheila couldn't imagine. Not aside from a rough childhood which she seemed to have come through fine. Better than fine.

But the killer was close. Close enough to know she'd be on the road at night, alone. Her body tensed and ached as she began to shudder reliving the terrifying moments of two nights ago. Someone was watching her. Watching and waiting.

Chapter Forty-Nine

Back in the saddle. Sheila had told herself she had to do an open mic again right away to get past her fear after the car accident. She equated enough random things with disasters. A comedy club couldn't be one more. She was back at The Laugh Track. No driving required. It was a full room with standbys closing out the waitlist. The emcee had told her she'd be in the first three to go up.

She sipped her tea. The emcee called the first name, and the guy behind her was so eager to run up that he bumped her elbow and knocked her cup of tea out onto the floor. "Clean up in aisle five," the guy next to her yelled to the emcee. The friends at his table laughed. Sheila put her hands over her ears to shut out the noise and focus on her set.

Then she was up.

As she felt the hot lights on her, she began to sweat. Her eyes weren't focusing, and she felt lightheaded. She made it to the setup line for "me, a Jewish girl from Iowa gets to New York" when her legs started to feel wobbly. Her brain registered that she was falling, but her body couldn't do anything about it. Only the emcee standing on the steps of the stage was able to stop her head from making hard contact with the wood floor. She'd righted herself and pulled some drunk jokes out of her ass. But she wasn't drunk. She'd barely had half her tea. She felt woozy and shaken. Her world had begun to feel out of control. As out of control as it had the summer that Sam had been killed.

Still clammy with sweat, Sheila treated herself to a taxi home. Her hand shook so badly she could barely get her key in the lock. Once inside the apartment, she felt almost safe with the new lock and chain on the door. She'd rearranged the scant furnishings to give her a more protected feeling. Instead of the sofa, she sat in her rocking chair tucked away in a nook behind a bookcase. She was hiding, curled up with a fresh cup of tea and two oatmeal cookies she had hidden from herself in the freezer. Was she getting sick? Was this an after effect from the car accident? She had been afraid. And now she was more afraid. Scared *shitless.* She was scaring herself. Would it help to call someone?

She thought of Marcus. But she hated the thought of calling him after their last conversation. It had left her feeling guilty and too vulnerable. Reassuring though his presence might be their relationship was still too new for her to lean on him repeatedly. She didn't want to call Mike—let him do his job and find the damned killer. He'd tell her it was normal to have a case of the nerves after what she'd been through, and he'd dismiss it as just that.

Like Billy had said, anyone could be in the wrong place at the wrong time. She wasn't about to argue with him. He was probably trying to downplay the incident so she wouldn't fall apart. Trying to protect her. *Poor, fragile Sheila.* If she hesitated or got emotional, Billy, ever the friend looking for benefits, would see it as an opportunity. *No, thank you.* All their joking and flirting aside, she didn't want him trying that again. She wanted to slap him or herself. Wake up!

This isn't about me being in the wrong place. This was personal. The break-in and her messed-with desk. Someone had tried to connect her to Sarah's death. It made her shiver. The car accident was no accident either. She didn't think it was Billy who had been targeted, even though she'd been driving his car. Someone had to have known she was driving it. Someone with motive and the means to follow her and force her off the road.

Rocking in her chair, she counted on the fingers of one hand everyone she knew who had a car. Also, a finger from the other hand. The image of Jane getting into her car after the funeral popped into her head. Then there were the other people at Craig's funeral—coworkers, friends, ex-girlfriends. She imagined Alfred Sienna (possibly the former Alvin Brown) had a car, probably an expensive one. There were people she worked with at Hummingbird and people at the writing center. Hell, Marcus had a car. Cars could be rented or even stolen. *Hard to believe I could have so many enemies to choose from.* That just sounded paranoid.

All the weird stuff had started after Craig's murder. If this had to do with Craig and his project, then she might not be the only one in danger. After all, Sarah had been murdered. Now that she thought about it, Billy and Jane could be targets too. Billy would pooh-pooh anything she said. He'd construe it as an attack on his masculinity. But she needed to talk to Jane. This couldn't wait.

Jane sounded pleased to hear from her. Sheila skipped the small talk. "Some weird things have happened to me recently, scary things. I think it might be connected to Craig's murder, and Sarah's. Frankly, I'm worried about you. Maybe you've noticed some strange stuff going on too."

"Nice of you to be concerned for me, but what are you talking about?"

"Sorry, I guess I'm not making much sense. Look, I'd prefer to discuss this in person. Meet me for a cup of coffee before work?"

"Okay, Chock Full o' Nuts, on Thirty-Fourth Street. Tomorrow morning, seven-thirty. Sheila, try to calm down, okay?"

***

Sheila had consumed half her date-nut bread and cream-cheese sand-wich when Jane sat down on the counter stool next to her. She held her container of coffee, studying Sheila. "Aren't you the early bird—I'm not late, am I? Didn't mean to keep you waiting. You sounded like a basket case last night. What's got you rattled?"

"Jane, Craig's murder has made me aware of the tightrope we walk between life and death every day."

Jane rolled her cool blue eyes. She furrowed her finely arched brows. Sheila didn't give her a chance to shut her down. "It made me see how connected we are without even realizing it. Since Craig and Sarah were killed my apartment's been broken into, and I was in a car accident."

Jane stirred her coffee. "Sorry, but I fail to see the connection. Craig and Sarah's deaths were horrible. But what happened to you, well. . ." She shrugged. "Sounds like bad luck." Jane raised the wooden stirrer to point at Sheila's bruised forehead. "I hope you didn't get a concussion. A blow to the head can have lasting effects—really mess with your mind. You should be home taking it easy." Jane gave her a sympathetic smile. She took a sip of coffee. "You know, Sheila, those things happen every day and not just in New York."

Exasperating. I wish I could say what I really want to say.

Jane took another sip, eyeing Sheila intently and said, "Was that why you called me?"

"You and I knew Craig. Is it so much of a stretch to think we know the person who killed him?"

Jane narrowed her eyes. Sheila continued while Jane sipped her coffee with an expression of skepticism that made Sheila want to dump the cup in her lap.

"Or that the murderer knows about us?"

Jane cocked her head and frowned.

"I think that makes us vulnerable. Us, as in you, me, and Billy. Has anything out of the ordinary happened to you in the last month or so? Even a little thing?"

Jane sighed and set her coffee on the counter. She pursed her lips and drummed her fingers on the counter. Sheila couldn't help looking at those long, red nails. She wondered incongruously; *how does she keep her nails so nice?*

"Okay. I suppose one little thing—a section of notes from a project I've been working on seems to be missing. They'll turn up. Certainly nothing for you to be concerned with." She cocked her head and looked Sheila in the eye. "Don't worry about me. I take care of myself. Always have." She eased herself off the stool and stood to go. "You should watch out. I think you're having some kind of post-traumatic stress reaction. Maybe you ought to see a doctor. We'll get together again soon, okay? See you."

Jane turned and shot Sheila a concerned, almost pitying look as she walked out the door.

Chapter Fifty

Mike and Duane had heard the call on their scanners. They'd been out on another case—a string of car thefts, one that had included an assault that had resulted in the death of the victim. Duane was ready to believe that this latest assault and attempted car theft was another in the same category. Only this one involved Billy Miller. He'd been taken to the ER unconscious.

The officers who'd been first on the scene when the attendant called it in said he'd found

Billy in a pool of blood. Next to his car, which had a flat tire. His briefcase looked like he had dropped it rather than set it down, but it was closed. They wouldn't know until he regained consciousness if anything was missing.

Please let him regain consciousness.

"Looked like he got hit in the head hard, but he was still breathing. I called an ambulance, and I didn't try to move him," the attendant explained.

The officers found his driver's license in his wallet, along with credit cards and cash.

The attendant had recognized Billy because he often stayed late.

"Poor guy really kept his nose to the grindstone. Must not have a family." The responding officers had noted this assessment in the report as if it was pertinent to the attack.

When Mike went over the scene, he was positive it wasn't a car theft. Billy's battered Chevette had a flat tire. Had the perp planned to fix the flat before stealing it? Billy hadn't even had a chance to reach for his Auto Club card. This had been planned. Someone knew Billy's routine. The layout of the place, and even the attendants' routines, wouldn't have posed a huge challenge. The attacker intended to hurt, if not kill, Billy, Mike was sure of it. And he was equally sure it was related to the Vitale case.

He'd have to tell Sheila. But not before he notified Billy's parents. Eileen and Bug Miller still lived in Delmont. This call would start a whole chain of calls. He'd try to get out in front of it by calling his dad as soon as he could. He needed to discuss some aspects of the case with him. He'd come to respect his father's handling of law enforcement in a small town more and more over the years. Joe Sloan walked a tightrope between concerned neighbor, adjudicator of minor infractions (even petty squabbles), and hardline enforcer in Delmont and the surrounding area. Mike didn't always see the same finesse used at home, but he had come to understand that too. His father was a fair man to whom life had not been especially fair. If he had seemed hardened or distant from time to time, well, Mike was learning that life and loss could do that to you.

The losses in Mike's life had been early and deep. First his brother, then Sam. Now, in the gay community, he and Ed had begun to experience more loss. A few acquaintances, friends of friends, had been diagnosed with a deadly form of pneumonia. More recently, a friend of Ed's from their Syracuse days. It was terrifying and depressing. Mike felt himself begin to put up the old protective walls, shutting down emotions before pain could get a foothold. But the wall that kept sadness at bay shut out intimacy too. Ed called him on it when Mike tried to shut him out. Mike told himself he must have done something good sometime to deserve Ed. These days he needed Ed more than ever. He looked forward to coming home to him tonight. After he made those phone calls.

He called Billy's parents, and they said they'd be out on the next available flight. Of course, they'd have to drive to Omaha or Des Moines and hope they didn't miss any connections. He hoped Billy had regained consciousness before then. He didn't let himself think of Billy taking a turn for the worse. He couldn't.

He called his own dad.

"Billy's connection to all this is more than I first thought," he told him.

"Don't jump to any conclusions, Mike. There could be plenty of reasons he was attacked. Didn't you just say there've been a string of car thefts in that area?"

"His car had a flat tire, Dad. What car thief is going to go for a car with a flat?"

"Only a stupid or desperate one, I guess," Joe Sloan answered. He sighed.

"I don't think our perp is stupid; desperate possibly," Mike said.

"A desperate criminal is a dangerous one, intelligence aside. Be careful, son."

Now he had to call Sheila. He'd pass on that bit of his dad's advice to her, in addition to plenty of his own. For all the good it would do.

"Sheila, it's Mike. No pleasant way to say this: Billy was attacked at work, outside at his parking lot a couple hours ago."

"Billy? My God, Mike Is he okay? Where is he?"

"He's unconscious at the hospital. Hopefully he'll come around soon. His condition is stable. I've notified his folks, and they're on their way here."

"What the hell happened?"

"We're trying to piece that together now."

"It's the killer, isn't it? It's the bastard who killed Craig and Sarah. The one who attacked me. The one who—"

"Sheila, hold on. Right now, we don't have any evidence. The attendant didn't get a good look at the attacker, and we won't know if Billy did either until he comes to."

"What about security? Don't they have cameras on that lot? For what they charge for parking in this city they damned well should!"

"We'll see. Hopefully the cameras were working, but the space Billy parks in isn't in the best view of the cameras. Those surveillance systems are only as good as the equipment and how well it's maintained. They probably relied on the attendant, and he was supposedly getting another car out of a tight spot when it happened. At least we got lucky there. If he hadn't come along..."

"Billy could have been killed. Mike, you have to tell me everything. And I mean *everything*. And if we're in full disclosure, I met Jane for coffee. When I pressed her, she said she was missing part of a project. If that means anything. I tried to warn her, but she said she can take care of herself. I believe her—about that anyway."

"You spoke to Jane, again? Damn." He didn't keep the surprise and irritation out of his voice. "She seems to be avoiding me. I'd like to know more about those missing pages she mentioned to you. I'll try her again. Then I'm heading home. You need to give it a rest."

It wasn't often that Sheila let Mike have the last word, especially when he'd given her a warning. Maybe his assurance that he'd check up on Jane had silenced her. For the moment. He tried the number he had for Jane and let the phone ring and ring. No answering machine came on. He tried Alfred Sienna. No answer on his office phone either. He should have been on it sooner. He hoped he wasn't too late.

Chapter Fifty-One

It had been Althorpe's parting shot that made Mike question Sienna's knowledge of Craig's fund.

"Craig's partner knew the kid had been into his business."

At first Mike had thought Althorpe had meant Craig had been raiding his partner's client list. He may have done that, but it was what Craig knew about Sienna's personal life. His other identity and his past. Somehow, Craig must have found out that Jane Brown was Sienna's daughter. Mike wasn't sure why, but Sienna seemed desperate to keep that secret. Family made Sienna vulnerable to ruthless people with scores to settle. The other thing that Althorpe had said about Sienna:

"Sienna isn't like Carl Vitale, nobody knows Sienna. Ask most of the Wall Street heavy hitters about Sienna, they'll say 'who'? But Sienna, *he* knows everything. Things about those people who you do not bullshit. And word is that he's done things."

Mike let his mind run through scenarios that would justify homicide to someone like that. Starting with the attempt on Billy. Had Billy covered his tracks while he was investigating Sienna for financial irregularities? Probably not well enough. Then Sarah, Craig's girlfriend. Craig might have let some of what he'd learned about Sienna slip.

People revealed all sorts of things to intimate partners. Mike always had to watch what he said to Ed, though he trusted him above anyone.

What about Sheila? Mike pictured a dark town car moving seamlessly through the night, forcing Billy's little Chevette with Sheila at the wheel off the road. He shuddered. Before that, there was the break-in at her apartment. *What had he been looking for in her desk?* He shook his head. He'd have to talk to her again.

As he tried to chain the murders back farther, he couldn't make sense of it. Sienna murdering the student poker player? No, that didn't make sense. Sienna might have had some unknown connection to the others through gambling, or drugs. But why Sam? What could Sam have done to Sienna? What could he have possibly done to anyone? He came up with nothing. He was trying to force the pieces to fit, and it wasn't working.

Then Mike thought of Jane's revelation about Jack Mahoney. Had Sienna somehow learned that Jack was abusing his daughter? Perhaps he had suspected that Jack had killed Mary and worried that Jane was in danger. Sienna could have made quick trips from the Quad Cities, even from Chicago back to Delmont. Sienna could have killed Jack and disposed of his body without being found out. He was, very likely, a professional killer.

***

Mike looked through records of unsolved murders and suspicious deaths in his precinct over the past five years. One struck him immediately: *Accursio Grasso*, known to his friends as *Little Gus*. No details were given, other than where his body had been found. Not more than half a mile from a bar. Named appropriately, *Bar*, Mike was familiar with the dark, tin ceilinged interior of the place that had survived Prohibition as a speakeasy. He and Duane had eased their way into the owner's good graces by regular off duty appearances and their assurance that they only wanted to keep the peace in the establishment.

"You think Louis is gonna give you anything?" Duane had scoffed. "Don't screw our working relationship with him. I've paid for too many watered-down drinks at that filthy place to start over. Not to mention gratuities."

"I want to confirm a hunch. I want to know who else was in the place the night Little Gus bought it."

"You think he's going to remember?"

"I'd remember if one of my connected customers got clipped after leaving my establishment."

"You're thinking of one of our suspects. Who's the lucky perp?"

"I don't want to jinx this, but my money's on Althorpe or Sienna."

Duane shook his head. "I know you think Althorpe is guilty of something and you're probably not wrong, but what good would making him for Grasso's death do? Or Sienna for that matter?"

"I'm sure at least one of them has done clean-up work for someone if not for Carl Vitale."

"Okay, I don't see what you're after, but I hope you find it. Bonnie and I have a Lamaze class tonight. She'll put a contract out on me if I miss this one."

***

The inside of *Bar* hadn't changed since Mike had last been there. And it had been at least a year. But Louis was still running the place. Skinny and pale, he leaned back in the corner of the long bar arms crossed over his aproned belly. His arms were ropey, and Mike could see a couple faded tattoos peeking out from under the black polo shirt he wore. Louis wore the shirt open at the neck, a gold chain with a horn dangled in his greying chest hair.

"To what do I owe the pleasure?" He said as Mike took a stool near him.

"I missed you?" Mike smiled, "And your fine establishment, of course."

Louis rolled his watery eyes heavenward. "What'll it be?"

"My usual. Whatever's on tap."

Louis set his beer in front of him, Mike put a fifty-dollar bill on the bar and said, "I need a few minutes of your time."

Louis had a nose like a boxer, flattened and asymmetrical. He wrinkled it with effort, curling his upper lip.

Mike continued, "Remember the night Little Gus was killed, not far from here?"

"Sure. What about it?"

"He'd been in here, right? Who else was working that night?"

"We been over this when it went down. Nobody working here had anything to do with it. Why you dredge this shit up again?"

"Inquiring minds want to know. Who was his waitress?"

"Our girls come and go. Mostly they go. That was what, five years ago? Like I should remember."

Mike pulled another bill out and put it on the bar. Louis reached for it.

"Okay. I don't remember her name; she had a great ass. Nice legs. Not much of a chest, but she was good looking. Real patient with the customers. Never lipped off."

"So, she doesn't work here anymore?"

"Hell no. She left a couple months later. Said she got a real job somewhere."

"Did she have any special customers, male friends maybe?'

"Hey, what you think I run here?"

"I don't mean that."

Louis gave an irritated snort. He sighed and looked around the bar. It was filling up.

"Did you see anyone watching Gus and this waitress?"

Now Louis's pale face took on an ashy cast. He swallowed. He leaned over the bar, his hollow eyes searched Mike's. "I don't know what you're after, but if I tell you what I know, you gotta leave. And stay away, okay?"

"Okay."

He whispered the words Mike had wanted to hear, wiped his face with the bar rag and turned away.

Chapter Fifty-Two

S heila had called Marcus in the morning, after the news about Billy's assault had made the morning paper. Though it wasn't front page news, Marcus had heard. Mike must have called him.

"Sheila, take a little time to feel for your friend Billy. Hey, I know this must be tough on you. We need to revisit all your meetings with Craig. There must be more to it."

"Thanks for nothing, Marcus."

Quit patronizing me, dammit! Of course, there was more to it.

"The connections you've made may be correct, but they seem tenuous at this moment. We need to build on evidence. I'm convinced you still have more to contribute by reviewing every bit of conversation you and Craig had as well as going through all your files one more time. That project was vital to Craig."

That project was deadly for Craig.

She had gone along with Billy's idea at first that Craig might have gotten mixed up with some bottom-feeders. But now she felt positive the answer was in the investment fund itself. Craig only let her see parts of it, but he had given her an extra folder the last time they'd met. She hadn't bothered to review it. Figured he'd explain if there was information she required for her verbiage. That folder was in a pile in the bottom drawer of her desk. Exactly what she hoped to find in that folder, she couldn't say.

But as my clients like to say, I'll know it when I see it.

***

The next day, Sheila finished work early. An end-of-day meeting her team was supposed to lead got canceled. She poured herself a cup of sludge from the pot before Danielle could dump it out. She took it back to her desk and opened Craig's folder.

The papers she was looking for were half-stuck together inside the folder's pocket. There were five pages of graphs with projected annual growth. Every page had notes written in red ink. The notes contained math-speak, which she didn't have to think about because the word *recalculate* appeared more than once. The handwriting wasn't Craig's.

Damn, I'm right.

Mike answered warily. "Before you ask, no, I haven't found any more hard evidence on Sienna or Alvin Brown. I did find something that confirms our suspicions about Jane's role in Craig's project. But Sienna seems to have known more, too. A lot more. There's something else I'm waiting to hear about. My guy in Davenport—"

Their conversation was interrupted by yelling in the background.

"Sorry, it's like rush hour here. I'm out the door to investigate another case. Tomorrow afternoon, bring this folder you discovered with any pertinent material. Since Billy's still on the mend, one of the detectives from the financial-crimes unit will join us."

At last. Help from an impartial expert. Should have gotten them involved earlier, maybe Billy would have been spared this ordeal. "Sounds good," was all she said. She knew Mike felt bad enough about Billy without any comments from her.

The attack on Billy had been far worse than her "accident." Anxiety, guilt, and fear were playing havoc with her concentration. She was in no shape to give new clients the attention they deserved. Now was a good time to take a few days off. They'd finished up the candy-bar campaign—and the rest of the sample Fit Bars too. Good riddance. Danielle was out of the office for the next two days as well. Kevin had told her he was planning to fill in on phones as he was under a campaign deadline. Sheila was grateful her supervisor and coworkers were flexible and understanding. She'd probably been a pain to work with lately.

She wouldn't leave any clients in the lurch, she just needed to get home, her brain was fried. She'd stop by in the morning and check in with Kevin before heading over to meet with Mike at the station.

***

She arrived at the office after a sleepless night. It was early morning, and the building was deserted. She started toward the stairs, then decided to take the elevator. She didn't think she had the energy to climb.

The office door was unlocked, but it was dark. *Right. No Danielle.* She flipped the light switch, a blue-white spark flickered, but the rows of fluorescent fixtures didn't come on.

Great.

Walking to her cubicle in the semi dark, she set her things down on the desk. She walked from the empty cubicle maze back down the hall to the kitchenette in search of coffee. The light wasn't working in the kitchen either.

What the hell?

She was irritated, then she was spooked.

She turned, ran back to her desk, and grabbed her things. She dashed out the door. Breathing hard, she walked to the elevator and pushed the button. *Please work.* The door opened, and her coworker Kevin stepped out holding a cup of coffee.

"Leaving so soon? Wait, what are you doing here anyway? Thought you were taking the day off."

"I am. Needed to grab the rest of my papers, and I wanted to touch base with you."

"That's very professional. Also, totally unnecessary. You look terrible, by the way."

"Thanks. You do know how to make a girl feel special."

"Sorry, Sheila, but I calls 'em like I sees 'em."

"Speaking of seeing, the lights are out in there." She gestured toward the room.

"I called maintenance this morning. They said they had no idea. Shocker, huh? Guess our Hummingbird nest will be extra quiet today. Supposedly they're working on it. Probably won't be fixed until tomorrow. I went down to the first floor for caffeine." He took a sip of coffee and made a face.

"Let's go get some good bad stuff," he offered.

"You go ahead. I'd like to use the phone in the conference room before I head out."

"Suit yourself. I'll get donuts."

"Thanks, but no thanks." Sheila smiled.

"Your choice."

They rode the elevator down in silence. She pushed open the door to the conference room and set her things down on one of the long tables. Kevin's briefcase was on the table across from it. He looked at what remained in the paper cup, tossed it in the trash, and jogged out the door.

Sheila sat staring at the table. She decided to call Mike.

"Mike, it's your hometown girl."

"Sheila, how are you doing?"

"I'm not sure. How's Billy? The hospital won't give me information on him or put me through to his room because I'm not family. That's some BS."

"I know how you feel, and I wanted to update you. His folks arrived on the red-eye and are on the way over to see him. Luckily, he's regained consciousness, but they've got him sedated because of his head injuries. No visitors for now, including me."

Sheila sighed.

"Marcus called me. He went over every concern he's had for you since the accident. By the way, if you haven't called your folks, you'd better do it before I do."

She was waiting to call her parents. Marcus had called Mike. She couldn't decide if she liked that or was annoyed. *Why am I the last to know who's calling who?*

"I promise. I just don't know if I can talk to them right now. It's too much. Mike, not to repeat myself, but that was no accident. Someone tried to run me off the road. I've been replaying it in my head. That car came out of nowhere and hit me hard enough to send my car across a lane into the guardrail. A little further down the highway, there's no rail, I would've gone over the embankment. And the car that hit me didn't stop."

"Did you recall anything more about the car or driver?"

"No. Only that it was a dark car, and it was big. Mike, I didn't say this to Billy or Marcus, but it's got to be the same person who killed

Craig and Sarah. I think his killer tried to kill me and now Billy. And as different as it all seems, I think its connected to Sam."

"Sheila, let's talk about this in person. I'll drive over and bring you down to the station. I want Marcus here too. You and I are going to go over everything we remember about what Sam was doing the day before he was killed. Yeah, we've done this a hundred times before, but there must be things we missed."

"Give me half an hour."

Sheila hung up as Kevin walked in with a fragrant bag of donuts and his cup of coffee.

"Seriously, my friend, you don't look so good," he said, squinting at her.

"I'm going, I'm going."

"I'll be around late if you need anything, I'll be working by camping lantern."

She grabbed her briefcase and stopped in front of the table where Kevin had set up his camp, chocolate donuts, and coffee on a cardboard tray in front of him, folders, pens, and notebooks fanned out around it.

"If anyone calls for me, I'll be back later today. I'm not sure when."

He reached out and grabbed her hand: "Take care of yourself, girl wonder."

"You too, Kevin. Thanks. I owe you."

"No shit."

***

Mike was waiting for her at the curb. His dark Crown Vic needed washing. She noticed strands of gray among his close-cropped, wavy, brown hair. Same boyish good looks that had made her swoon whenever he came to see Sam. Mike caught her looking at him and smiled.

"Mike, let's make a deal not to call my parents yet. I promise I will, but do you honestly feel they need to hear about me being in a car accident? Not to mention the circumstances. And now poor Billy. That's a long list of bad things that have happened since I left Delmont for New York."

Mike's forehead wrinkled in concern. He gave her the side-eye and said, "They're going to hear something through the Delmont grapevine. No way Billy's parents aren't going to be talking to people even before they get back. How's silence from you going to go over with your folks?"

Sheila sighed and rubbed her temples. Mike was right.

Not ready to let her off the hook, Mike continued, "When we wrap things up, when this killer is in a holding cell, I expect you to square things with them, and I mean in person. You don't get back there nearly enough. Don't bullshit me about finances and time."

Sheila cleared her throat and changed the subject, "I've been thinking about Jane. At first, I thought she might be in danger." Sheila shook her head. "That folder I've got with me has corrections and notes that aren't in Craig's handwriting. I'd bet my typewriter it's Jane's. She's downplayed her connection to Craig and that project of his."

"Sienna is involved, too. I think you were right; I'm sure he is Jane's father."

Sheila wanted to gloat. She'd been right. But then the hairs on the back of her neck rose. She felt a flood of apprehension. The bad feeling. Her head began to throb. *What did this all mean?*

Sheila saw Marcus's silver Buick Skylark pull into a parking space near the station as she and Mike entered the building. Mike led her to a table in a fishbowl conference room. Miniblinds covered the windows, but she could look out onto the busy station house. She put her messenger bag on the table, Craig's folder, and her notes inside it.

Marcus strode into the station house. Duane followed not five minutes later carrying bags of sandwiches and sides from Katz's deli. He put a Styrofoam container in front of Sheila.

"Mike ordered this for you—chicken soup. You need this. Eat."

Sheila gave Mike a wry smile. "Thanks, Mom."

They ate as Mike spread reports and photos on the tables. Sheila finished her soup and closed her eyes. She listened to the conversation around her. She wanted to organize her thoughts before she said word one.

I looked at every person as a potential murderer. Especially anyone at Tractor Supply. That made the most sense, then. But after Mike and I went back a year later, there was no one. As for school, no weirdo teachers, or at least none we talked about as suspects. Sam didn't have a secret life. What does Mike have for a conclusion today?

Mike had copies from the murder book, as well as other reports his father and other law-enforcement agencies had filed around the time of Sam's death. After two hours, they had put together a picture of the summer Sam was killed. Nearly. There were still important missing pieces: mainly why?

Marcus left them for a lecture he had scheduled and appointments with students.

"I'll be back for the wrap-up and to take Sheila home."

Sheila went to the restroom and pressed wet paper towels to her forehead. Her head was throbbing again. She thought of Jane that day in high school, standing at the restroom sink washing her hands, toweling her face. Sheila suddenly felt cold, as if she'd been splashed with ice water. She began to shake. Then anger ran through her. She knew. She didn't know how she was going to prove it.

Mike and Duane waited with coffee. Mike offered her the bag of cookies. She pulled out a black and white and set it down on a napkin. *To hell with the calories. I need this.*

"How are you holding up, Sheila?" Mike asked. "I don't want to wait to finish our collective take on this."

"I'm good to go," she said and took a sip of coffee and nibbled at the chocolate side of the cookie. Buying time. She could feel him looking at her, but she didn't give him a chance to contradict her.

She opened her messenger bag and pulled out Craig's folder and her notes.

"I'd faxed copies of earlier notes to Billy before he—" Her breath caught; images of Billy prone in a pool of blood that Mike had shared with her filled her mind. "Before he was attacked. He'd faxed something back to me, but I hadn't gotten around to looking at it yet."

A note with her name caught Sheila's eye.

Billy had scrawled on the margins of two of the sheets: *Proposal is bs. Legals, financials. Same stuff my office's been after. Look at A. F. Sienna now—claims made to investors?*

Sheila was furious. She thought back to their first meeting.

"I have doubts about my ability when it comes to making sense of the projections," she'd told him.

"That's not why I came to you. You'll make sense of the larger picture. You'll be the forest. I've got other people for the trees."

Craig had used her. She didn't need to make sense of the projections; Craig hadn't wanted her to. But someone had known exactly what it was."

Mike answered the phone and hung up after a conversation that lasted only a few sentences.

"Damn, our grand-larceny guy was called out on another case. I'll send him copies of what we've got, but we don't get his expertise now. In the meantime, Duane and I have a theory about Sienna's involvement. We like him for Craig's murder and that's not all."

Sheila's jaw dropped. "Sienna? But Jane is most likely the numbers person. I know I'm the one who was talking about Sienna's family ties to crime and his connection to Iowa, but I think you're barking up the wrong part of that family tree."

"Evidence is what counts, and we still don't have enough for either murder."

Sheila and Duane caught Marcus up on where the information they'd pieced together had led them. Marcus said, "Seems Craig's investment strategy as was as much about who he knew *about* as much as what he knew. He overestimated his hand when it came to risk. You're saying Jane worked with the numbers and knew his scheme was smoke and mirrors. But money wasn't the only thing Craig's murder was all about, was it?" Marcus didn't wait for a response. "There was a case I came across. The killer was trying to restore balance in his life. His mother deserted him when he was young, and he killed to take away from others what he had lost. Killed because he feared exposure, and more loss. And killing was a release for all the anger.

There are elements we know nothing about. What we do know is that our suspect is organized, acts on opportunities that provide a release for an emotional need. But it's carefully channeled rage, not passion, not like stabbing someone during a bar brawl. I'm not telling you anything you haven't considered, Mike, but when you do catch up to this psychopath, don't count on any cooperation. Most serial killers won't give you an inch unless they know they've run out of choices."

Listening to Marcus was exhausting.

"I can't do this anymore today," Sheila said.

Mike got up and gave her a hug. "You've done good, kid. Now it's up to Duane and me. Go home and get some rest."

Marcus helped her gather up her files and notes and stuff them back into her bag.

"Let's hit the diner, feed you a little before I take you home," Marcus said.

"Best offer I've had all day."

Marcus took her hand after he ordered a deluxe tuna melt for them to share. "What's the Sheila weather report?"

"What do you mean?"

"You're crystal clear, foggy, ice cold, or steamy. I like the steamy. But what you need, lovely Sheila, is clarity. On a clear day, what do you see for yourself? So much of your life has been in the shadow of Sam. You've got a whole lifetime ahead of you after his killer's in prison."

"Prison? Hard to believe that."

"Believe it. I feel positive Mike is going to catch our killer—and soon. What are you going to do for your next act?"

"I'm not sure my imagination can expand that far." *Let him in.* "You're part of my future. Our comedy future, now." She looked into his eyes. "I'd like it to be more." She moved the salt and pepper shakers behind the ketchup bottle. "You ordered a Diet Coke for me, didn't you?"

"Why are you so quick to change the subject?"

"Marcus, I'm not avoiding the subject of you and me. At this moment, it's hard to think that far ahead. Please don't interpret that as 'I don't want to.' And why are you the only one asking the questions? What about your plans—do they include me?" Sheila put her hand to his cheek, waiting for an answer. She pulled it away and smacked her palm to her forehead as she remembered a different folder she'd left at work. "Crap! Marcus, I left something else I meant to give Mike at work. Run me over there? Ten minutes extra, tops."

Chapter Fifty-Three

Marcus let her out and pulled in between two No Parking signs. "I'll be right back, promise."

"I've got my motor running," Marcus said, giving her a wink.

Sheila took the elevator up to two and walked to the conference room. The door was locked. Damn. Since she was here, she'd check if Kevin had put any of her forgotten files and notes upstairs in her cubicle. She pressed the up button and waited.

Just one floor. Might as well take the stairs—my ass will thank me.

She pushed open the heavy fire door. Her footsteps echoed as she climbed the two flights. The hall was empty. A light was on in the Hummingbird office.

At least they fixed the electrical problem.

She pushed open the door.

"Kevin? You still here?"

She walked to her desk and set down her briefcase, looking over the divider into Kevin's cubicle. He was lolling in his chair, head turned to the wall, arms hanging stiffly off the armrests, his legs splayed.

"Kevin?"

A scream rose in her throat as her eyes caught a loop of wire circling his neck.

"Oh, Kevin, no! No!"

She searched for a pulse in his wrist and neck but couldn't feel one. She picked up the phone to call 911. No dial tone. She ran to her desk, tried her phone.

Nothing.

She heard a pop and smelled burning wire. Most of the room went dark. The hairs on the back of her neck rose. The hallway threw a runner of light under the door. A shadow fell across it. A slim figure stood in front of the door.

"You don't want to go now, Sheila. We need to talk, and I won't have time for coffee tomorrow. Neither will you." Jane held her arm out as she closed the distance between them in a few steps. She was holding a gun. "Not sorry about your friend."

"You didn't have to kill Kevin."

"You're right. I didn't have to, but I did. Now, you... you I have to kill. Stupid Sheila, in my way, up in my business. Unbelievable. I've worked my ass off—made my own good luck everywhere I went, every way. Then, I hit Craig's funeral, and who do I run into? You, Billy, and Mike Sloan. Sam's very good buddy. And now he's a cop. Not just a cop, a detective. What are the odds? Don't try to answer. You still suck at math. Guess I didn't get far enough away. I will not make that mistake again."

Jane's tone sent a chill down Sheila's spine. She felt her legs turning to jelly.

I've got to keep her talking while I think. Hell, I've got to say something, anything.

Sheila blurted, "You've made plenty of mistakes, Jane. You've just been lucky. You've gotten away with so much for so long." Calmed by her own bravado, Sheila went on. "Card shark like you, I bet you know the saying, 'Luck never gives, it only lends.' Well, your luck is over."

Jane's face showed a trace of hesitation. Then she narrowed her eyes, and her mouth became a hard line, as if she were performing some calculation.

Marcus. Does Jane know he's out there waiting? Oh God, has she hurt him, maybe even killed him? All my fault. Why in hell didn't we just go home?

Sheila could feel tears begin to sting her eyes. *Stop it. I'll be damned if I'll cry.*

"Sheila, I want Craig's file. Everything he gave you, his notes, your notes, the pitch deck, and pamphlet mockups."

Sheila looked up in amazement. "That's what this is all about? That's what you tried to kill me for?"

"Not just you. What an ego! No wonder you fell for my trick. You believed the guy I paid to tell you you'd won a spot at that club in Younkers. But I was hoping Billy, your loyal pal would drive you out there. He was closing in on me. His fraud investigations. At first, I thought it was Billy driving his cheap, little car. Could have been a two-for-one. Oh well, I got you. Luck of the draw."

"You killed Sarah, and you tried to implicate me."

"Craig's plastic girlfriend got in the way. She saw me talking to him one night when they were out to dinner. I'd followed them to the restaurant. He slipped away from their cozy little table and we argued. I knew Craig recorded conversations at home and at the office. I'd seen him do it when we met at his place one night. Thought he was being clever. I got the tape, but I couldn't take a chance on Sarah identifying me."

"Then you tried to kill Billy—again."

"Almost got him. He's one lucky bastard," Jane said, smiling.

"You killed Kevin. Just for Craig's proposal?"

"I killed Kevin because it felt good, and it wasn't *Craig's* proposal," Jane growled. "It was never *his* proposal. My father... no, you wouldn't understand. It's *my* proposal. My work: the numbers, the projections. The only parts that count. That was my plan, a big score, winner take all. Then, I'd disappear. But you show up ruining everything, again and again. Enough. The file, Sheila. Now."

"M-my messenger bag, next to my desk." Sheila cocked her head toward her workspace.

Jane walked over to Sheila's desk and picked up the bag, keeping the gun levelled at Sheila's chest. She stepped closer to the door and stopped, listening.

"We've got company. Probably building security. I've got a meeting. You're coming along."

Jane kept the gun against Sheila's back as she pushed her through the door, steering her down the stairs. Their steps made a hollow echo that sounded like a death march. A side door led from the stairwell to the alley next to the building. Jane's car was waiting, hidden in the building's shadow.

"Hurry up, open it," Jane commanded and gave Sheila a nudge with the gun. Sheila's hand was slippery with sweat as she wrestled the door open. She wanted to cry out, to yell "fire," anything to draw someone's attention, but Jane's voice was deadly calm as she bent to Sheila's ear: "Don't even think about it, bitch. Get in."

Jane shoved her into the black Lincoln Town Car, got in, and locked all the doors.

"Kiddie locks. Don't bother to try."

They drove toward Lower Manhattan, and Sheila's mind raced: *Marcus won't have a clue where we're headed. Is there a way to draw the attention of the police, alert Mike?*

Jane was handling the big car expertly with one hand, while keeping the gun aimed at Sheila.

Power steering. Crap. How can I get her to lose control? If I can, will I be able to get anyone's attention before she kills me? If she crashes the car and I die at least I'll take her with me. Not great options, but here goes.

Sheila kicked at Jane's foot, knocking it off the gas pedal. Jane swerved a bit, recovered, and dug the gun into Sheila's ribs.

"Don't try that again." she said through clenched teeth. "I can shoot you while I drive. Believe me."

Oh, I believe you.

She tried to stay calm, but her thoughts were racing—from Craig to Kevin and back to Sam, always back to Sam. She couldn't keep quiet any longer, she had to ask. She had to know.

"Why did you kill him, Jane? What did he ever do to you?"

Jane drove on, staring ahead, her forehead creased. Finally, she said, "You mean Sam? He knew too much. He would have figured it out. I couldn't let him. I couldn't let that happen."

"What? He didn't know anything about you. What was there to know? He didn't care about you. You're delusional."

"Wrong. He knew. He saw me going into the Mahoneys' cellar the day I killed Jack. I had wire in the bag, along with all the cleaning stuff I bought at Tractor Supply. Then he found that ring. He could put two and two together. He was a lot smarter than you. So much better than you. You never deserved someone as good as him. His bad luck to get you for his sister."

Ignore that. "What about the others?"

"If you mean Mary, Jack killed her. I helped him bury her in their own cellar. Wasn't that convenient? I borrowed her identity for a while. And her money. She didn't need it anymore."

"So, Jack really is dead. You killed him."

Jane didn't answer. The streetlights let Sheila glimpse Jane's face half in shadow. She smiled as if she was reliving a particularly satisfying moment.

She nodded. "Oh, yes."

And Jane proceeded to share some of the details of Jack's murder with her.

There had been no struggle. Jack hadn't had time to react when Jane had come up behind him swinging the length of steel pipe that he kept under the seat like a Louisville Slugger. He'd been getting blankets out of the back of his truck in preparation for a "celebration." They'd finished transferring the last of Mary's savings and closed out her account the day before. Jane had let him think she wanted this. She'd even let him touch her with his filthy hands. Only thinking about what she'd do to *him* had kept her from retching.

He'd driven them out to a secluded area in an overgrown field. Cottonwood trees and scrubby mulberry partially obscured the weathered outbuilding. It stood a few yards from where he'd parked his rusted truck. It was where he brought some of the women he picked up at dive bars. Like the biker bar outside of Delmont. He'd told her about it one night when he was drunk out of his mind. He'd drop a lude into the woman's drink when she wasn't looking and wait for it to get her sloppy. Sometimes he'd have to nearly carry her to his truck. Jane didn't have to ask what came next. But Jack kept running his mouth while her rage grew. He'd figured it didn't matter what he told her; she'd keep his secrets—they were partners. Well, this was one she would keep.

The release she felt delivering that blow had nearly been enough. He was slumped over the truck's tailgate, unconscious. She could have left it, left him for dead. But she wanted to feel life draining out of

Jack's body, pulsing through the wire into her hands as she had pulled the loop of wire tight crushing Jack's windpipe.

The steel wire had cut into the skin, enough to make it ooze blood. A thin line of bright red that turned dark as it dried. Not as much of a mess as the whack to his skull with that pipe. She'd had to drag his body into that dilapidated shed and bury it. Even dead, Jack still made messes she had to clean up.

Jane chuckled as she recounted how he'd landed on the outspread tarp with a satisfying thud. How his head bounced once before coming to rest with his face upturned. His mouth gaped open: surprised as any animal at being caught. Her gloved hands picked up the length of pipe from where it had fallen, and she removed the wire from around Jack's neck. She'd taken his wallet and keys. There'd been nothing identifying about his worn work shirt and faded jeans. She'd taken his army jacket with her.

"Then I buried him in that old, nasty shed. The ground was soft, and I dug a shallow hole. Fitting place for him. Probably not much left after all this time."

Sheila shuddered. She hadn't wanted to listen, but she knew Jane was giving her information Mike would want. If she lived to see him again. She asked Jane more questions.

"What about Jay and those other men in Iowa?"

"What about them? Why the hell do you care? You didn't know any of those men. Believe me, they weren't worth caring about. Sam was the only one who was. And *not* because he was your brother. He was smart and he was nice to me. He was never going to stay with Janice. Not after they graduated. He cheated on her. Bet you didn't know that. We could have had something."

Sheila felt sick. Anger and nausea were duking it out in her gut. She tried not to think about Jane's confessions. Especially what she'd said about Sam. For whatever perverse reasons, Jane may have chosen to tell Sheila the truth about Jack, Jay and Sam, but she was still a liar. And a killer.

"How could you kill all those people so easily?"

"Stupid, little Sheila. You think it was easy? Well, it wasn't. It took careful planning. No one appreciates all the moving parts involved in a thoughtful murder. You have to consider every step; you can't make any mistakes. It's like an elegant equation and a high-stakes poker game all rolled up into one."

Jane's not a mystery. She's a monster.

Jane pulled her car into an underground parking garage. The gleaming towers. Craig's office. Jane forced Sheila to empty her briefcase and transfer the contents to Jane's messenger bag. Then she opened the door and motioned for her to get out. Jane kept the gun pressed to Sheila's back as they rode the elevator.

"Craig called you Einstein. Frankenstein is more like it." Sheila kept up a chatter during their ascent. Risky as it was, she was trying to say something annoying to throw Jane off balance.

"Bitch, shut up. You used to be more quiet."

"You used to be more human. Or am I wrong about that too?"

"I said, shut up! Who the hell are you to judge me? You're nothing but a gutless, pathetic loser."

The elevator doors opened onto the seventy-fifth floor. Jane used the gun to nudge Sheila out of the elevator.

"Here we are. Down the hall to the left. We're right on time."

They walked through a door that had "Sienna and Vitale, Investments, LLC" in gold letters.

A tall, balding man was seated at a glass desk. His eyes were the same icy color as Jane's. His face wore the same hard expression. She could see the woman in the grainy, old photo reflected in those eyes and that mouth, with its sardonic smile.

"Who's this? And what is she doing here?"

Jane looked at him. She tipped her head and pushed Sheila into a chair in front of the desk. She nudged Sheila's shoulder with the gun.

"A temporary inconvenience from Delmont days. Not important. I'll take care of it once we finish."

Sheila studied him. *Jane's father, I presume.*

"I brought it," Jane said, lifting the messenger bag. "Now, your part of the deal."

"Let's see the contents first, daughter."

Chapter Fifty-Four

Marcus called Mike from a lobby phone, "I wanted to come in with Sheila, but she said she only wanted to grab some folders. She's been gone twenty minutes."

"Okay, Marcus, don't panic. You know Sheila, she probably got distracted. Decided to check her messages, then return a call." As soon as he'd said it, he could feel his own unease grow. And the fact that Marcus had called him, again. Marcus had lost his cool.

"I'm not just sitting here," Marcus said. "The security guard and I are going up."

"Hold on. We'll be there in five minutes."

The siren blared as they drove, weaving in and out of traffic. Mike silenced it off as they approached the building. He jumped out of the car, not waiting for Duane, and ran into the front door of the building.

Marcus and a security guard were waiting for him.

They led him to the office. When they'd gone upstairs in search of Sheila, they'd found Kevin's body.

"Sheila said she only wanted to get a folder. How could I have let her out of my sight? She wouldn't have left on her own. But how in hell would she have left without me seeing her? And if she didn't leave on her own, who the hell would have taken her?"

"I'm not sure how, Marcus, but I'm positive Jane has taken her. I don't know what her endgame is, but right now the question is, where are they?"

Mike's work on Jane last night had proved fruitful. He'd found out about a few of her gaming haunts in the Midwest and who she'd played with. Then he discovered her apartment building was only a few blocks away from Craig's fancy high-rise. She wouldn't go there. Not to her place.

Craig's office. Of course.

"I'm betting they're headed to Sienna and Vitale in the World Trade Center. Marcus, Alfred Sienna is Jane's father."

Craig's father had been instrumental in setting up Sienna Investments. Mr. Vitale wanted his little boy's name on the door. Funny how well both had come out of the financial crisis.

"Duane and I will head there now. I'm calling for backup. Marcus, you can ride with us, but I need you to stay out of the way."

***

Mike entered the tower with Duane. He flashed his badge at security and ran for the elevator. Seventy-five floors up to the office of Alfred Sienna. The elevator was empty and silent but for the two of them, each steeling themselves for what they might find.

Finally, Mike asked, "There a back way in?"

Duane nodded.

They stopped on the seventy-fourth floor and took the stairs. Mike looked down the hall. A light was on in the office.

Duane whispered, "This way." He motioned to a door leading to a utility hall. "Saw it when we paid a visit to Sienna."

The door they wanted was second from the end. Mike removed a pry bar from his duty belt. He moved to wedge it in the door under the lock.

Duane stopped him. "Take the door off the hinges—just as quick."

There was no quiet way to do this. He only hoped that they wouldn't draw attention before they could storm in. They loosened the hinge pins and pushed on the door. It gave up a weak groan as they moved it aside. It was hollow.

Here's to crap construction.

Mike could hear a woman and man talking, their voices getting louder. He thought he heard Sheila, but he didn't get what she said. At least she was still alive. He drew his gun.

Alfred Sienna had his back to the hallway. Mike pressed himself against the wall in shadow. He motioned for Duane to wait. Mike could see Sheila, frozen in a chair in front of the desk. Jane stood over her, the butt of her gun raised over Sheila's head. A folder lay on the desk, papers spilling from it.

"You stupid bitch! I told you I needed *everything* Craig gave you."

"That *is everything.*"

A trickle of blood ran from Sheila's scalp onto her forehead.

"Jane. It doesn't matter," Sienna said. "You've got what I need, and I've got what I promised you. And a little extra."

He held something up between his thumb and forefinger, and Mike guessed it was a microcassette.

"From Craig's desk. After our phone call I wanted to make sure you didn't have this; Craig recorded your conversations too. He thought he was being smart."

Jane's face turned white. The corners of her mouth turned down. Her anger took over, and she turned the gun from Sheila to her father.

"*Your* part of the deal, Father. I want all of it. It should be *my* fund. Give me the passbook for the account, and I want those bearer bonds. Everything you promised me. And that tape. Now, or I swear to God, I'll kill you too."

"You're bluffing, my ice princess. See, I know my girls. You like taking risks, like me, but really Jane, I'm disappointed." He shook his head. "You can't walk away. You should, but you won't. You'll keep playing until you've lost everything, and I can't let you do that. You're out of control. You're on tilt. I know you want to take me down, but that doesn't matter. It will never happen. You have no idea what I've done for you."

Jane stared at him. She was shaking. *Was it anger or another emotion? Did Jane know her father had killed Little Gus for her? Was it enough to make up for his abandonment?*

"Look, I'm giving you what you want.

Sienna's hand moved under the desk as he spoke. Something glinted in the light as his hand returned to the desktop. He held a gun. Then he motioned to Sheila with it. "Go now, Jane." He rose pushing a stack of envelopes across the desk with one hand, the gun in his other hand still pointing at Sheila. "I'll take care of your friend here. It'll be quick and clean. You don't have to thank me."

Sheila spat out, "Thank you in hell," and swept an arm across the desk scattering the envelopes.

Jane shrieked at her in rage, "I'll kill you!"

Where was their backup? No time to wait. Mike emerged from the shadows, gun drawn and pointed at Jane.

"Police. Drop your weapons. Both of you."

Jane shifted her aim to Mike. Sheila reared back in her chair, her head butting into Jane just as she fired, throwing her off balance. Jane missed. The bullet whizzed past him and embedded in a wall. Mike ran toward Jane as she regained her balance and advanced, recalibrating her aim at him.

"Jane, don't be stupid," Sienna shouted. He moved his gun from Sheila to Mike. "You can get away. He's not going to stop you, are you, Detective?"

Mike didn't lower his gun, but he stopped in his tracks. Two guns were trained on him.

He looked from Sienna to Jane but kept his gun pointed at Jane.

Jane had a wild look in her eyes. She moved her gun in the direction of her gaze. Her eyes met Mike's. Her arm was rigid, her face a mask. Mike held his breath. In that split second, he thought he heard footsteps and prayed it was his partner.

A shot rang out from Jane's gun—pain seared Mike's right shoulder. Grazed, he felt blood seep from the burning wound. Jane leveled her gun again. Mike steadied his shaking arm.

"Jane don't do this. Drop your gun. It's over," he said.

Duane burst from the back and yelled for Jane and Sienna to drop their weapons. In surprise, she looked away from Mike to Duane. Then she looked back to Mike and smiled as she aimed the gun at Sheila.

"Shoot me, and Sam's sister dies. Quicker than he did, but she'll be just as dead." Jane didn't stop smiling as she looked from Mike to Sheila. Mike looked at her cold eyes, searching her face for a trace of doubt, regret, anything. She stared back at him, those pale eyes burning with malice.

Blood pounded in Mike's head; his ears were ringing. Time slowed, and he could hear the hollow sound of a basketball bouncing on a court, thump-wump, thump-wump. He was on the court with Sam. He shot.

He heard a bullet explode, unsure from where, but it was followed by another. The first brushed Sheila's ear, drawing blood. The second bullet was his; he felt the recoil. It hit Jane just below her collarbone, knocking her back. *That's for Sam.*

Chapter Fifty-Five

Jane didn't look back as she ran from Jack, her heart still beating fast, face flushed. He'd hurt her again. She felt sick. She had to numb the feeling. She stumbled across the field, hugging herself with one arm, keeping her other hand in her pocket. She rubbed the piece of rabbit tail and felt for the tissue with the rabbit-foot he'd given her. It felt sticky at one end.

The rabbit's powder-puff tail was her trophy, but what to do with the foot? Nobody in her class shared her fascination with things like that. At least none of the girls. That thought made her smile. She'd put it in that new girl's desk. Sheila. *Stuck-up snot from Minnesota. Thinks she's cool, always giggling with Nancy. Laugh at this, bitch.*

In her head, the knife's dull chink against the wood of the worktable echoed. The metallic tang of blood lingered in her nose. She felt the small claws of the foot with her finger, and her mind flitted back to the first time she'd seen a rabbit caught in a snare.

The memory was vivid. Walking among the tall weeds and saplings at the back of the field between her house and the Mahoney's. She saw the red cloth marking the snare fluttering midway down the length of a sapling. A rabbit's head had caught in the wire loop as it hopped through an opening between the weedy trees. Its struggles to free itself only tightened the wire noose. She heard the rabbit scream as the wire cut into its neck; it was an eerie sound. A thin smear of red had appeared around the rabbit's neck. She'd stood and watched until the creature had stopped moving; it hadn't taken very long.

Jane's ears buzzed, and her heart had beat fast. It had been a rush—she'd wanted the feeling to last. She needed it to last. It shut out everything else in that moment. It set something free inside her. But now it was all fading. It had been Jack who had set the trap. Now in her last moments, Jane realized she'd been caught, right along with that rabbit.

Chapter Fifty-Six

Jane's father stood stunned. He rocked on his feet as if he had taken the bullet. His face crumpled. His head bowed. His motionless hand gripped the gun loosely now.

Duane pulled the gun from Alvin's hand and cuffed him. He was just Alvin, now. His carefully crafted persona ebbing away with his daughter's life.

Mike knelt over Jane, trying to staunch the wound. She lay sprawled on the floor. Bleeding out. Four officers stormed through the open back door.

Mike shouted, "Call for a bus."

Duane radioed for the ambulance.

The EMTs were through the front door in minutes. They put Jane on a gurney. She was so pale and still. Mike looked at the stain that spread through the blanket across Jane's chest. His hands were sticky with her blood.

Two officers escorted Alvin Brown out the door. He was nearly as pale as his daughter.

Marcus, it seemed, hadn't listened to Mike. At what point during the chaos of shots being fired had he entered the building? He stood over Sheila, arms protectively around her shoulders. She was shivering.

"Over here!" Marcus called. "She needs medical attention; she's going into shock."

Marcus wrapped his sport coat around her and held a handkerchief to her bloody head. Mike pushed a wheeled office chair over to Sheila, and Marcus helped him transfer her to it. A paramedic handed Sheila a paper cone of water, and she drank while he assessed her and Mike.

"Those wounds need attention, and you both better plan on a night in the hospital for observation," the paramedic told them.

"I won't fight you on that," Sheila said.

Sheila's gaze rested on the empty messenger bag. Its contents lay scattered across the glass desktop.

A token balanced on the edge of the desk. Sheila pointed at it with a shaky finger.

Mike examined what seemed to be an ordinary poker chip; imprinted on its face: *DEALER*.

Was it proof that Jane had been with Jay the night he'd died all those years ago? Why on earth had she kept it? Maybe she thought of it as a good-luck piece. Or a souvenir of another kill.

Mike called Duane over. "You need to bag this."

The office was cordoned off with yellow tape. It was a crime scene now. Mike wanted to go to the ER with Sheila, but Marcus was with her. Marcus would do more for her than Mike could.

The wound Mike hadn't acknowledged during the standoff had his attention now. It felt like a hot coal pressed to the flesh, and his fingers felt stiff. Blood saturated his sleeve, and cloth stuck to his arm as the blood dried.

Duane was talking to him, but he was having trouble making out his words. Finally, Duane steered Mike to the elevator and said loudly, "I'm taking you to the ER—don't mess up the car." Then Duane held out his hand. "Sorry, Mike. I need your gun." Mike complied, and Duane bagged and tagged it. "Mike, it's going to be okay."

Mike didn't say anything—what could he say?

After his wound was cleaned and dressed, he rode back to the station with Duane. He'd have to make a statement, and someone from internal affairs would interrogate him. Probably more than *one* someone. He'd be on leave, undergo a psychological evaluation and several sessions with a counselor. Maybe that wouldn't be so bad.

Mike talked to his dad. He knew he'd had to kill in the line of duty once. It helped to talk to him and his mom too. They reminded him that although he was a cop, and a good one, he was more than that. He was human. He could feel anger, rage, hatred even, and he could feel regret, guilt, and compassion. Sometimes all jumbled together.

"Don't shut Ed out," his mom said. "That's the toughest thing your father and I had to learn. We may not be able to control what happens in this life, we can't fix things, but we don't have to be alone."

"You two come visit when you can take time off," his dad said. "I know the Rosses would love to see you and meet Ed too."

Chapter Fifty-Seven

Sheila picked up the phone and dialed her parents. She wanted to do it before Mike did. There was a script in her head, but she couldn't stick to it.

"Mom, Dad, we got Sam's killer," She blurted.

Her mother sobbed.

Her father's voice sounded like it was coming from farther away than Delmont: "Who, Sheila, who?"

"Jane," she sobbed, "Jane Brown." And then, she had to stop talking. She was choking trying to control her sobs. They took turns crying into the phone. Marcus was right, their family did have an emotional structure.

"Mike asked his dad to come to your house today. It will be in the paper and on the news tomorrow. Chief Sloan will try to protect you from the creeps. But you need to be ready. I'm coming home for a visit, but I can't be there right now, when we need each other most, and I'm sorry. So sorry. Not just for this time, but for all the times I shut you out, even though we needed each other. It just hurt too much."

"We know, darling," her father said. "We all did the best we could all these years."

Sheila said, "I love you."

  E.G. RUTLEDGE

There was only a moment in between disconnecting from her parents before she phoned Nancy.

"It's been way too long," Sheila said, afraid she would begin to cry or even laugh. "But I needed to hear your voice so I could say, 'You won't believe this.'"

In the aftermath of Jane's death, Shelia felt as if a funeral cloth had been placed over a mirror. Years ago, she had felt something of herself reflected in Jane—her anger, isolation, even jealousy. It had scared her, and she had tried to push it away. Then, a new Jane had appeared in her life, a polished improved version. Sheila had thought they could be friends. But that had been a disguise. A part of Jane's plan. Now, whatever it was that had bound them was gone. There was nothing to mourn about Jane, but plenty that would take time to forget. Would she ever be able to forgive Jane? She could hear Jane saying Sam was the only one worth caring about. Yet she had killed him. To forgive Jane would she have to understand her? Some things were beyond Sheila's comprehension. She was fine with that.

Chapter Fifty-Eight

They met for brunch at Pearl Diner. It seemed fitting to meet there in the Financial District. Over eggs, pancakes, and plenty of coffee, they told each other the stories they hadn't yet shared. Mike talked about Jane's troubled past with her abuser, Jack Mahoney and what he guessed had pushed her over the edge.

"We'll never know exactly how Mary died, but I believe Jane was telling the truth when she told Sheila. Jack killed Mary. Jane helped him cover up Mary's death, then steal her money. Jane was helping herself to Mary's money as well. Either Jack didn't know, or he didn't care. But she finally decided she had to kill him."

"He was a sick bastard," Billy said. "Jane had to be pretty sick too."

"I'll leave that judgment to Marcus. Jane killed Jack. I think that was the first time she killed. There's no evidence she did again until Sam." Mike closed his eyes. "I went over and over that with my father. Why would she kill Sam? He told me that the best he could figure, and Sheila confirmed, it was because Sam had seen her going into Jack's cellar. My father wasn't sure if it was before or after she'd killed Jack, but she was worried that Sam knew enough to tie her to Mary's disappearance and to Jack, at the very least. Enough to interfere with her plans."

Mike looked at Sheila and continued. "Jane had big plans. I don't know when she found out about where her father was, but at some point, he became part of that plan. She killed those men in Iowa while she was in school—Gary, Jay, and Cory—probably won't ever be able to prove if those murders were premeditated or crimes of opportunity. We think there was someone she killed in Moline too, after she left Iowa City."

Sheila looked at Mike and Billy. She said, "Then she wound up in New York, with Craig Vitale and her father. And us. How strange that our lives kept intersecting like that. Jane told me the project Craig was working on was really hers. I don't know if that was true or boast and a way for her to rationalize what she did. Poor Sarah, she was collateral damage."

"Yes," Mike said. "Poor Sarah. Jane must have thought she had a tape Craig made of their conversations. Even though she found out Sarah didn't have it, she knew Sarah could have identified her as having argued with Craig that night she saw them at the restaurant. So, Jane brought her a drink, overdosed her, and tried to make it look like suicide. Writing Sheila's name in her appointment book was to cover her own. After the crime lab looked at the page, they found Jane's name written after the six o'clock slot. Jane erased it and decided to mess with Sheila by writing her name instead." Mike shook his head.

"That crazy bitch," Sheila said, her face flushed with anger. "Then she broke into my apartment looking for Craig's files. I guess she was afraid I'd take them to Billy or you. I didn't know Craig's hot project was a scheme to defraud investors, but Jane knew exactly what she was doing. She didn't want Craig to mess up her own plan. Billy, she was afraid you were on to her. That's why she came after me; she thought it was you driving your car away from my open mic that night."

Billy said, "I was on to Craig and Jane's father too. I wasn't the only one. Federal investigators were interested in him, so I had to be careful not to tread all over their case." Billy ran his fingers over his healed head wounds where the hair was growing in unevenly. "Not that it mattered in the end. They'll have plenty of time to talk to Jane's father from behind bars. But I have to admit that Jane wasn't on my radar."

Sheila said, "What I found in the newspaper morgue paid off."

Mike raised his brows at Sheila, and Billy groaned. But Marcus smiled.

Sheila continued. "Hey, it's all public record. Even though Jane was the killer, not her father, would you have taken him in and questioned him without my discovery of Frankie 'Fishhooks' Sienna? Jane had wanted to set her father up as the fall guy, but she hadn't yet gotten what she wanted from him. She was afraid he'd use the tape Craig made at the office to implicate her. It forced Jane's hand, didn't it, Marcus?"

Marcus said: "I think Jane's father, Alfred, Alvin, whatever you want to call him, played a larger part in this than any of us realised. He was her mentor and her target. He protected her, but she never knew it. What did she want more, his approval or revenge on the father who walked out on her? She chose a path that might have given her both if she hadn't been so out of control. I don't know what other experiences shaped her, but I'd guess Mahoney's early and continuing abuse was a major contributor. She was hurt, numb and scarred. And she was filled with rage."

"Looking back on how isolated and aloof she seemed to me, that makes sense," Sheila said. "I always thought it was that her father had left them, but there was much more."

Marcus nodded agreement, "Everyone reacts to loss in their own way, but abuse on top of that only isolated her more, I think. Shame and anger are natural responses to that sort of abuse. It set her on a path of destruction. I think that killing, instead of diminishing her rage, intensified it."

"But she was so smart, so good at what she did. She fooled so many people for a long time. Including me," Sheila said.

Marcus added, "She was as skilled at manipulating people as she was at manipulating numbers. I wonder if Alvin knew she was going to make him the fall guy, and beat him at his own game? How well did he really know his daughter?"

"When she confronted her father," Sheila's voice wavered, reliving the terror, "he told her she was on tilt, that she was out of control."

"I think she had been for a long time," Marcus said.

Had Jane's father known what she was? Had it mattered? In the end it had been too late. Jane had left a long trail of death and deceit beginning in Delmont, but it had ended. Mike had ended it.

"He'll have a long time to think about all of it," Mike said. "You know, I feel bad for Jane's sister, Peggy. My mom still works in Glenwood at the library, and she sees her now and then. She's given her the names of some local therapists. It would be a good place for her to start." He looked at Sheila. "Losing a sibling is tough, no matter the circumstances. Jane sort of raised Peggy. I can only imagine what that must have been like."

"I guess I was lucky," Sheila said. "I used to say Sam and I had a love-hate relationship, but from where I am now, it looks mostly like love."

When they had drained their cups, Billy paid their bill. He hugged Sheila and Mike. He shook Marcus's hand. Sheila nudged elbows with Billy as they walked him to the door.

"Thanks again for your call," Mike said quietly to Marcus.

The day after the shooting Marcus had called him.

"I'm sure your lieutenant has you shrink-wrapped or in process," Marcus had begun, "but you've always got my listening ear, if you need it."

"Thanks. In process, most definitely. Had the initial evaluation, and I'm scheduled for counseling sessions. My chief says he thinks IAB will clear me, but it might be a while before I can return to duty." Mike had sighed, then asked, "Do you ever get over killing someone?"

"I can only speculate, but my guess is no," Marcus had said.

"I needed to stop Jane but not like that. Don't know if I'll ever be able to stop seeing the replay."

"Time to start healing, for Sheila and for you. You've got closure now, but my offer stands."

But did they have closure? Was it closure that he felt? Something had changed in him. Being grazed by a bullet had punctured a thin, brittle shell he'd encased himself in. Shooting Jane had shattered it, and he felt both defenceless and unbound. Knowledge of Sam's killer mostly left him feeling sad. Had there been a way to have stopped Jane without a bullet? IAB had determined that his use of deadly force had been warranted. But he would have to ask and answer the question a few hundred more times for himself.

Sheila seemed different too, somehow. After the shock of what they'd been through began to wear off, she had looked spent but calm, like a runner at the end of a marathon.

Mike watched Marcus come up behind Sheila and put his arm around her waist. She turned her head toward Marcus and smiled, her face flushed.

Mike figured it was his cue to leave. He needed to stop at D'Agostino's anyway. Ed had asked him to pick up fresh mushrooms, parsley, and sour cream on the way home. Duane and Bonnie were coming for dinner, and Ed was making beef stroganoff.

Sheila grabbed Mike's elbow and took Marcus's hand in hers.

"Mike, I don't think I've actually said it. Thank you. You saved my life, and you got Sam's killer."

"*We* did, Sheila. *We* kept our promise."

Sheila nodded. "I'm going back to Delmont for a visit. You've been on me to get back there. It was hard for me to visit and feel Sam's absence, but it was damn selfish of me to have stayed away." She pursed her lips, "Tough on my parents. It'll be ten years to the month since Sam was murdered. I need to visit his grave with my mom and dad."

"That's good. Really good. Give them my love, okay?"

"Give it to them yourself. You need to go home for a visit too."

"Right, don't start cutting me any slack now." Mike smiled and gave Sheila a hug.

A smile spread across her face and she hugged him back. Mike felt warmth spread through him with that hug. He could feel Sam, here with them in that hug. It would be a while before all the ghosts were lain to rest. Even so, Mike thought that he could go back to Delmont for a visit now. But he wasn't sure it was still home. He had the part of Delmont he wanted to keep with him. The scent of spring in Iowa: turned earth, the green, grassy smell of weeds competing with linden and lilac trees. Images of a family picnic on a summer day, smiles on their faces. Those were the memories of home that he wanted to keep. That was then, and that was all it was. Now he had Ed. He had the life they had built here. New York City was his home now.

Looking at Billy, and Sheila with Marcus, Mike thought they all looked at home, too. The four of them walked out of the diner together into the heady scent of automobile exhaust, hot asphalt, and steaming hot dogs.

Acknowledgements

This book would not have been possible without the support and contributions of so many people. Here are a few: My sisters, who have the best sister: Gayle, Joyce, Evelyn, Tina, and Sue; Family and chosen family: John, Beth, Jesse, Zev, Raviv, Aaron, Christine, Charlotte, Ty, Jennifer, John, Talia, Ethan, Ben, Sam, Dan, Shelly, Bert, Leslie, Morgan, Drew, Mark, Wendy and Avery. Friends, especially those conscripted as beta readers: Maya and Barry Lippman, Jane O'Connor, Pam Friday, Davina Katz, Bernard McNally, Horace Batson, Ph.D., Michelle Halprin, Sibby Wolfson, Judi Busboom, Robin Zagurski, Sara Samet; members of the Thursday night Writer's Roundtable, and Write Out Loud. In Edinbugh, Scotland: Rogue Writers, and Edinburgh Creative Writers. Special thank you to editor: Jonathan Starke

Admired authors—those living as well as those who live on only in their works: Carolyn Keene, Agatha Christie, Truman Capote, Lawrence Saunders, Ruth Rendell, Thomas Harris, and Sigmund Freud.

* 9 7 9 8 9 8 9 2 8 8 4 2 7 *